SHADES OF DEATH

Catrin Surovell Mysteries
Book One

Angela Ranson

SHADES OF
DEATH

Published by Sapere Books.

24 Trafalgar Road, Ilkley, LS29 8HH

saperebooks.com

ISBN: 978-0-85495-131-4

To Ruby, Sarah, Andrew, Elaine, Paul, Kimberly, Isaac, Colin, Rachel, and the rest of my beautiful family. You are like that first cup of tea in the morning — strong, sweet, greatly appreciated and much loved.

ACKNOWLEDGEMENTS

I have been blessed with many incredible people in my life, and each one of them has contributed to this book in one way or another. It would be impossible to name them all, but there are some who must be mentioned.

My teachers, who first drew out my love of writing: Miss Brown, Mrs Boyne, and Mrs Shannon. What an inspiration you were — and still are.

My supervisors, who made the Tudor era live and breathe for me while I did my postgraduate work: Dr Krista Kesselring and Dr John Cooper.

My wonderful, lovely friends, who have been there whenever I need them and always provided tea and chocolate. Especially Nia and Andrew Passmore, Sally O'Connor, Casey Smedberg and Louise Hampson.

My delightful colleagues at the University of York, who have cheered me on every step of the way.

The team at Sapere Books, including my fellow authors. What a wealth of knowledge and imagination you have!

Thanks for everything.

CAST OF CHARACTERS

Queen Elizabeth I, daughter of King Henry VIII and heir to her sister Queen Mary

Robert Dudley, her favourite courtier

William Cecil, Secretary of State

Ladies of the Bedchamber, companions to the queen:

Catrin Surovell, stepdaughter to the Earl of Ashbourne

Lucretia ('Lucy') Howard, her closest friend

Mary Sidney, sister to Lord Robert Dudley

Kat Ashley, the queen's former governess and current friend

Blanche Parry, personal attendant of the queen

Assorted other ladies

Katherine Grey, granddaughter of the queen's aunt

Mary Grey, her sister

At the Queen's Court

Roger Surovell, Earl of Ashbourne, Catrin's stepfather

Nicolas Swann, heir to viscount D'Alloway, a suitor of Catrin's

Francis Russell, the Earl of Bedford, a suitor of Catrin's

Thomas Howard, the Duke of Norfolk, a friend of the queen

Francis Talbot, Earl of Shrewsbury, a suitor of Catrin's

Lord Talbot, his son and heir

Sir William Paulet, Marquess of Winchester

Residents of Cumnor Place

Amy Dudley, wife of Lord Robert Dudley

Bowes, her servant
Picto, her lady's maid
Gryse, her servant
Master Forster, the gentleman who rented Cumnor Place
Mrs Odingsells, a guest of Master Forster
Richard Verney, a frequent visitor and friend of Master Forster

Others
Thomas Blount, Lord Robert's steward
Beatrice Drury
John Drury, her husband
Grisel, her daughter
Rose Kene, a chamberer

PROLOGUE

10 September, 1560

The four of them descended into the cellar, leaving all life behind. The familiar sounds of a busy manor house abruptly stopped as the door fell shut, leaving them wrapped in a heavy, unnatural silence. Lady Catrin Surovell noticed her friend shudder.

"Fare you well, Lucy?"

Lady Lucy Howard swallowed hard. "Well enough."

"It will be over soon, I promise," Catrin murmured, and they followed the coroner to the centre of the room. He stopped beside a plain wooden table and they all gathered around him, looking down on the body of a young woman wearing only a linen shift. Her arms lay straight at her sides and her bare feet stuck out from the bottom hem, toes turned up to heaven. Lucy looked away.

The fourth person in the party, Master Thomas Blount, leaned closer and fixed his eyes on the woman's delicate features. She had bow-shaped lips, now faintly blue, and a nose that came to a point. It was a pretty face, turned grotesque by the extreme twist that made her head hang loose on her shoulders.

Master Blount grunted. "Aye, that is Lady Amy Dudley. And her neck is broken."

Catrin reached out and set her hand against the woman's stiff curled fingers. "There is no doubt about how she died, good Blount."

"No, the question is *why* she died," Lucy murmured.

"Aye, and a terrible question it is," Catrin said. "The wrong answer could force the queen from her throne."

CHAPTER ONE

Two days earlier

Catrin could see Lucy's fingers shaking when she brought Queen Elizabeth a basin of water, but fortunately the queen herself did not notice. "Thank you, Lucy," the queen said absently, and picked up a piece of Castile soap that released the scent of fragrant oil into the air as she washed. Then she used a special cloth to clean her teeth, dipping it in a mixture of white wine and vinegar, boiled with honey. She left the cloth on a silver tray, and Lady Mary Sidney whisked it out of sight.

Catrin took the basin out to the privy chamber so that one of the chamberers could take it away. Several people were already there, including the Earl of Bedford and Sir William Cecil, the queen's young and brilliant Secretary of State. Sir William was pacing back and forth, impatient to begin the day's work, but the Earl stood still in silent worship. His eyes, comically small in his overlarge head, followed Catrin's every move as she went to the privy chamber door and accepted a package wrapped in linen from one of the yeomen of the guard. She turned, saw the earl watching her, and offered him her sweetest smile. "Good my lord, is there a stain on my gown?"

His eyes travelled down over her slim figure in its black taffeta. "Nay indeed, my lady."

She gazed limpidly at him for a long moment, and then demurely lowered her lashes. "Is my hood askew?"

This made him run his eyes over the gleaming black hair the French hood just barely displayed. "No, my lady. Why do you ask?"

"I could think of no other reason for you to gaze at me so intensely," she said in mock innocence, and slipped back into the bedchamber before he could untangle his tongue.

Lucy was in the doorway, giggling. "For shame, Catrin. He may not recover for hours."

"That is well; 'tis good to befuddle them once in a while. I have Her Majesty's fresh neck and wrist ruffs; have you collected the jewels?"

Lucy nearly fainted then and there. "I forgot!"

"Do not upset yourself, petal, it merely makes it worse." Catrin handed her the linen package. "The yeoman is surely still waiting in the presence chamber with the coffer; I will simply collect them now."

Catrin returned to the privy chamber, but her task was not as easy as expected. The room was full of strutting peacocks in satin finery, all hoping to see the queen. They gave way without fuss when the Duke of Norfolk strode in. Then the duke altered his path and stopped before Catrin. "My lady."

"Good morning, your grace," she said, and tried to see around him. Where was the yeoman? She hoped he hadn't taken the coffer back to the wardrobe.

"Has the queen arisen yet?"

"Yes, your grace, but she is not granting audiences yet."

"How is her mood?"

Catrin caught sight of the yeoman, standing by the wall with the coffer held tightly in both hands. "Fair, but the storm will soon gather if we are late."

The duke's lip quirked. "A brave maid you are, to answer so freely."

She smiled innocently. "Did I misspeak, your grace?"

"Not at all." He gave a slight bow and turned toward the privy chamber door. "You have told me exactly what I needed to know."

Stretched along the north front of Windsor Castle was a terrace commonly known as the 'new wharf'. It was not so new, having been built during the reign of Henry VIII, but it was still beautiful. Thus, once the queen was closeted with her privy councillors and busy with the day's work, Catrin always went outside to enjoy it. Lucy often went with her, and on that day she was more eager to go than usual.

"Have you heard what people are saying about the treaty Sir William made in Scotland?" Lucy asked, as soon as they were alone.

"I fear not," Catrin said absently, her eyes on the birds that swirled overhead.

"Sir William did well to get it agreed and signed. It is as good as we could possibly hope for, considering our circumstances. And yet people are grumbling about it!"

Catrin wrapped her cloak more tightly around herself. "People always grumble."

"I know, but surely they should be able to see that Sir William would only ever do what is best."

Catrin sent her an amused look. "What a saint he is."

"A saint, no. But a great statesman, yes. I can't help but think —"

A tall skinny figure loomed into view before them. "What-ho! Catrin!"

Catrin tensed, but she kept her smile firmly in place. "Why, 'tis my stepfather. What a surprise."

He lifted his chin and looked down his nose at her, trying to give the impression that he was far taller than he was. "You should address me as 'my lord'."

"Perhaps I should," Catrin said. "Have you met Lucy — I should say, Lady Lucretia — Howard? She is a niece of Lord William Howard of Effingham. Lady Lucy, my stepfather, the Earl of Ashbourne."

Lord Ashbourne sketched a bow in Lucy's direction and then folded his arms across his chest. "Have you petitioned the queen to grant me the lands around Ashbourne Abbey?"

"No," Catrin said calmly, and started to walk past him. "I said I would not, and I have kept my word."

Lord Ashbourne's fingers latched onto her arm like talons, dragging her to a stop. "Useless wench! Your only purpose is to promote my family, and you fail at every turn!"

Catrin wrenched her arm away. "I have my own purpose, *my lord*, and it does not include putting my status with the queen at risk by assisting *you*."

"But those lands border my manor house, as you well know, and if you are as well acquainted with the queen as you claim to be —"

"I make no claims and do only what I say I will do." Catrin touched the fingers of her right hand to her left wrist and stared at him. "No more, no less."

He squinted at her fingers and immediately backed away, his lip curled up in a snarl. "Do not forget that you are here by my gift alone. If you do not become more helpful, I will take back all your fine clothes and turn you out in your petticoat."

Fear made Catrin's heart flutter, but her voice remained icily calm. "And if you do, the queen will hear of it. That I promise you."

He had no answer to that, so Catrin left him behind. She walked to the edge of the terrace, over the Thames, and deliberately turned her back on him. Lord Ashbourne strode away, back toward the castle, and Lucy joined her friend by the water. "He's an unpleasant fellow, isn't he?"

"He has tormented my mother and I since my father was killed."

Lucy made a face at Lord Ashbourne's retreating back. "I am surprised that your mother agreed to marry him."

Catrin watched a seagull catch a fish and knew just how the fish felt. "I have always assumed it was out of necessity alone. He came along at a low ebb in our family fortunes."

"A common tale, I fear. But I believe it will have a happy ending, dearest." Lucy patted her arm. "When you marry, your husband will protect you from him."

"When I marry, I will gain the means to protect myself," Catrin said, and took tight hold of the wooden balustrade. "And I will do so as quickly as possible."

Catrin paused in the doorway of the privy chamber and absorbed the musky scent of many bodies packed into a small space, overlaid with woodsmoke and the tang of rich red wine. Across the room, the Duke of Norfolk was playing at dice with a baron and two of the maids of honour ——. who were winning, judging from their squeals of joy. Just in front of the fireplace, Lord Robert Dudley was playing cards with the queen and two of her ladies, and it seemed a merry game indeed. In the corner opposite the fire, a group of musicians played a sprightly tune on the drums, tambor and lute. Two or three couples had found the space to dance, adding the rustling of heavy taffeta and the swish of slippers against the floor to the cacophony of noise.

Lucy arrived by her side.

"Let us consider the possibilities," Catrin said. "One of those earls over there is a widower, but the queen does not trust him or his Catholic sympathies, so there would be no advantage to that match. Methinks a far better choice is the Earl of Shrewsbury."

Lucy set her hands on her hips. "Catrin, he's four times your age and not far from the grave!"

"True, but eligible in all other ways." Catrin caught his eye across the room and smiled, and he lifted his chest and smiled back. "I will speak to you later," she said to Lucy, but before she took a step a figure swirled out of the ring of dancers and manifested directly in her path.

"My lovely Lady Catrin!"

Catrin sighed. "Sir Nicolas."

Sir Nicolas Swann effected a sweeping bow and did not notice that he nearly knocked the cup from a passing lady's hand. Lucy failed to stifle a giggle. "It is the greatest joy of my life to set eyes on you, good lady. Prithee grant me the honour of a dance."

"I'm afraid I —"

A new tune burst out from the corner and Sir Nicolas beamed. "A galliard! We cannot miss it," he said, and all but dragged Catrin into the column of dancers.

A lute joined in with the drumbeat, and then a recorder added its clear sweet melody and the dancers all started to move along with it. Catrin took a light but stately step across the dance space, moving closer and closer to Sir Nicolas until they crossed paths and took hold of each other's hands. Steps forward, steps back, the fabric of Catrin's skirt swirling around her ankles and the feather on Nicolas' cap fluttering in the breeze.

Sir Nicolas dropped to one knee. Catrin circled him as the dance decreed, but her eye was on the Earl of Shrewsbury. Then Sir Nicolas started to rise to his feet, caught the hem of his own cloak with his foot and tumbled back to the floor with a hearty thud. A chorus of laughter arose and his face flushed flaming red. He pushed himself upright and fled, leaving Catrin alone on the floor.

The musicians continued with but a single sour note, and Catrin let her embarrassment show, hoping the earl would come to her rescue. And he may well have done, but he did not have a chance. Lord Robert Dudley himself, the queen's favourite, fell smoothly into the step instead. He moved around her in a graceful circle; she bent her arm and tilted her head, and on went the galliard.

The evening wore on. The page boys standing ready along the walls started yawning, and the candles burned low. The youthful maids of honour became annoyingly giddy, and many people were swaying somewhat from too much wine, but the queen was steady. She withdrew to her bedchamber without fuss, with Mistress Blanche and Lady Mary Sidney by her side.

Catrin was busy talking to the elderly Earl of Shrewsbury when Lucy appeared at her side.

The laughter faded from Catrin's face. "You look pale, dearling; are you weary?"

Lucy blinked away tears. "Quite."

"Then let us retire." She sent the earl an alluring smile and sunk into a curtsy. "Until tomorrow, my lord?"

"If I can wait so long," the earl said gallantly, and bowed low in return. Then he watched them leave, which Catrin pretended not to notice as they moved away from him through the crush.

The corridor outside was a cool, empty haven. Lucy leaned against the wall to catch her breath, and Catrin took a moment to smooth her skirts and straighten her hood. "All well, dearling?"

Lucy started to speak but then stopped. "No," she said. "But I cannot speak of it further."

Catrin had seen Lucy conversing with Sir William Cecil and suspected her friend may be lovesick, but she would not press her if she was unwilling.

"Very well. Let us depart."

They set off toward the ladies' chamber, where they slept when the queen did not need them, and Catrin linked her hands in front of her. "Did you see — the earl would not let Sir Nicolas reclaim my attentions; he kept me by his side. I consider that a fair sign that I have gained his interest."

"I'm sure it is."

"And did you hear the queen speaking to the Spanish ambassador? She mentioned again that Lord Robert's wife is ill. I wonder why he does not go to visit her."

"That is simple," Lucy said. "The queen will not let him leave her side."

Catrin's attention was caught by the two men standing in the meeting-place of two corridors. "It seems that is not true," she murmured. "For there is Lord Robert, and the queen is behind us, asleep in her chamber."

"Who is he talking to?"

"One of his servants. Laneham, I think his name is."

They drew closer, in time to see Lord Robert snatch his cap from his head in a gesture of frustration. "You have no idea of the strain I am under," he hissed, and stabbed his fingers through his hair. "Timing is everything — a minute too late might as well be a year."

Master Laneham hung his head. "Yes, my lord, I understand."

"Then do ensure that the deed is done. Immediately. If he won't oblige me, then find someone else. It is life or death in more than one way — do you hear?"

"Yes, my lord."

Lord Robert turned abruptly and walked down the corridor, away from Lucy and Catrin. Master Laneham stayed where he was, his head bent and his eyes on the ground.

Catrin acknowledged him with a shallow bow as they passed, and then promptly forgot about him. It was only later that she saw his face in her mind's eye ... and wondered.

CHAPTER TWO

Queen Elizabeth, as she often said herself, was not fond of mornings. In truth, nor was Catrin. They were both fond of the gardens and the park, but the queen's fondness led her to walk out with her ladies before she was even dressed sometimes, which was something Catrin would not even consider.

It was fortunate that the queen had decided to dress first that day. If she had not, and Nicolas Swann had appeared as he did, he would have ended his career at court in that moment.

When it all started, Catrin was walking beside Lucy, who had good tidings to share. "I heard that the Earl of Shrewsbury is still talking about you," she said, "and how beautifully you dance La Volta."

"Is he?" Catrin smoothed a stray lock of hair under her hood. "How kind of him to notice."

"He was not the only one," Lucy said. "The earl's son and heir, Lord Talbot, is said to be quite annoyed at the attention you received from the earl."

"That, too, bodes well for my prospects."

Lucy started to agree, but broke off when Sir Nicolas vaulted over one of the railed shrubberies and landed in a heap before the queen.

"Your Majesty," he cried. "I beg an audience!"

The queen stared at him in astonishment. His sudden appearance irritated her enough to revert to the royal 'we', which she usually used only when she spoke for the realm.

"Who is this," she demanded, "who so disturbs our progressing?"

Sir Nicolas clasped his hands together. "A man broken by love, Your Majesty!"

Mistress Ashley rolled her eyes. "Sir Nicolas Swann, Your Majesty. Heir to Viscount D'Alloway."

The queen surveyed his prone figure in its striped, yellow breeches and scarlet doublet. "New to court, we assume?"

"Aye, Your Majesty," Sir Nicolas said. "And already I love so deeply, so fully — I must petition you to help me."

A faint smile touched the queen's lips. "And whom do you love, young stripling?"

"You, Your Majesty! If you do not have me, I may perish." He blinked long lashes and rose to his knees. "I pray thee, consider my suit."

The queen burst out laughing. "Foolish boy. You know full well the queen of England cannot marry a man-child such as yourself."

Sir Nicolas drooped in dramatic dejection. "'Tis true, Your Majesty, I am young and foolish. Love has overwhelmed me to the point where I can neither think nor act properly."

"Now that we do believe," the queen said tartly. "You need a governess for a wife, not a queen. What say you, Blanche? Perhaps you could keep this young man in line."

"Pray excuse me, Your Majesty," Mistress Blanche said. "I fear he would take too much of my time from your service."

"True. Perhaps we must find him a lady who can bring him to his knees in no time at all," the queen said thoughtfully, and Catrin knew at once what she was thinking. "Ah — the perfect lady has come to mind. Just the thing!"

"Your Majesty?" Sir Nicolas asked hopefully.

"You may marry Lady Catrin. Forsooth, you have already fallen for her," the queen said mischievously.

The ladies tittered, reminded of Sir Nicolas' undignified exit the night before, but Sir Nicolas did not even have the grace to blush. He scrambled to his feet sure that he had won.

"Truly, Your Majesty? You would allow me to marry one of your ladies?"

"Of course," the queen said generously. "Provided, of course, that she has no objection."

"You are the greatest and kindest of sovereigns, Your Majesty." Sir Nicolas turned to Catrin, his face a study in hope and adoration and great satisfaction at his own cleverness. "What say you, lovely lady?"

"I fear I must object," Catrin said. "I cannot marry a man who has so recently declared his love for someone else."

Sir Nicolas' jaw dropped; evidently he had not thought of that.

The queen laughed merrily. "Alas, once again young love is cruelly thwarted," she said. "Come now, ladies, let us return to the castle. It is time to go riding."

Dressed in her riding-costume, with her hat tilted jauntily over one eye, Catrin stood next to a roan mare amongst a dozen other people similarly prepared. They had been waiting so long that even the horses were stamping with impatience. But the queen was annoyed that someone had mislaid her favourite riding-gloves, and insisted that they be found before they departed. That she had another twenty pairs, she chose not to remember.

Two of the maids of honour passed by: Lady Katherine Grey and a redheaded girl who had only recently taken a place at court. Catrin inclined her head politely, but they pretended they didn't see it.

"That's the one," Katherine Grey whispered. "Her mother ran off with a local shopkeeper and is living in sin in London."

Oh, is she? Catrin rolled her eyes, too used to such rumours to be upset. At first she had checked every story, just in case her mother actually *was* in London with a shopkeeper or in Dublin with the stableboy or hiding from her debts in Paris. Now she knew better, but still knew nothing more than anyone else. And that was simply this: soon after Catrin had taken a place at court, her mother had gone out riding and vanished, like the morning mist in the sun.

Catrin felt for the crackle of parchment in the purse attached to her belt. There was no need to draw it out; she knew every letter and number and symbol on it. What she did not know was what they meant. It was her mother's last letter, and Catrin could not read it.

Angharad Surovell had always loved secret messages, learning about the methods the ancients had used and creating her own. As Catrin had grown older, they had spent many a merry hour in a lonely hollow in the forest, trying to confuse each other with new methods. This was by far the most complex message her mother had ever created, making Catrin think she had had a vital message to relay, but so far she had failed to decipher it.

Perhaps it held the answer to the questions that often tore Catrin out of a sound sleep and echoed sadly in every silence.

Where had her mother gone?

And would she ever return?

Lucy had the pale wine ready when they returned, watered down as the queen liked it. Judging from the lack of steam arising from the jugs, she had even remembered to let the boiled water cool before she added it this time. There were cups ready, and silver plates of candied fruit, so she had done everything properly. It was strange, therefore, that she looked so anxious.

Sir William was there with her, and behind him hovered a man in rough, dusty travel clothes whose face was deeply grooved — whether by weather, work or sorrow, Catrin could not tell. He did not look up when they all arrived in a great rush and noise, with the queen and her favourite in the middle of it all, flushed and laughing at a joke no one else had heard.

Sir William stepped forward and pitched his voice above the babble. "I must speak with you, Your Majesty."

Something in his face made the queen's laughter die at once. "Leave us, all of you," she said, and then raised a hand. "Not you, Robin. Or little Lucy — or Catrin; I must have my talisman."

Sir William waited for the crowd to filter out, and then waved his companion forward. The goodman fell to his knees before the queen, wringing his cap in his hand. "I am a servant of the good Lady Dudley," he said, and then stopped, as if something had caught in his throat.

"I know who you are, Bowes," Lord Robert said, and cast himself down on a pile of cushions before he reached for wine. "What news? Does my dear wife long for gold buttons for her new russet gown?"

"No, your lordship. She longs for nothing."

Lord Robert paused, looked up. "Has the malady in her breast gotten worse? Is she suffering?"

"No, my lord." Tears filled Bowes' eyes and spilled over. "There is no suffering now. She is dead."

A cry tore from the queen's lips, and she stopped it by pressing the back of her hand to her mouth.

Lord Robert jumped to his feet, his face flushed red. "You lie."

"I — I swear I do not, my lord."

"How do you know? Did you see her?" Lord Robert strode over and hauled Bowes to his feet. "Answer me, man! Did you see her, or are you reporting idle stories?"

"I s-s-saw her." The man's tears turned to sobs. "At the bottom of the stairs outside her chamber, white as snow, limp as a broken reed. My poor lady! I saw her."

"The stairs?" the queen asked sharply. "She did not die in her bed?"

"Nay, indeed, Your Majesty. Her neck was broken," Bowes said. "We do not know how or why, but a coroner has already begun to investigate."

"Poor sweet Amy." Lord Robert seemed to bow in on himself, covering his face with both hands. "Have mercy, O God, and take her into your kingdom."

"Amen," the queen murmured.

A faint 'Amen' came from Bowes, but not Sir William. "This is a scandal, Your Majesty," he said instead. "It will taint your reign from its infancy if you do not act quickly."

A series of oaths exploded from Lord Robert. "Is that all you can say, Sir William? Is that your only concern? By God, man—"

"Robin." The queen drew herself up to her full height. "Sweet Robin. You know he is right. This death is suspicious, and the prattling tongues of this court will blame us both."

Lord Robert picked up the jug of wine and flung it against the wall. "Damn them all to hell for their gossip!"

The queen did not flinch. "You must leave the court until you are proven innocent."

"I will not be forced to flee like a common knave!"

"Yes, you will." Wine dripped down a tapestry of Eve in the garden of Eden and there came a shout of alarm from the yeoman guards outside, but the queen ignored it all. Her dark eyes caught and held Lord Robert's, and they gazed at each other as if they were the only ones in the room. "For both our sakes, you must leave now."

Lord Robert got control of himself with difficulty. "As you wish, Your Majesty," he said tightly. "I will go to Kew House. And I will send my cousin and steward Thomas Blount to ensure the investigation into my wife's death is thorough."

"A well-seeming plan, my lord," Sir William said. "Let it begin now."

Lord Robert shot him a look of disgust and then bowed before the queen. "Farewell, Your Majesty."

"Until we meet again, Robin," the queen said, with surprising calm. She even managed to send him a reassuring smile. It was only when the door shut behind him that she burst into tears.

CHAPTER THREE

"Lord Robert!"

He already had one foot in the stirrup, but he paused at the sound of Catrin's voice and waited for her to join him. "Yes, my lady?"

She couldn't believe the change in him. His face, usually so merry, was drawn and grey. "The queen sends you this," she said, and handed over the velvet pouch she carried. "A token of her unwavering affection."

Pain flickered in his eyes. "Is Her Highness well?"

"She is … recovering," Catrin said. "She wishes to know if you are well."

He took a deep, sharp breath as if to steady himself. "I met Amy when I was a boy of sixteen. I was commanding my first company of foot soldiers, and we were billeted at her father's house. She used to climb the apple trees and sing to herself … a great musician was my Amy."

The horse whinnied and Catrin stroked a hand over his neck. "I did not know that."

"No one did; she was very shy." His shoulders slumped. "I cannot believe she is dead."

"It is a great shock."

"Was her pain such that she could not bear it? Was it simply a misstep? Or…" His hands clenched around the pouch and something inside clinked and rattled. "I cannot help but wonder … the queen grows impatient at times…"

Catrin stepped smartly backward. "Lord Robert, that is a very dangerous thing to say."

"I know," he said thoughtfully. "Dangerous — and foolish. Surely it is but a fantasy — surely Elizabeth would not —"

"Lord *Robert*."

He shook his head as if breaking out of a dream. "I do apologise, my lady," he said formally, and put his foot back in the stirrup. "May I ask you not to repeat what I have said?"

"You need not ask, my lord," she said dryly. "Unlike you, I have a sense of self-preservation."

A faint smile touched his lips. "Then I will simply thank you for extending it to me." He swung himself up onto the horse. "Farewell, my lady."

"Farewell, Lord Robert."

He urged his horse into a trot and was soon out of sight. Catrin lifted her skirts and picked her way carefully back into the castle, where she couldn't help but notice that the path back to the queen's chambers resembled the beehives she had once cared for at Ashbourne Manor. People were standing about in groups, buzzing with the news, while others darted between them anxious for any fresh juicy morsels to add to their hoard. She heard snippets as she passed.

"She must have been pushed —"

"I hear it was Lord Robert —"

"They say her neck was broken, but her hood was undisturbed —"

"Perhaps the queen —"

"Tush! No, it was Dudley himself —"

"Would he be so bold?"

"Of course! He wants to be king!"

"A wife is a small sacrifice for a kingdom."

"It must be Dudley. Did anyone see him in the castle yesterday?"

"The queen knows it's him. She sent him away."

"Dudley killed his wife —"

" — to be king."

"The queen's 'sweet Robin' has claws."

"Dudley — it was Dudley."

The opinion of the court had tried and condemned him already. Not a single soul was even considering that others might have reasons to want Lady Dudley dead. It was the same in the presence chamber — the maids of honour were aghast with delighted horror that the queen's favourite had killed his wife.

No matter — it was none of Catrin's concern. Others would unravel this spider's web; her involvement would end when she gave Lord Robert's message to the queen.

Catrin passed into the privy chamber, where Lady Mary Sidney stood at the window, her eyes rimmed with red. The queen sat limply on a low chair by the fire, with Lucy on a stool by her side and Sir William and Bowes kneeling before her. Bowes was drooping with exhaustion, but Sir William was annoyingly pert. His beard was positively twitching with excitement. "It is good that you sent Lord Robert away, but we must decide what to do next," he was saying. "It would be good to show favour to others, Your Majesty. Too much largesse to one man alone breeds contempt and jealousy."

The queen ignored him. "Is my lord well, Catrin?"

"Aye, Your Highness. He has just now departed."

"As I should, Your Highness," Bowes said tentatively. "I am needed by the coroner in his investigation."

The queen frowned. "We wish to know all, Bowes. Every piece of evidence, every word from witnesses. Can you provide us with that?"

Bowes looked terrified at the very thought, and Sir William cleared his throat. "Your Highness, he is not … ah, qualified, for such a task."

"Then I must send someone else. Norfolk? Bedford? Nay, they are needed here."

"As am I, Your Majesty," Sir William said, as if to remind her.

The queen made a small noise of consent, and Catrin noticed Lucy smile.

The queen glanced around the room. "Shrewsbury is too old — Swann is too young…"

And she would get no coherent response from either of them, Catrin thought. They would be too wary of the queen's wrath to tell the truth. Nay, this situation needed someone who could think for themselves. Someone who could look at all that Amy Dudley had left behind and understand what it meant.

Lady Mary Sidney crossed from the window to Catrin's side. "Her Highness should not send a man," she murmured. "A man will not understand."

"I was just thinking the same thing," Catrin returned. "It requires someone clever and insightful, such as yourself."

"I cannot go; I am Amy's sister-in-law." Fresh tears rose in Lady Mary's eyes. "Was. I was her sister-in-law."

Of course. Catrin had nearly forgotten that Lady Mary was Lord Robert's sister. "Who else then?"

Lady Mary gazed at her intently. Catrin caught her thought and held out a protesting hand. "Nay, not I. I am needed at court."

"And my brother needs the truth, or he may suffer for it."

"Unlikely, considering how greatly the queen favours him."

"Favourites have died at the hands of their sovereigns many times before." Lady Mary caught her breath. "Whether they were guilty or not."

A shame, but there it is. "I'm sorry, but —"

"If you go, I promise to give you information about your mother."

Catrin's eyes narrowed. "We have known each other for two years, but only now do you tell me that you know something about my mother?"

"Knowledge is best kept till it is most useful; that is how it works at court," Lady Mary said frankly. "But I will tell you if you go to Cumnor and discover all you can."

Catrin sent her an icy glance and raised her voice, so she could be heard above Bowes' anxious mutterings. "I will go, Your Highness."

The queen abruptly stopped her deliberations and stared at her.

Bowes' eyes narrowed. "Forgive me, Your Majesty, but that is a foolish notion," he said. "What can she contribute to a coroner's inquest? I wager she has never even seen a corpse."

The flash of an axe blade in her mind's eye rendered Catrin speechless for a moment, until Lucy's hand slid into hers. "Catrin has seen more terrible things than you can imagine, Master Bowes, and survived to tell the tale," she said stoutly. "And Her Majesty knows how clever and capable she is."

"That is so," the queen agreed, and smiled fondly at Lucy. "Dear little Lucy, you are as loyal as a puppy, and just as brave. You will go with Catrin to Cumnor."

Lucy's eyes went round, and Bowes shook his head. "I could not take charge of such highborn ladies, Your Majesty — and I must needs go right away. How long would it take for them to prepare?"

"Not long," the queen said briskly. "Lady Mary will help them."

"I must protest," Sir William said. "This is all wildly out of joint."

"Yes, you are right, Sir William," the queen said sharply. "The death of Lady Dudley is in every way against nature. We must do all we can to restore order. *All* we can."

Sir William subsided. Reluctantly. "Yes, Your Majesty."

A half-dozen people helped Catrin and Lucy collect all they would need for travelling. It was all a rush and a flurry, and Catrin did not have time to answer the question that stood out so clearly in Lucy's eyes. And Lucy didn't ask, until they were scurrying down the corridor on their way back to the queen. Then it burst out of her as if it could no longer be contained.

"Why are you so keen to find out the cause of this death, Catrin? Were you particularly fond of Lady Dudley?"

"Not really. I met her once, when she was last at court," Catrin said, and quickened her pace so she could keep up with Lady Mary, who was escorting them back to the queen's rooms. "She came when Lord Robert was made a Knight of the Garter."

"That was a long time ago," Lucy said breathlessly. "Why do you care what happens now?"

"I have my reasons."

"But what if someone killed her?"

"Then his punishment should be the loss of his own life."

Lucy stopped short. "You say that so coolly. It's as if you had never seen such a law in action." She started walking again, but slowly. "I thought you did not approve of executions."

"It is not that I believe the axe should never fall, Lucy," Catrin said. "I just want the blade to land on the right neck."

Catrin stepped into the queen's chamber with Lucy close behind. The scene remained the same. Bowes was wringing his hat, and Sir William was still protesting.

"They are gentle ladies, Your Highness. They do not know enough of the world to make sense of this," Sir William said. "It will do naught but cause them distress."

Lucy glanced at Catrin. "He might be right."

"I doubt it. Not everyone who blows a horn is a huntsman." Catrin lifted her chin. "We are ready, Your Majesty."

Sir William actually moved to block the door. "Tarry but a moment; give Her Majesty time to consider. Prithee, mighty sovereign —"

"Oh, by God's heart, William, move aside," the queen ordered. "They barely have enough time to make it to a decent inn before nightfall as it is."

People obeyed at once when the queen used that tone — one could hear the echo of old King Henry within it. Sir William was no exception, and his hasty jump away from the door amused Catrin a great deal.

"We will return with news as soon as we can, Your Highness," Catrin said.

"So you shall," the queen replied, and waved her hand toward the door. "May God go with you."

Hours later, the silence of the road and the steady clop-clop-clop of the horses' hooves was lulling them all to sleep. Bowes trotted along ahead of Catrin, setting an even and steady pace. Lucy was on her right, her head nodding, her eyes closed more often than open.

Catrin pressed her fingers to her left wrist, and the touch of cold steel under the lace of her cuff immediately brought her back to full wakefulness. She drew the knife slowly from its hidden sheath, but knew better than to test the blade. It was an Italian knife known as a *stiletto*, one of her father's collection. She had chosen it because it was so thin, so sharp, and so easily hidden. Most ladies did not carry such a weapon, but then again most ladies were protected by their fathers and brothers. She had no such champion and had learned when very young that she had to protect herself. Since then, carrying a hidden knife had saved her from a man's overzealous attentions several times, and once from a highwayman after her purse.

Lucy rose up in her saddle and stretched, holding her eyes wide open as if to take in as much of the fading light as she could. "Where are we?"

"Nowhere in particular," Catrin said. "But I am glad you are here."

Lucy sighed. "You tease. Both of us know I will be of little use."

"Nay, indeed, I wager you will contribute greatly." Catrin slid the knife back into its sheath. "Right now, for instance, it would be useful for me to talk to someone about what may have happened."

"All we know is that Lady Amy fell down the stairs," Lucy said. "It could simply have been an accident."

"Or she could have meant to harm herself."

Lucy gasped. "Surely not."

Catrin let the thought pass. "Or someone harmed her."

"But who would do such a thing?"

"That is the question. The obvious candidates are Lord Robert, the queen herself, and Sir William."

Lucy's cheeks immediately turned pink with anger. "Sir William is a good and honourable man. He would never harm a woman with whom he had no quarrel."

Catrin kept her gaze steady on the horizon. "What if it was her husband with whom he had the quarrel?"

Lucy's clear blue eyes filled with tears, and then she shook her head with such vehemence her hat wobbled on her head. "He wouldn't. He *wouldn't*."

Catrin held her gaze, wishing for more than one reason that she knew what was weighing on Lucy's mind. "He wouldn't what, dearling?"

"Nothing," Lucy said firmly, and looked away. "Nothing at all."

Whether it was from shyness or displeasure, Bowes had not spoken a single word to Catrin or Lucy since the three of them took to horse. Catrin had tried to start a conversation with him and failed, so she and Lucy had simply conversed between themselves. Now, as Bowes led them into the yard of a timber-framed inn with sagging walls of mouldy plaster, Lucy spoke up. "Master Bowes, what is this?"

"'Tis the Old Swan, my lady," he said. "We can rest the horses and find refreshment here."

Lucy looked at the stones of the yard, covered with more than a day's worth of muck, and her rosebud lips puckered. "Must we?"

"Tush, dearling," Catrin murmured. "'I wager there are no better choices."

Lucy did not look convinced, and she was all the less so when they went into the common room. It smelled musty and sour, like old reeds and stale ale, and it was brimming with men singing bawdy songs, while serving-maids with tired eyes wove among them in low-cut kirtles.

Lucy crowded close to Catrin and Bowes stomped in behind them, carrying the packs into which they had bundled all their personal items. "Sit down somewhere and they'll bring you food," he grunted, and stomped on by.

The motion of his feet made the smell of the reeds on the floor all the stronger, and Lucy took a silver pomander from her belt and held it near her nose.

"This way," Catrin said, and wove between groups of people who were all trying to talk above the singing men.

The noise was incredible — worse than the echoing banquet-hall at Hampton Court. And they all believed passionately in what they were saying: the first group debated the value of horseflesh and declared that any horse thief should be hanged without trial. The second group argued over which of them was better with the longbow. The third was talking about the queen, and as they passed the biggest man declared that the queen was pregnant with a bastard child.

"'Tis that knave Dudley what fathered it," the man said. "And it's not her first, either."

"That's why she travels every summer," another man said, and took a great slurp from his cup. "She has the child far from court and hides it in a hedgerow."

Lucy's hand tightened on Catrin's arm, but she said nothing aloud until they made it to a table in a secluded corner. Then she drew her cloak closer around her and glared at each man in turn. "How dare they say such things about their sovereign?"

"It's just talk," Catrin said. "The interesting thing is that no one has mentioned Lady Dudley. Perhaps the news hasn't reached this far."

Bowes came in and dropped into a seat next to Catrin. "You two have a room at the top of the stairs on the right," he said, and waved a hand to get the attention of the nearest serving-maid. "I'll sleep with the horses, since they are of a finer sort than most found around here and might tempt a jack or two."

"Thank you, Bowes," Catrin said, and folded her hands in her lap as a serving-maid walked up to them with wide eyes. "Good evening, goodwife."

"Good evening, my lady." The serving-maid ran her eyes over the fine velvet of Catrin's travelling-cloak in evident envy. "We don't get much of your sort here, I must say. Are you lost?"

"Aye, and thirsty," Catrin said innocently. "Two cups of red wine, if you please, and what will you have, Bowes?"

"Pint of ale," Bowes said, and then his head suddenly jerked in the direction of the door. "By our lady, it's himself."

Catrin followed his gaze. A man was framed in the doorway who looked just as disgusted as Lucy. He was certainly a gentleman, based on the cut of his doublet and the snowy white of his shirt, but he was not a courtier or she would have recognized him. "Who is that?"

"Thomas Blount, Lord Robert's steward," Bowes said. "He must have received Lord Robert's message."

Master Blount noticed them then and strode across the room as if he expected everyone to move out of his way. Not everyone did, and that caused no small conflict with other patrons, but he finally sat down at their table just as the wine and ale arrived.

"The messenger told me Her Majesty had sent you along," Master Blount said, and asked the serving-maid for small beer. "'Tis a waste of time, I say. The woman killed herself. She had a strange mind."

Lucy frowned at him. "Prithee, Master Blount, do not say that. Remember: she cannot be buried in sacred ground if she killed herself."

"Aye, and the preachers say that you will lose your soul if you die by your own hand. Whether or not that is true, she was devout and may well have believed it," Catrin said. "That makes suicide less likely."

Master Blount had a thin, straw-like beard that seemed to emphasise his double chin, and he drew his fingers down it as he sent Catrin an oily smile. "Do you think she had an accident, then, my lady?" he asked. Catrin gazed at him limpidly and said nothing. After an age of silence, he cleared his throat. "Accident or suicide. Surely those are the only two options you are thinking of."

"I am not thinking of anything, my lord," Catrin said, and took a delicate sip of wine. "Yet."

CHAPTER FOUR

The next day, Catrin was standing in a cold cellar before the body of Amy Dudley, with Lucy and the coroner on one side and Master Blount on the other. Bowes had disappeared as soon as they had safely arrived, immensely relieved that his responsibilities were over.

Master Blount glanced at Catrin and then shifted to face the coroner and began to speak in Latin. The words were a string of nonsense to Catrin, but Master Blount was not hiding information as well as he thought he was, for Lucy spoke Latin. Catrin would soon know all that Master Blount knew — unless Lucy *told* him she understood, and she seemed about to do so then and there. Catrin pressed the toe of her riding-boot against Lucy's with a gentle but insistent pressure and shook her head when Lucy glanced at her. To her relief, Lucy sent her a comprehending wink and put on an expression of blank incomprehension.

The coroner rubbed the stubble on his cheek before he responded, also in Latin, and the two men spoke for several minutes. Then Master Blount's cheeks suddenly swelled with satisfaction. "Of course she did," he said, in English. "Thank you, Master Smith. I believe we are finished here."

Master Smith agreed with obvious relief and led them out of the cellar.

They emerged into the warmer world above, with the scent of woodsmoke and baking bread from the nearby kitchens swirling around them. Cumnor Place was constructed in a square — two storeys of irregular grey stone surrounding a central courtyard. It was a friendly-looking place, with arched diamond-paned windows looking down on the courtyard with the benevolent indulgence of a dog watching her puppies play. However, there was also a tinge of fear and uncertainty in the air. Catrin could see it in the way the servants avoided the eastern wing, and the staircase next to the chapel.

Master Blount dismissed the coroner and decided that he needed to speak to Picto, Amy Dudley's maid. That meant they had to climb that very staircase, and Catrin saw Lucy shudder when she first put her foot on the stair. She fully understood: after all, it was here that Lady Dudley had met her end. Here, on this dog-leg staircase with its stone steps and age-hardened oak balustrade.

Catrin hung back to see whether she could find anything that might be useful, but no trace of Lady Dudley remained and there was no sign of damage to the stairs. Her only recourse was to follow as Master Blount pressed onward — or rather, upward — and walked through the open door of Amy Dudley's chamber.

Picto was there, folding gowns between sheets of linen while tears slid slowly down her face. Master Blount ignored the tears, and did not even bother to greet her properly. "So, Goodwife Picto, what do you think of this matter?"

She smoothed a fold of linen over a russet gown with hands that looked worn thin with work. "I do not know what you mean, Master Blount."

Master Blount folded his portly frame into a chair. "You knew your mistress well. Do you think she died by chance or by her own hand?"

"By chance," Picto said stoutly. "It was done neither by man nor herself."

Master Blount stroked his hand down his beard. "You seem very sure."

"She was a good virtuous gentlewoman, and daily would pray upon her knees." Fresh tears scored the wrinkled cheeks. "Diverse times I heard her ask God to deliver her from desperation ... praise be that He has answered her."

"Desperation, you say?" Master Blount's plump fingers started to pick at the armrest. "Perhaps she had an evil toy in her mind."

Picto stiffened, and for the first time her hands went still. "No, sir. Do not judge so of my words," she said firmly. "If you should so gather, I am sorry I said so much."

"Aye, but so you said," Master Blount said, and rose from his chair. "I must write to my Lord Robert. Until supper, ladies."

He strode away, and Picto started to cry in earnest. "He is going to speak ill of my lady, isn't he?"

Lucy hurried to the woman's side, drawing her thin bent frame into her arms and making soothing noises.

Catrin wandered over to a shelf in the corner of the room, where a half-dozen books lay flat with their gilt titles facing outward. "Perhaps he will," she said, and flicked a finger over the ribbon placeholders sticking out of the pages. "But we will not, and it is we who must report to the queen. Is there anything else you can tell us?"

"Nay, indeed," Picto sobbed. "I went to the fair that day. How I wish I had stayed with her!"

"To the fair?" Catrin asked. "Why did you go to the fair?"

"Lady Dudley insisted that they all go to the fair that day; or at least that is what the coroner told Master Blount while they were speaking in Latin," Lucy said. "When they returned, they found Lady Dudley at the bottom of the stairs, already cold."

"Do you know why she asked you all to go, Picto?" Catrin asked.

"No, but she wanted the house to be empty," Picto said. "She even asked Mrs Odingsells to go."

"Who is Mrs Odingsells?" Lucy asked. Picto looked up at her to answer, and Catrin took advantage of her distraction to remove one of the books from the shelf and hide it in the folds of her skirt.

"Mrs Odingsells is another guest of Master Forster's," Picto said. "Her relative owns the manor; Master Forster himself merely leases it. Mrs Odingsells refused to go to the fair because she did not think a gentlewoman should attend on the Sabbath. My lady was angry that Mrs Odingsells refused, but she could not change her mind."

"I wonder why she wanted everyone to go," Catrin murmured. "It does seem strange."

Picto straightened, drying her tears with her apron. "This is a small house, and my lady was very shy. Oftentimes she asked to be alone — especially in the last few months."

"A fair point, that," Catrin said wryly, thinking of the crowds at court that were so difficult to escape. "We will leave you be — thank you very much."

Lucy followed Catrin out of the room. "Are you sure we should leave her in such distress?"

"We must find out all we can before Master Blount tries to stop us," Catrin said. "What else did the coroner say?"

"Only that Amy had two dints in her head — one was half a thumb deep, the other two thumbs deep. Master Blount was sure that they were sustained in the fall, but the coroner suggested that they might be separate injuries."

"That," Catrin said, and immediately started down the stairs, "is significant."

"Why? Do you have an idea of what happened?"

"None at all. But I am sure of one thing — the truth is like a jewel." Catrin paused on the landing and looked thoughtfully upward. "It has many facets, and the right light makes each one shine."

Catrin and Lucy had had neither time nor space to pack additional gowns, so they simply brushed their skirts clean of dust before they went to the evening meal in the grandly named great hall. Catrin thought it fortuitous that they had not changed, once they saw the neighbours and friends Master Anthony Forster had invited. Each of them was obviously dressed in his or her best, and their best was not up to the standards of court. If Catrin and Lucy had worn their usual evening finery, they may well have embarrassed their host. As it was, they fit in quite nicely with the ladies in their simple brocade and the men in woollen breeches, and Master Forster was obviously pleased to offer such illustrious visitors to his guests. He introduced them both in tones as reverent as if they had been the queen herself.

They were about to settle down to the feast when a man appeared in the doorway to the hall. Immediately Master Forster's expression soured, and he marched over quivering with indignation. The two men began arguing, quietly but with such ferocity that Catrin was not the only one to notice. She saw another guest looking their way, and moved closer so she could ask, "Who is our host talking to?"

"Master Richard Verney. An old friend, but a new drunkard," the man said sadly. "I have seen them argue several times over the past few days. Poor Master Forster is always telling Master Verney that he has gotten in over his head and it will be the death of him someday."

By the third course, Catrin could tell that Lucy was bored. She had admirers who strove mightily to entertain her, but they could talk of nothing but the harvest and breeding sheep. Not topics that interested Lucy. Catrin was not surprised when Lucy removed herself from the crowd and went to admire the carvings on the lintels and the tapestries on the walls.

It was growing dark, and the light from the beeswax candles on the table did not extend to the furthest corners of the hall. But there was something there; Catrin could see a shape in the shadows.

She excused herself from her tablemate and circled the hall, stepping as lightly as she would in a dance. Finally she slid into a hiding spot behind a tapestry, and from that vantage point she could see that the shadow had eyes. Lucy saw too, and jumped back with a gasp. "Who is there?"

A small dark-skinned figure emerged. Catrin recognized him as the young servant boy who had taken their packs inside when they arrived. "Just me, my lady."

Lucy pressed a hand to her heart. "Why were you hiding there?"

"Not hiding, my lady, just waiting." He removed his cap, revealing a head of tight black curls, and bowed a quick nervous bow. "I need to speak with you, my lady."

"Of course," Lucy said in her sweet, gentle voice. "Say whatever you like."

The boy cast down his gaze and sniffed back tears. "I am my lady's boy — Lady Dudley — I want to help her."

"I see. What is your name?"

He blinked, as if he hadn't expected her to ask. "Gryse."

"That sounds like a Welsh name."

His dark skin suggested that he came from far further afield than Wales, but he nodded. "I lived there long ago, my lady. When I was a child."

"I see. Do go on."

The boy nodded and bowed several times, and only then found the courage to continue. "I have been with Lady Dudley for a long time," he said. "She is a good lady … that man Master Blount, he says bad things about her, but she is a good lady."

"I'm sure she was." Lucy fingered the pomander swinging on its chain at her hip. "Do you know something that would show that Master Blount is wrong?"

"Perhaps." He started wringing his cap. "Lady Dudley was with a man, my lady. A man came to see her."

"When?"

"Many times, but the last time was on the day she died." A burst of laughter from the crowd around the table made him jump. "I should go."

"Wait — wait — do you know who the man is?"

"I only saw him once, and only his back. Ask Mrs Odingsells." His voice twisted with dislike on the name, but he nodded. "Mrs Odingsells, she saw him too."

"All right. Thank you, Gryse."

He bowed again. "Thank you, my lady," he said, and retreated back into the shadows.

Catrin emerged from her hiding place, quite satisfied.

Lucy nearly leapt out of her skin. "How do you *do* that?"

Catrin quirked her lip. "I don't know what you mean."

Lucy huffed out a breath. "You move like a cat."

"When necessary. Now, let us go." Catrin led her friend out of the hall. "It seems we must speak to Mrs Odingsells."

CHAPTER FIVE

"Mrs Odingsells," Catrin began, and sent the old lady her best enticing smile. "We had hoped to meet you at supper, but when you did not come, we thought we would see you here."

The woman sniffed. "I would have no part of those foolish people doing foolish things," she said. "Forster did not think about how it would look, to invite guests tonight."

Catrin nodded solemnly. "You should all be in mourning still."

"Of course we should. Amy Dudley was one of the premiere ladies of the realm and deserves to be remembered in a way that befits her station."

"Yes, she does." Catrin bowed a heavy head. "She was so young … too young for such a death."

"She was young and silly." Mrs Odingsells adjusted her stiff gable hood so it sat more firmly over her ears. "And she had quite the temper."

"We heard that she was angry with you when you would not go to the fair," Catrin said. "I do wonder why she wanted to be alone so badly."

Mrs Odingsells' gaze drifted up and away, but a sour smile twisted her lip. "I cannot say."

Lucy looked disappointed. "You can't? But —"

Catrin sent her a warning look and waved a dismissive hand. "Of course you cannot. You are not one to gossip, are you?"

"No, never." Mrs Odingsells shook a warning finger. "I know the danger of idle tongues."

"Oh, indeed. It is so easy to damage reputations," Catrin said. "But Lady Dudley, I'm told, was spotless. An ideal wife,

48

staying innocently in the country so her beloved husband could advance at court."

"Ha!"

Catrin blinked. "Is that not true?"

"I know little of her husband's advance, but innocent she was not," Mrs Odingsells said, and hunched her shawl around her shoulders. "I saw her meeting a man in the deer park. Walking with him, holding his arm, accepting gifts."

Lucy's face lit up. "Do you know his name?"

She snorted. "Do you think I *spoke* to the blackguard? Nay, indeed, I kept my distance. I know only that he was missing an earlobe."

Catrin's fingers clenched at this piece of information. "Are you sure?"

"Of course! I'm old, but my eyes are as good as they ever were. And I saw him often enough to remember him." She sniffed again. "I even saw him talking to Richard Verney."

"Was Master Verney close with Lady Dudley?" Catrin asked.

"Richard Verney is a friend of the Dudley family, and a friend of Master Forster," Mrs Odingsells said. "Lady Amy stayed with him for several months, but the silly woman thought he was poisoning her, so she left and came here. Which proves that he *wasn't* poisoning her, by the way."

Lucy looked puzzled. "How so?"

"Richard Verney is here so often that if he was poisoning her there, then he could have kept poisoning her here."

"Indeed; methinks he's here now," Catrin said. "I saw him arguing with Master Forster."

Mrs Odingsells shrugged. "They argue all the time."

"Over Lady Amy?"

"Perhaps. I cannot say." She wagged her finger again. "But I can tell you that there was nothing wrong with Amy Dudley.

She was just fine, for all that she complained of illness in her breast. She was fine. That is all I know."

With that, Mrs Odingsells shut her mouth tight, and wouldn't say another word.

Catrin rose and thanked her politely, then followed Lucy out of the room.

"That was … interesting," Lucy said tentatively, and fidgeted with her pomander. "We now know who was meeting with Lady Amy."

"We do, and this facet of the truth could be dangerous," Catrin said. "We may have to limit where the light shines."

Catrin waited until she and Lucy were in their bed and protected from the night air by a thick coverlet before she placed the book she had secreted earlier from Lady Dudley's chamber delicately between them. "So," she said, and ran a finger over the leather binding. "What do you think?"

Lucy glanced at the title. *The Wholesome and Catholic Doctrine Concerning the Seven Sacraments.* It was a Catholic text from the reign of Queen Mary. "I've never read it."

"Nor have I, but don't you think it's an odd choice for a woman to have in her chamber now, fully two years after Catholic Mary's death?"

"Perhaps," Lucy said. "But there might be some other reason she was reading it."

"I don't think she was reading it at all," Catrin said, and flicked a finger at a green ribbon page marker protruding from the bottom. "My mother taught me that a contrasting coloured ribbon is often a marker for a coded message. See? They are all blue, except that one."

Lucy snuggled down deeper into the blankets. "Oooh — a secret message. That would be interesting."

"I thought so too." Catrin opened the book with a protesting creak that supported her theory that it hadn't been well-read and started searching. She tried substituting letters in the text, to see if it yielded another meaning. Nothing. Then she looked for patterns and anagrams and came up with a string of nonsense phrases.

Lucy yawned as Catrin worked, and her eyes were fully closed by the time Catrin let out a victory cry.

Lucy sat bolt upright and grabbed a cup to use as a weapon. "What is it? Who is here?"

"Tush, you'll wake the house," Catrin said. "I'm sorry I frightened you. All at once I saw how they made the cipher, that's all." She held up the book near the candle, so Lucy could see tiny points of light shining through the page.

"Pinpricks?"

"Pinpricks," Catrin said triumphantly. "Have you a quill and ink?"

Lucy did, and rather reluctantly left the warm bed to collect and prepare them. It was a long process, so Catrin used the time to examine the page. By the time Lucy finally had a full quill poised over a piece of paper, Catrin could read out the message in full. "O-a-k — t-h-r-e-e — x-i."

Lucy surveyed the letters doubtfully. "I'm not sure that makes sense."

"Yet." Catrin looked at the scribbles, brow furrowed. "Let's start with the obvious: oak as in tree, three as in the number. The third oak."

"It sounds like the name of an inn or a farm."

"Yes it does. Now … xi. Roman numerals for eleven?"

"If so, why write out three and put eleven in Roman numerals?"

"I assume they had to work with the letters they had on the page ... but why this page?" Catrin hastily flipped through the rest of the book, testing each page against the candlelight. "It's the only one with pinpricks."

Lucy took the book and counted, since the pages weren't numbered. "And it's the eighth page, if that matters."

"It does." Catrin smoothed a wrinkle from her pillow and leaned back. "Amy Dudley died on the eighth of September."

Lucy dropped the book like a hot ember. "It predicted her death! Maybe it's cursed!"

"That's a foolish notion," Catrin said impatiently. "You sound like a superstitious old woman."

Lucy made a face at her. "And you sound like some sort of soothsayer, making connections without proof."

"These connections will lead to the proof," Catrin said. "Methinks the message was sent to Lady Dudley to tell her when and where to meet."

"Eleven o'clock on the eighth of September by the third oak."

"Aye." Catrin traced a finger down the page. "I doubt that she knew that death was coming, but killing her may well have been the plan on the other side from the moment this message was created."

Lucy corked her ink bottle and set aside the quill. "What other side?"

"Whomever sent the message, of course."

Lucy cleared her throat and fixed her gaze on a point above Catrin's right shoulder. "I thought we had guessed who sent the message, because Mrs Odingsells said she saw Lady Dudley meeting with a man who was missing an earlobe."

"No, that tells us only the man who delivered it, not who sent it." Catrin set the book aside and slid down under the covers. "And I hope to God they are not one and the same."

Lucy shivered. "So what do we do now?"

"Now, we sleep," Catrin murmured, and let her eyes close. "Tomorrow, we find the third oak."

CHAPTER SIX

The house was barely stirring when Catrin and Lucy entered the courtyard. Chamberers were cleaning the rooms, so the air smelled of vinegar, and noises from the direction of the kitchen heralded the preparation of the midmorning meal. Of the other residents, such as Master Forster and Mrs Odingsells, there was no sign.

Catrin linked her hands in front of her. "Hm. Now, dear Lucy, where do you think one would find several oaks together in the bustling village of Cumnor?"

A shadow behind the open door of the chapel jumped as if in response to the question, and Lucy smiled. "Gryse would know, I wager."

"An excellent point." Catrin waved the young boy out and he came eagerly. "Young Gryse, we are looking for oak trees," she said. "Probably not too far from the house, but not too close either."

"Yes, my lady. Come with me," Gryse said, and scurried off. He headed directly south, past the deadly staircase that led to Lady Dudley's chamber and out onto the terrace. Catrin half-expected him to stop in the gardens, for there were trees dotted throughout its pebbled paths, but he kept going, past the fishponds and through the gated entrance of the deer park. Catrin grew quite breathless trotting along after him.

He circled a large open meadow where a lone doe was nibbling at birch leaves, and once on the far side he followed the dip of a shallow hill. It was like a large bowl of earth, holding a thick growth of trees in its deepest part. "Here are the only oaks in the park," he said. "They grow slowly."

"Thank you so much, Gryse — we would never have found this ourselves," Catrin said.

Delighted, Gryse bowed so low he almost toppled over. Lucy caught him, which set them both to laughing.

Catrin left them to their merriment and started circling the trees. "Did you ever see Lady Dudley come out here, Gryse?"

He bowed again but kept his balance this time. "Yes, my lady walked here often."

"Did you see the man here?"

"No, my lady. Only in the garden. He brought her a big book with ribbons."

Catrin raised one eyebrow. "When was this?"

He screwed his eyes up tight and thought hard. "On the Feast-Day. St. Giles."

"That's the first of September," Lucy said.

"Leaving the perfect amount of time to ensure the message was received before the meeting took place on the eighth." Catrin paused beside one towering oak and looked up at the thick green leaves that were just beginning to turn autumn orange. "Why did Amy Dudley die?" she murmured, mostly to herself. "Was it suicide, accident or murder?"

"Methinks we have reason enough by now to say it was not suicide," Lucy said, and great relief crossed Gryse's face. "But it could still have been an accident. She had a malady in her breast; perhaps she grew faint at the top of the stairs and simply fell."

"And perhaps…" Catrin saw something among the moss and small plants at the base of the largest tree and drew it out. Gryse and Lucy moved closer just in time to see a blade flash in the dappled light as she raised her hand. "Perhaps it was murder."

Lucy stared at the long thin piece of steel, which had a lethal tip at one end and a diagonal break at the other. No hilt, no sheath. "It's a ballock knife. But Lady Amy wasn't killed by a ballock knife."

"No, she wasn't … possibly because the knife broke before the deed could be done," Catrin said, and handed the blade to Lucy before she went searching amongst the plants again. A duller gleam this time, and she pulled out her hand to find herself holding a square metal button.

Lucy took it from her, and a worry line appeared between her brows. "I've seen that design before, I know I have. But I cannot say where or when."

"For now it is enough to suggest that there was someone else with Lady Dudley on the day she died," Catrin said. "I wager that person met her here, went back to the empty house with her, and hit her on the head with the hilt of the knife that had lost its blade here in the forest. Then he pushed her down the stairs, to make it look like an accident."

Gryse's face crumpled. "But why, my lady? Why?"

"I don't know." Catrin raised one shoulder and let it fall. "That is a question for someone else to answer. All we can do is report to the queen."

"Where have you been?" The voice echoed around the courtyard, making it hard to determine a source until Catrin saw Master Blount stomping his way towards them, quivering like an arrow with fury.

Gryse ran away on fleet feet, and Catrin shifted slightly to block Lucy from the man's advance. "In the deer park, good Master Blount," she said. "'Tis a fine morning for a walk."

"You're interfering. You're muddying waters that must — simply *must* — run clear," Master Blount said. "I know that you spoke to Picto and Mrs Odingsells without my presence. I know that you have been interrogating the servants. Why are you so determined to complicate this situation?"

"We are not complicating anything," Catrin exclaimed. "We are merely fulfilling the task that Her Majesty herself gave us."

"Silly creature! You do not even realise that she has asked for something she does not truly want to have," Master Blount said. "You would be wise to stop your meddling and return to your embroidery."

"But we found something in the park," Lucy said. Catrin pressed her foot against hers again, but this time Lucy ignored the hint. Instead, she drew her handkerchief out of her sleeve and unwrapped it, releasing the scent of perfume and the sight of the blade and the button, which she had carefully wrapped while they were in the park. "See? This suggests someone could have been there on the day Lady Dudley died."

"Those items could have been there for years," Master Blount said, but they all knew that the shining blade belied that notion. To be so rust-free, it could not have been lying in the woodland more than a few days. "And there is no proof that whoever it was came to see Lady Dudley."

Lucy shifted away from the additional pressure Catrin put on her foot. "But we found —"

"Tush," Catrin hissed.

Master Blount snatched the handkerchief and its contents. "I care not what you have found," he said. "You are a disgrace, both of you. Pack your things this moment; I am taking you back to court."

Dismayed, Lucy watched him stuff the handkerchief into the purse on his belt. "But won't you try —"

"Defy me not." His voice rose to a bellow. "Go!"

"As you wish," Catrin said coolly, and led Lucy across the courtyard and back to their room.

Catrin started folding their nightclothes and collecting their things, but Lucy stayed frozen in the doorway.

"Catrin — the book is gone!"

CHAPTER SEVEN

A certain fair-haired courtier was waiting for them when they finally rode through the giant stone arches of King Henry VIII's gate at Windsor, and for some reason his very presence irritated Master Blount. "Who is that young whelp?"

Lucy giggled. "His name is Sir Nicolas Swann."

"You know him?"

"I do."

"Then convince him to let us pass."

"'Tis not I who can persuade him, Master Blount, but our Lady Catrin," Lucy said mischievously. "For her, he would do anything."

"*Except* get out of my way," Catrin murmured. "So perhaps I cannot help after all."

Lucy laughed, and Master Blount started muttering angrily to himself, as if her merriment was a personal insult. Meanwhile, Sir Nicolas ran to help Catrin down from her horse, his face flushed with delight.

Catrin found herself trapped between intense hostility and overwhelming enthusiasm, and it was difficult to decide which was the more wearing.

"Greetings, Lady Catrin!" Sir Nicolas said. "I am bold to say that the court has been dark and cold without you — as if it lost its sun."

Catrin winced. "Do not say such things, Sir Nicolas — the queen will be displeased."

Evidently that possibility had not occurred to Sir Nicolas; he looked askance at Master Blount, who scowled back. "I meant no insult. I am a loyal subject."

"Oh, of course you are." Catrin stripped off her riding-gloves. "But that does make one wonder why you are here instead of attending upon the queen."

Sir Nicolas practically danced with excitement. "I have learned something that may influence your audience with the queen regarding Lady Dudley."

"Do tell us, then," Master Blount demanded, and remembered at the last second to add, "my lord."

Sir Nicolas ignored him, his gaze fixed firmly on Catrin. "My lady, I have discovered that one of Sir William's secretaries has been absent from court since we arrived here."

Lucy's brow furrowed with puzzlement. "Is that important?"

"Well … I thought so. After all, Sir William wanted to prevent Lord Robert from marrying the queen, and everyone says that someone killed Lady Dudley for a reason…" His shoulders slumped. "Perhaps it does not matter."

"And perhaps it does," Catrin said. "One never knows what might prove relevant, Sir Nicolas."

His face lit up. "Thank you. Your kindness is one of many reasons why I live for your service, Lady Catrin. And now may I escort you fine ladies to your rooms?"

Catrin restrained a sigh. "Of course."

Mistress Rose Kene was singing to herself in the ladies' chamber when they arrived. She looked up from her sweeping with a smile. "Lady Lucretia! I hear you had an important commission from the queen," she said, her dark eyes round. "What was it like?"

"Cold and uncomfortable," Lucy said, and a guilty look crossed her face. "I do not think I am meant for a life of intrigue."

Mistress Rose giggled. "The court may not be the best place for you, then, my lady."

Catrin would have rebuked such boldness from a chamberer, but Lucy just laughed. "It's a far better place for me than Cumnor, though. Especially since we were forced to travel with Master Blount — a more unpleasant man I have yet to meet."

Mistress Rose dropped her voice. "That is his reputation among us chamberers as well. Strange that such a highborn man as Lord Robert would have such a steward."

"I am hoping that we will soon be rid of him, but first we must present our findings to the queen," Lucy said. "What has been happening here since we have been gone?"

"The Duke of Norfolk and Sir William Cecil are vying for the queen's attention, and the maids of honour were scolded for idleness."

"So nothing has changed," Lucy said. "That is somewhat comforting."

"But that is not all." Mistress Rose lowered her voice yet more. "Everyone is talking about who killed Lady Dudley, but they have to be careful. When the queen heard the Earl of Shrewsbury arguing with the Duke of Norfolk about it, she banned discussion of the matter in her presence."

Lucy bit her lip. "Oh, woe. I wish we had better tidings for her."

Mistress Rose looked interested, and Catrin suspected that the girl was going to forget her place and ask what those tidings were. So she stepped closer, eyebrows raised, and sure enough Mistress Rose visibly changed her mind. "Oh, whatever the tidings are, my lady, I'm sure all will be well."

"We can only hope," Catrin said. "But now we should prepare ourselves to see the queen, Lucy — so we can leave before Sir Nicolas finds an excuse to return. Do you have time to help us, Mistress Rose?"

"By all means, my lady." The girl set aside her broom. "I will fetch you some washing-water."

A few steps from the privy chamber door, Master Blount put his hands on the back of Catrin and Lucy's necks and squeezed. "If you breathe even a word about your false proofs, I'll see you are punished for it," he hissed, then let them go as abruptly as he had taken hold and pushed past them into the chamber.

Catrin rubbed the back of her neck, where five stinging spots were sure to become bruises. "Weasel."

Lucy's lip trembled. "And we are the mice he has trapped."

"Nay, we are the goshawks who will overpower him," Catrin said grimly, and followed him into the room.

Master Blount was already bowing before the queen, who stood with her fists clenched in front of the fire. Sir William stood to her right and the Duke of Norfolk to her left, and several ladies stood about, watching. Still, it looked strangely empty without Lord Robert, and Catrin did not hear any of the usual laughter or chatter.

"What tidings?" the queen demanded.

Master Blount's dark eyes swept the length of the room. "Would you not prefer to speak where we cannot be overheard, Your Majesty?"

The queen lifted her voice. "Remain if you speak only English; otherwise, depart," she said.

Lady Mary Sidney, who spoke fluent Italian, subtly retreated. Another lady Catrin did not know went with her, and one of the maids of honour scurried after them both. Sir William and the duke reluctantly withdrew as well.

Lucy started to follow them, but a glance from the queen kept her still.

"And now only you and I are privy to our conversation," the queen said. "What do you speak? Italian? French?"

Master Blount smoothed his hair back from his face, making his widow's peak all the more pronounced. "Latin, Your Majesty."

The queen switched to that language with ease, and asked again what they had learned.

Master Blount started to talk, and the queen listened carefully, but her eyes flickered in Lucy's direction more than once. Catrin wanted to do the same, but to do so risked spilling Lucy's secret. So she waited, gazing demurely at the floor, until Master Blount switched back to English at last.

"The coroner has yet to deliver his verdict, Your Majesty," he said, "but I feel sure it will match with my findings."

"We give you hearty thanks, good Blount," the queen said. "Now go and take your ease, and we will speak again at supper."

"Yes, Your Majesty."

He bowed low and backed out of the room, and the queen beckoned Lucy and Catrin forward. "He says it was suicide. Should I believe him, Lady Lucy?"

"No, Your Majesty," Lucy said. "He did not tell a single lie, but he also did not tell the truth."

"Nor, I wager, did he mention what we found," Catrin said.

Lucy shook her head miserably. "I think he destroyed it all, so there would be no evidence to counter what he has told you, Your Majesty."

"And we cannot prove his findings incorrect," Catrin said. "Even though we hold a very different view."

The queen's jaw tightened with anger. "Tell me: if that evidence still existed, would it point to an accident, suicide, or murder?"

"Murder," Catrin said, and told her first about the injuries to Lady Dudley's head. Then she talked about the book, the discovery of the code, and the items they had found in the forest. She finished with the visit to Mrs Odingsells. "Through her, we discovered that Lady Dudley had been meeting with a man," she said at last. Lucy caught her breath and looked away, and Catrin took a moment to gather her courage. "And I think the man she met with may have been my stepfather."

Lucy let out the breath. The queen's eyes narrowed. "Based on what?"

"Mrs Odingsells remembered that he was missing an earlobe."

"Not a common injury, that," the queen said, and raised her voice. "Bring Lord Ashbourne here at once."

A page darted out the door, and Catrin dropped her gaze. "Your Majesty, by your leave?"

"Speak freely, my talisman."

"If Lord Ashbourne had anything to do with this … I pray thee know that I neither condone his acts nor hold the same prejudices."

The queen burst out into a laugh, so suddenly it made Lucy jump. "I know that. If it were not so, you would be in chains by now, and my talisman no longer." She raised her voice again and resumed her formal speaking style. "Sir William, we have need of thee."

Sir William returned to her side with all speed, his long robe rustling along the plank floor. "Yes, Your Majesty?"

The queen took a seat in a wooden chair that was shaped like a curved 'x' and padded with thick velvet. "Lord Ashbourne has a secret, and we wish to know what it is."

A spark lit in Sir William's eye. "Yes, Your Majesty."

The queen waved Catrin and Lucy away, and they retreated further from the fire but not so far that they could not hear what was happening. The faint buzz of conversation returned to the room, and one or two people dared to drift closer to the queen. She and Sir William were talking quietly, and Catrin could hear enough to know she was telling him everything.

"An ill wind," a voice muttered behind them, and Catrin turned to find Mistress Ashley hunched in the window-seat, her embroidery on her lap. "This business … 'tis an ill wind indeed."

Lucy nodded agreement, but Catrin just stood still and waited, hoping that no one noticed how her knees trembled when Lord Ashbourne came in. He was walking on his tiptoes as always, and wearing a smile of smug self-satisfaction.

He stopped before the queen, swept his hat from his head and bowed low. "Your Highness. How good of you to summon me. I am at your service."

"Yes, you are," the queen said tartly. "Or at least, you should be."

Lord Ashbourne lowered himself cautiously to his knees. "Have I displeased —"

"Do not speak to Her Majesty again," Sir William barked. "She does not converse with traitors."

Lord Ashbourne turned a sickly shade of green. "My good lord, I am not a traitor. By God's wounds, I swear it."

"With such oaths do traitors swear," Sir William said dryly. "I shall need more than that to counter the intelligence I have recently received."

"Intelligence?" He glanced in Catrin's direction and hate flared in his eyes. "I pray thee, take not the word of a worthless child like my wayward stepdaughter, Your Majesty. She seeks only petty revenge."

"I did not say the knowledge came from her," Sir William said, and his voice rose to a mighty thunder. "I said only that you have committed acts of treason."

"I — I — did not —"

"Do not deny it!" Sir William swooped closer, robe flapping like the wings of a great owl as it descended on an unsuspecting mouse. "You were seen, man!"

Lord Ashbourne cowered. "It is not treason to deliver gifts, and that is all I did! On my own soul, I swear! That is all I did!"

Sir William hovered mere inches above him. "What gifts?"

"A — a book on the seven sacraments. A set of brass buttons marked with the Dudley crest. A barrel of beer. Writing-paper, with a quill and ink. A s-small chest."

"Such important goods," Sir William said sarcastically. "Only an earl could deliver such treasures. Did you not have a servant to make these deliveries?"

"I had to ensure that they were received."

Sir William leaned closer so he was almost nose to nose. "And who received them?"

"Lady Amy Dudley."

It was the merest whisper, but the significance of those words echoed through the room. Lucy took Catrin's hand and held on tight. The queen sat rigid on her chair, and Sir William abruptly lowered his voice to something like a croon.

"And why, good Ashbourne? Why were you so kind as to deliver goods to this poor lost lady?"

The sudden change in Sir William's tone seemed to unnerve Lord Ashbourne completely. As, of course, it was meant to. "I — I was paid."

"By whom?" the queen demanded, her hands holding tight to the arm of her chair. "Who paid you to deliver these gifts?"

"I do not know his name."

"Do you know anything of him?" Sir William asked, still in that soft crooning voice. "Any information would be helpful, Ashbourne."

"He-he was a servant, I think. He wore a brown tunic." Lord Ashbourne sunk further into a heap on the floor. "And on his left arm, a livery badge."

Sir William stood over him, waiting. The silence stretched taut and Lord Ashbourne started to shake. It was not long before he broke. "It was … the b-bear and ragged staff." He gulped. "The badge of Lord Robert Dudley."

CHAPTER EIGHT

"I will not believe it. I will not!" The queen charged up and down the length of her bedchamber, her chest heaving against the restraints of her bodice. Her rage was such that the maids of honour cowered as one, their white gowns blending together so that they looked like a cloud that had fallen to earth. In another corner, a smaller group of women represented the few ladies of the bedchamber who had not withdrawn until the storm had passed.

Catrin and Lucy, meanwhile, had stayed by the queen. As had Mistress Ashley, who was wringing her hands.

"Perhaps the gifts and favours you have given him made him greedy for more, Your Majesty. Men do strange things when their minds are filled with gold."

The queen stopped short, her face suffused with rage. "Kat, you try me sorely. Know your long service will not spare you from my wrath."

Mistress Ashley withered, leaving Mistress Blanche to make a second attempt. "Any man would wish to be king, Your Majesty," she said. "And most would do whatever it took to achieve that wish."

The queen spun in her direction, flinging out one arm as if to ward her off. "Nor you, Blanche!"

"We know that very well, Your Majesty," Mistress Ashley said miserably. "But we both pray that our long service lets us tell our beloved queen the truth."

"You do not speak the truth!" the queen cried. "The truth is that my sweet Robin would not commit murder."

"Your Highness, take heed!" Mistress Ashley lowered herself to her knees, trembling. "There is no way to prove that Lord Robert did not commit this crime."

"Neither is there any proof that he did!"

"He had reason to wish himself free of his wife, and for many people that is enough." Mistress Ashley's voice wobbled. "I pray thee — I beg thee — for the sake of your safety and your throne, distance yourself from him. You must distance yourself from him."

"I cannot," the queen said, and her voice broke. "I cannot."

Tears stood out in Mistress Ashley's eyes. "Then you condemn us all."

A terrible silence fell. Lucy pressed her fingers to her lips, as if afraid that even her breathing would break it. Catrin, however, felt no such fear. "Your Majesty, there may be no proof, but there is still logic," she said quietly. "Why would Lord Robert send secret gifts and messages to his own wife?"

The red flush faded from the queen's cheeks. "A good question, that. After all, he could write to her or visit her openly whenever he wished."

One of the maids of honour tittered. "If *she* would let him go." It was a whisper, but nowhere near quiet enough. The queen heard, and fresh fury stiffened her spine.

"Katherine Grey, you impertinent wench, do you dare mock a queen in her own chamber? By God, I'll have you in the Tower!"

The other maids subtly drew back from Katherine, leaving her alone in the midst of a crowd. She was an empty-headed girl with pale eyes that protruded slightly, giving her a permanent expression of faint surprise. Catrin found her irritating.

"I — I am sorry, Your Majesty," Katherine said, and glanced at her sister Mary for help. "I meant it only in jest."

Her sister, a short and twisted woman with a pronounced hump in her back, rolled her eyes. "Prithee forgive her, Your Majesty," she said. "She has always responded with such terrible humour when she is nervous. Why, she once asked a man with a wooden leg to dance with her!"

Two of the other maids giggled at that, and the thunder in the queen's face faded into weariness. "Both of you return to your chamber," she said. "You will not show your faces again today — is that clear?"

"Yes, Your Majesty."

The two girls withdrew with all speed.

The queen passed a hand over her eyes. "Leave this chamber, all of you. I must think."

The others scattered about the palace in search of diversion; Catrin went directly to the dancing-chamber, where Lady Mary Sidney was watching over the delivery of some of the queen's gowns from the Great Wardrobe. Catrin waited in the shadow of the open door whilst sleeves, petticoats and skirts were checked and counted, and stepped forward only when Lady Mary turned to leave. She jumped at Catrin's sudden appearance, fumbling the ledger she carried and losing her quill altogether.

"You must be the only person in England who can hide in an open space," she said. "Why have you come?"

"Surely you can guess," Catrin said coolly. "I have paid your price, after all."

"I suppose you have." Lady Mary retrieved her quill and folded it carefully inside the ledger. "I do not know where your mother is now, Lady Catrin. Or if she is even alive."

"Then what do you know?"

"On the day before Her Majesty's coronation, your mother arrived in London and came to court uninvited and unannounced. Sir William Paulet, the Marquess of Winchester, granted her an audience."

She went to Sir William Paulet? Why did she not come to her? Catrin kept the question locked within her, refusing to give it voice. Refusing to feel the hurt. "And what did she say?"

"I'm afraid I don't know. All I know is that Sir William gave her money and told her to take refuge in West Drayton."

"He told her to leave London for a tiny village? Why?"

Lady Mary's gaze dropped to the floor. "Once again, I don't know."

"Surely she would have been safer with my stepfather in his London home — or with her friends."

"I thought the same; that is why I remember her visit." Lady Mary rested a comforting hand on Catrin's shoulder. "But that is all I know, I'm afraid. I cannot help you further."

"That's all right, Lady Mary." Catrin stepped backward so that the comforting hand fell away. "I am well acquainted with helping myself."

It was not their night to sleep in the queen's bedchamber, so Catrin and Lucy went back to the ladies' bedchamber. Often they chatted before they fell asleep, but that night Lucy fell asleep almost immediately, exhausted by the long ride and the drama that had followed it. Catrin closed her eyes and drifted into drowsiness, but real sleep did not come. When someone came into the room, she was immediately wide awake.

"Lady Mary? Is that you?"

"It is." Lady Mary paused at the end of the bed, the candle she held casting patterns of shadows and light on her face. "The queen has need of you both."

"We will come now, my lady," Catrin said, and shook Lucy's shoulder before she slid out of bed.

Lucy whimpered. "What? Surely it is not morning. Prithee, let me be."

"Wake up, dearling," Catrin whispered, and pulled a heavy dressing-gown over her nightclothes. "The queen has need of us."

"How do you know?" Lucy pushed herself upright, and her bleary eyes focused on Lady Mary. "Alas. Very well then."

"Quietly," Lady Mary murmured, and held the light up so Lucy could find her dressing-gown. They shod their feet in thick woollen slippers, and then all three of them shuffled out of the chamber and into a darkened corridor. Wood panelling gleamed dully in the candlelight, and the dour faces of long-dead nobles loomed into view and faded out again as they passed them by.

Lucy shivered. "It's like their eyes are following us."

"Tush," Lady Mary said sharply, and glanced from side to side before she opened a panel in the wall. It led to a tiny antechamber lined with thick woven panels to block out sound. It was devoid of furniture but for a small writing-desk, where three candles in a single pewter holder cast a circle of shivering light into the room. "I will return," Lady Mary said, and shut the door carefully behind her.

"It is so small — like a prison cell." Lucy moved closer to Catrin. "Do you think we are in danger?"

"No more than usual." Catrin said it lightly so she did not frighten Lucy, but there was a prickling in her spine that she could not dismiss. Something was out of joint.

Another panel creaked open across the tiny room, and the queen herself slipped inside. "Good evening — or rather, a very early good morning," she said calmly, as if this were not highly unusual. "I must ask that you tell no one about this gathering, upon pain of death."

Catrin understood then. This was a council of war, with a murderer as the target. "Of course, Your Majesty," Catrin said. "And when will Lord Robert be joining us?"

The queen chuckled. "You have puzzled it out already? I am not surprised. And, to answer your question: any moment now."

On the heel of her words, another panel slid open. Lord Robert stepped inside, his doublet gleaming dull silver in the light. He saw the queen and dropped to his knees, and she let him take her hands, bending close to him in a way that made Lucy press her hand to her heart, her face awash with sentiment.

"Rise, sweet Robin." The queen straightened. "Tell him what you have discovered, my talisman."

Once again, Catrin went through the story, but this time she included how Master Blount had tried to hide information by speaking in Latin, and how he had taken the evidence, and how he had threatened them when they returned to the queen.

Lord Robert listened carefully, his face drawn and pale, and when she had finished he rubbed a hand over his eyes. "Poor foolish Blount — in his attempt to exonerate me, he has condemned me."

"Did you know of any of this?" the queen asked, with an edge to her voice.

"Nay, indeed. I will show you his letters — they mention only that he expects the verdict to be death by misadventure." He sighed. "And that he felt that Amy was not right in her mind, which I cannot believe to be true. She was so sensible, so dutiful … she handled my estates when I could not, ensured that debts were paid, convinced men to do their duty."

"You forget that she was also receiving men bearing gifts," the queen said sharply. "What of that?"

He winced. "I do not know."

"So you did not send them?"

Lord Robert straightened to his full height. "Of course not."

"And what of the livery badge?"

"Anyone could have stolen one of my badges from the laundry. Even the best of servants are occasionally careless."

"Tell me about those servants. Could any of them have paid Lord Ashbourne to send these gifts? Were any of them missing on the eighth of September?"

"No, Your Majesty," Lord Robert said coolly. "What of yours?"

Fire lit in the queen's eyes. "You dare speak so to the queen of England?"

"I dare because you have the same cause for this crime as I, and yet men do not question *you* day and night."

"There is a difference between us," the queen said icily. "*I* have no need to murder to gain a throne."

"And I had no reason to murder to gain a wife," Lord Robert snapped.

They glared at each other with such ferocity that the air sizzled, and Catrin thought it wise to step between them. "Very good; that answers many of our questions," she said. "Let us assume, then, that neither of you killed Lady Amy, shall we? It will allow us to focus our attentions on who did."

The tension held for a moment more, and then the queen released it with a long sigh. "Agreed," she said, and held out her hand. "I regret your loss, Robin. Truly, I do."

"Thank you, Your Majesty." He said it stiffly, but he took her hand and bent over it. "And I … I regret the distress and disruption this has caused."

"Think of that no more, Robin. Let us work together." The queen closed her hand around his. "Do any of these discoveries give you a hint as to who did this?"

"The button intrigues me; its shape and size sounds familiar, but without being able to see it I cannot say for sure," Lord Robert said. "Shall I speak to Blount?"

The queen shook her head. "You are not supposed to know of any evidence, lost or otherwise," she said. "Unless it is from you yourself."

"I know nothing. It has been nearly a year since I last saw Amy," Lord Robert said, and his voice grew thick with unshed tears. "We wrote often, though I rarely kept the letters. All seemed well, although over the last few months she spoke less about what she was doing and more about Forster and that Odingsells woman. She spoke of Gryse, the boy she had befriended, and the gowns she was making with the fabric I sent. At the last full moon I suggested that she might want to move on — perhaps establish our own household — but she said she was not ready to leave Cumnor Place yet."

"Did she mention any visitors, my lord?" Catrin asked.

"No, but that is not unexpected, if she was cuckolding me," Lord Robert said bitterly, and that possibility sparked a new thought. "God's mercy, do you think she was killed by her lover?"

"Surely not," Lucy said. "You said she was a good and faithful wife."

"So I thought," Lord Robert said. "But what if…?"

"Such musings will not help, my lord," Catrin said.

"True. We need proof, not speculation," the queen said. "Go now back to your mourning-house, sweet Robin. I will summon you again once we have brought order from this chaos."

He bowed low. "Yes, Your Majesty," he said hollowly, and left the same way he had come.

The queen gazed for a long time at the panel that had shut behind him. "Catrin," she said at last, "tomorrow I will send you and the Duke of Norfolk back to Cumnor Place. You must search thoroughly for anything — testimony, documents, anything — that will reveal the truth about this tragedy."

Catrin tilted her head. "You wish for me to deal further in this matter, Your Majesty?"

"Aye. If indeed it was murder and not an accident, the murderer must be caught. Otherwise, Lord Robert will torment himself about that woman's fate for the rest of his days." Suddenly her eyes glittered. "Do you object?"

Catrin rather wished she could, but she knew better. "Nay, indeed, Your Majesty," she said. "I merely thought my task was done."

"The task is not done until we know all," the queen said. "And this time, Norfolk will be there to ensure that no evidence disappears."

Lucy started to speak. "But what if..." She stopped and swallowed. "Pardon, Your Majesty."

The queen's eyes narrowed, and Catrin knew that she had already guessed what Lucy had been about to say. "Ask your question, Lady Lucy."

"What if..." Lucy dug her toe into the floor beneath her. "What if the evidence points toward Lord Robert?"

The queen's jaw tightened. "That would change nothing. Lady Catrin must still bring it here, and I will determine what to do next."

Lucy curtsied. "Yes, Your Majesty."

"Very good. Now go to bed, both of you." The queen sighed. "It all begins again tomorrow, and we shall need our strength."

CHAPTER NINE

Catrin's mother was sitting at the end of her bed, humming the haunting Welsh songs that had always lulled Catrin to sleep. But Catrin did not want to sleep; she wanted to gaze at her mother, to watch her glossy black hair gleam in the candlelight, to reach out and touch the soft warmth of her cheek.

"Where are you?" Catrin whispered. "What are you doing?"

Her mother dipped her head low, her lashes falling over her eyes. "Do not follow me, kitten. Do not follow."

"Follow I will, as soon as I can get to the village of West Drayton," Catrin said fiercely. "I will not let you go so easily."

"But that is just what you must do." Her mother reached out a hand that turned to mist just as the fingertips touched her cheek. "You must let me go."

"No! Mother!" Catrin's own voice woke her. For a long time after that she lay still in the dark, her cheeks wet with tears.

A few hours later, Lucy was folding linens for Catrin to pack, but her mind was not on the task. Something was troubling her; the furrows on her brow made that easy to tell. But Catrin knew better than to force a confidence. Lucy, for all her sweetness, could be stubborn.

"I do not need much, dearling." Catrin let her hair loosen and fall free of its bindings. "I will return as soon as I can; my own plans have suffered enough of a delay."

"You may not need to make your own plans after this," Lucy said. "Helping the queen may lead to a reward."

"That is by no means certain; the queen might quickly forget any help I provide." Catrin pulled a comb through the thick ebony strands of her hair. "You seem quiet this morning; are you still tired?"

"Yes." Lucy focused most intently on the linens, avoiding Catrin's gaze. "And I think this is a fruitless errand. The murderer is at Kew House, not at Cumnor."

"So you suspect Lord Robert?"

"I have since we met last night. He could so easily have ordered Master Blount to destroy all evidence."

"Yes, he could have." Catrin gazed at Lucy for a moment, the comb still in her hand. "And perhaps you would prefer to think of him as a killer, rather than Sir William Cecil, who would become the queen's favourite if Lord Robert was disgraced."

"Sir William would not harm a soul," Lucy declared, but she shivered as she said it. Catrin suspected that she spoke from blind loyalty, not real conviction. "And do you remember what Lord Robert said to Master Laneham?"

Catrin resumed brushing her hair. "Aye … I have been thinking on that."

"The very day after he ordered his man to find someone to take on a task that was 'life or death in more than one way', his wife was dead."

"True." Catrin set the comb aside and began to bind up her hair again. "But by then the book had been in Lady Dudley's possession for days."

"Perhaps the book was just a gift from a friend and had nothing to do with her death."

"And perhaps there are mermaids in the Thames."

Lucy's eyes sparked. "You're as bad as Master Blount."

"Am I?"

"Yes — you think it's Sir William Cecil, and you will not listen to any other possibility."

Catrin chose not to respond, focusing instead on fitting her hood into place.

Lucy stamped her foot in frustration. "I cannot believe you would listen to gossip from Sir Nicolas over my —"

A strange sound reached Catrin's ears. "Tush," she said suddenly, and turned toward the door. The sound came again, and this time she recognized it as the floorboards outside, creaking faintly.

Catrin crossed the room on tiptoes and flung the door open. A rush of air made the fabric of her hood flutter, and there was a gasp and the pitter-patter of slippered feet. By the time Catrin rushed out into the corridor, it was empty.

"The court is full of spies, and one came to pay us a visit," Catrin said. "Little did they know, we have naught to tell them."

A guilty look passed over Lucy's face, and her anger vanished. "You're right. Nothing at all."

A new rustle of cloth made Catrin tense. She put her finger to her lips to warn Lucy and waited, watching the corridor as the sound grew louder.

Then Lady Mary Sidney walked serenely into view. "Good morrow, ladies."

Lucy let out a long, tense breath. "Good morrow."

"Lady Catrin, I bring you a message from the queen."

"Oh?" Catrin raised one eyebrow. "May I guess?"

Lady Mary chuckled. "If you wish."

"I wager she has changed her mind, and my day's journey is over before it begins."

Lady Mary smiled. "Aye, my lady, that she has. She has decided to wait until the coroner's report has come before she takes her next steps."

"As Her Majesty wishes," Catrin said, and tried to hide how pleased she was. "I am sure that I can find something else to occupy my time."

Once Lucy had left for the mid-morning meal, Catrin moved quickly. She changed into her riding-costume in the empty ladies' chamber with a chamberer to help her, took a side route out of the castle to the stables and saddled the roan mare herself when she found no stableboys about. There was no time to lose — if the queen found out that she had left the court without permission, she could very well lose her place. But she had to go; she needed answers to the questions that hummed in her veins. Why was her mother sent to West Drayton? Had she asked to leave the city? Could she possibly still be hiding in that village, two years later?

Catrin used a mounting-block to mount her horse, set her thigh around the pommel, and urged the mare out into the cobbled courtyard.

"Lady Catrin!"

She nearly jumped out of her skin. Sir Nicolas was trotting toward her on a dappled grey stallion, his hair a twisted mess from the wind. "God's heart, Sir Nicolas, you startled me."

Sir Nicolas chuckled and held his horse back so he stayed next to her. "You have a guilty flush to your cheek, my lady. Are you planning devilment?"

"I am planning to go riding. Do excuse me."

"A lady cannot ride alone," Sir Nicolas said solemnly. "I will go with you."

"I have no need of an escort."

"A companion, then." He grinned at her. "You will not shake me off, my lady."

"Perhaps not." Catrin urged her horse to a gallop. "But I will try."

Five miles into the ride, Catrin had to accept that Sir Nicolas could keep pace easily. His stallion was a fine match for her mare, and she found herself enjoying the challenge. Riding with the queen had taught her to appreciate the heady recklessness of speed.

However, there were things that must be said, so she reined in and waited until Sir Nicolas had brought his stallion under control and cantered back to her side.

"Are you well, Lady Catrin?"

"Quite. And you?"

He looked around at golden fields and dark green trees and raised his face to the clear blue sky. "Aye, well indeed."

"And are you trustworthy?"

His youthful jaw with its downy fuzz set firmly. "I am an honourable man, Lady Catrin."

"Which means that you will keep my confidence?"

He set a hand against his heart. "To the death."

"Then I will tell you my purpose," Catrin said, and immediately regretted it. For all that he was five years older than she, he was still young. How seriously would he take her quest? Could he even understand her need to know?

Sir Nicolas circled her on his horse, hooves thudding gently on the dirt road. "You need not tell me if you do not wish to do so," he said quietly. "I am content merely to escort you, Lady Catrin, and happy to keep your secrets."

Catrin lifted her chin. "So be it, then."

"Aye, so be it." He urged his horse back to a canter. "Lead on, my lady, lead on."

The second half of their ride was as fast as the first, and Catrin enjoyed it all the more. Once they arrived in West Drayton, however, sense prevailed. She brought the horse down to a walk so she could easily avoid slow-moving carts and plodding workhorses and started looking around for an inn. Innkeepers were always the best sources of information.

Sir Nicolas reined in and surveyed the scene with disfavour. "Is this our journey's end?" he asked. "I must say, it is singularly unimpressive."

Catrin could not disagree. The wattle and daub houses were dingy, their wooden frames cracked and pitted. There was one church, a thing of squares and rectangles in dull grey stone. Next to it was the only spot of colour: a red brick gatehouse. It looked like the entrance to a manor house, and for a second her heart quickened. "But there are redeeming qualities."

"Only the manor," Sir Nicolas said, as if he knew what she was thinking. "But no one is at home."

"How do you know?"

"This is the country seat of Sir William Paulet, Marquess of Winchester, and he is at Windsor Castle. I saw him just yesterday."

Catrin held in a sigh. "We must find an inn — the horses need to rest."

"Aye, and I need to quench my thirst," Sir Nicolas said, and turned his horse to the right at the next cross-street. A wooden sign on the largest building declared it to be the Sword and Crown Inn, and a busy stable sat next to it. They released the horses to the stableboys, ordered them well cared for and retreated to the common-room. It was warm in there and smelled pleasantly of roasting meat.

Catrin asked Sir Nicolas to find a seat at a table and he removed himself with good grace. A second later the innkeeper came in. He was a tall man with massive hands, and Catrin was not surprised that he was moving a barrel of beer on his own; he seemed capable of moving the building itself. "Good morrow, my lady," he said, and wiped his hands on a towel. "What can I get for you?"

"A pint of your best ale, and a cup of your best wine," Catrin said. "And a pint for yourself — with the pleasure of your company."

The innkeeper looked at her in surprise, but Catrin did not explain. She let the barmaid take the ale to Sir Nicolas' table, then settled in a seat by the window. The innkeeper brought their drinks and settled in somewhat uneasily across from her. He did not take a drink until Catrin had.

"I am looking for someone," Catrin said without preamble, acutely aware of the passage of time. "She was here two years ago."

A slow smile spread over his face. "Did she look just like you?"

Catrin's heart ached. "Some say so, but no one could be as beautiful as she."

"Aye, beautiful she was, and a lady like yourself," the innkeeper said. "I remember — it was during the coronation of our sovereign queen. She stayed two nights."

"So she is gone?" Catrin had known … of course she had known … that her mother wouldn't still be there. And yet, she was disappointed. "Do you know where she went after that?"

"A grand gentleman of the court came late in the evening, and she left with him," the innkeeper said.

"Did she seem frightened of him? Did it seem that she was in danger?"

"Nay, she was pleased and relieved to see him, and happy to go." He took another hearty drink from his tankard. "They did leave quickly, though. So quickly that she left some of her things behind."

Catrin carefully schooled her voice so he did not hear her eagerness. "Do you still have them?"

"Aye, I wager I do." He pushed himself to his feet. "If you would wait but a moment, my lady."

"Of course," Catrin said, and took another sip of wine while he walked away. Her hand was shaking, she noticed, and could not steady it. Possibilities were swirling about within her. Could these things contain the secret to interpreting the letter? Could her mother have left a clue about her destination?

The innkeeper returned quickly, carrying a small wooden box. Catrin itched to open it then and there, but she managed to simply thank him calmly and address herself to her wine. The innkeeper left with a courtly bow, and Sir Nicolas shifted over to join her.

"Success, my lady?"

"Perhaps," she said, and looked up in surprise when an elderly man came up to the table and sketched out an uncertain bow. "Good morrow, goodman."

"Good morrow, my lady." He snatched the cap from his head as if just remembering that he wore it. "I could not help but overhear. Are you looking for the lady you spoke of?"

Her breath caught in her throat. "I may be," she said lightly. "Do you have news of her?"

"There's a lady that walks the parapet at the manor-house," the man said, and leaned close enough for her to see the small red veins criss-crossing his skin. "Hair dark as night. Skin like snow."

Catrin's hands clenched around the box. "Have you seen her?"

"Aye, many a time. I deliver flour from the mill to the manor."

"Could you take me to her?"

"Not now, no. She don't come out when the old lord is away. I think he locks her up."

Catrin fished some coins from her purse and dropped them into the man's gnarled old hand. "Thank you," she said. "Sir Nicolas, I believe it is time to go."

To his credit, Sir Nicolas didn't ask questions. "I'll have the horses brought round," he said, and left the table.

The old man tottered away calling for ale, and Catrin drained her wine. She wanted to go to the manor immediately, but knew there was no point. She would never gain admittance without the permission of its lord, and he was back at Windsor. That was where she needed to be.

Sir Nicolas returned to report that all was ready. "Are we bound for more adventures, my lady?"

Catrin stood, hoping her trembling knees would hold her. "No; we must return to court, before the queen realises we are missing."

"A wise plan, my lady." Sir Nicolas swung open the door and let her leave first. "To horse, with all haste."

CHAPTER TEN

Catrin abandoned Sir Nicolas without ceremony when they returned and took the box to the ladies' chamber. It seemed prudent to change into her gown before she looked at it, for fear someone would ask for her and find her dressed for riding. It strained her patience to its end, though, to tie ribbons and tighten laces while that small wooden box sat silent on the bed.

She sent away the chamberer who had helped her and sat down next to the box. It opened using a simple latch, and the lid did not creak as she raised it. Somehow that seemed ominous … surely the key to a two-year-old quest should not yield so easily?

The key. Catrin found herself suddenly breathless. Some of her mother's secret messages had used a keyword or phrase; once one knew the phrase, it was possible to decode the message. Why had she never thought of that before? She would have to try that method as soon as possible, but first she had to know what her mother had left behind.

A piece of linen covered the contents of the box, and Catrin took it out and spread it out on the bed for protection. Then she lifted out a piece of parchment and caught her breath when she realised it was one of her own letters, sent soon after she had first arrived at court. She had written about her meetings with various courtiers, and one of the names she had mentioned was Lord Robert Dudley's. Her mother had drawn a small hand in the margin of the letter, with the index finger pointing at Lord Robert's name.

Catrin next drew out a boxwood comb, which made tears rush to her eyes. She had seen that comb every day, all through her childhood. Inlaid with ivory in an intricate floral pattern, it was as delicate and complicated as her mother was.

She laid the comb gently on the linen, and then drew out a golden case. It seemed designed to fit onto a belt, but the loop at the top was broken and the case itself seemed loose. Catrin opened it carefully, and this time the tears flowed free. Inside was a miniature portrait of her father, his mouth set in that quirky smile she remembered so well.

She forced herself to set the portrait aside and lifted out the last item: a silver pomander with etchings of birds in flight, still full of delicate dried petals of faded pink. She held it to her nose and drew in the scent, remembering in sudden vivid clarity the time she had spent with her mother in their favourite nook in the forest, surrounded by wild climbing roses.

Slowly, she put the items back in the box, then took them to the chest at the end of the bed where she locked away all her personal items. Only once it was safely hidden amongst her linens did she take out her mother's letter and her own quill and move to one of the writing-desks.

What could the key be? Her mother had often made a grid of letters and numbers to encode her messages, and the key was always placed at the beginning. Catrin took some paper and tried to recreate it, and then tried a variety of keys. 'Dafydd', for her father. No. 'Catrin', then. That produced only gibberish. 'Cecil'? Her mother had gone to him for help, after all. Nothing.

She caught her breath, remembering that tiny drawing of a hand next to Lord Robert's name. Could it be? Hastily she filled in 'Robert' at the top of the grid and started to translate.

"Lady Catrin?"

She jumped to her feet, catching her bottle of ink just in time to save it from crashing to the floor. Lady Mary Sidney was in the doorway, obviously startled by Catrin's reaction. "Are you quite well?"

"Of course," Catrin said, and hastily gathered up the papers. "I am just writing a letter."

"I see." Lady Mary folded her hands in front of her. "The queen has asked for you."

"Thank you." Catrin wanted to kick the table in frustration, but instead she rose to her feet. "I will attend her at once."

When Catrin arrived in the royal lodgings, Lucy was sitting in the privy chamber, trying to see her embroidery by the light of the fire. Her efforts were blocked by the aged Sir William Paulet, Marquess of Winchester and Lord of the Manor in West Drayton, and the Earl of Bedford. They were sitting even closer to the fire and did not seem to see her. It was an odd pairing; the venerated marquess with the youthful and somewhat simple-headed earl, and stranger still was that they were both too intent on their conversation to notice the lady in their midst.

Catrin could not help but draw close enough to the fire to catch the earl's words. "Lord Robert's wife has died in suspicious circumstances, and so will he if he keeps the queen from marrying," he said. "And if it is discovered that he did poison his wife —"

"Do not talk of poison," the marquess hissed. "Lady Amy *fell* to her death."

Bedford shook his head. "I heard Lord Robert had been poisoning Lady Amy for months via his man, Richard Verney.

Perhaps that was taking too long, so Verney pushed her down the stairs."

The marquess' thick white eyebrows drew down until they formed a single line across his forehead. "That is a foolish and dangerous thing to say."

"I believe it is the truth, my lord," Bedford snapped. "The queen herself said Lady Amy had a malady of the breast, but I have since been told that she recovered once she left Verney's home and moved to Cumnor Place."

"One does not recover from a malady of the breast."

"That is why I think her illness was poison, not a disease," Bedford said, and then appeared to notice Lucy for the first time. "Do you agree, my lady?"

Lucy considered. "Poison would have weakened the lady and made her more susceptible to a fatal injury when she fell, so it seems an effective way to make a death look natural," she said, and let her embroidery fall to her lap. "How do we find out if it's true?"

The marquess rose to his feet with a grunt. "If we are wise, we do not meddle any further," he said shortly. "And I for one will entertain the thought of murder no longer."

He stalked away, and Catrin resumed her journey to the queen's bedchamber. She found the queen at her writing-desk, looking very royal in a taffeta gown of Tudor green, with pearls around her neck and diamonds glittering in her hair. Sir William Cecil was nearby, a sheaf of papers in his hand, his brows drawn together in concentration. Several clerks were sitting cross-legged on the floor, writing hastily on paper braced on pieces of wood.

"Ah, Lady Catrin, my talisman," the queen said, and set down her quill. "There is a wooden box in the drawer of the table by the bed; bring it here."

Catrin curtsied. "As you wish, Your Majesty," she said, and retrieved the box. Something rattled as she drew it out, so she held it very steady as she carried it back across the room.

"I wish to show you something," the queen said.

Catrin curtsied again, and waited while the queen retrieved a small key from a chain around her neck and used it to open the box. Inside, Catrin could see a miniature portrait of Lord Robert, a large unset emerald, a piece of parchment, and a necklace. It was this that the queen drew out of the box, and rested against the back of her hand to show Catrin a golden 'B' with three hanging pearls.

Catrin went breathless. "Your Majesty — is that —"

"Yes. It is my mother's necklace." The queen settled it carefully back into the box. "Saved with great difficulty when her perils began."

Her perils … the term reminded Catrin that the queen, too, knew what it was like to lose a parent on Tower Hill. "It's beautiful, Your Majesty."

"It's dangerous." The queen carefully locked the box and returned the key to its safe place beneath her bodice. "Looking into the past leads only to trouble, Lady Catrin. 'Tis far better to live in the present."

Startled, Catrin looked up and was immediately caught in the queen's gaze. She knew. Somehow, the queen knew what she had done. "Your Majesty, I only wish to know what happened to my mother."

"Mine own experience says that it is best not to know," the queen said. "I suggest you search no more."

Catrin swallowed hard. "As you wish, Your Majesty."

"Good. Now return this box to its place and take up your daily duties."

"Yes, Your Majesty." Catrin returned the box to its drawer and hastened out of the room, where her knees went suddenly weak. She leaned against the wall, breathing hard.

What to do now?

First she had to find a safer spot for her mother's things. If the queen felt that having them was dangerous, she would not hesitate to remove them.

Second, she needed to make a copy — several copies — of her mother's letter. It, too, could vanish. Like that broken blade, that coded book.

She hurried back to the ladies' chamber and searched every corner and cupboard until she found a domed coffer large enough to fit every item. Then she left the palace for the gardens, forcing herself to move at a measured pace, as if it was a normal day and she was completing her usual round of tasks.

The enforced slowness suddenly reminded her of the day she met Lucy. They had carried the queen's train in the procession during the coronation festivities: an honour, but a tedious task that Catrin had expected to lead to nothing but sore shoulders and blistered feet. Instead, fortune had favoured her. A man had approached the queen with a knife, and Lucy had seen it in time for Catrin to trip the man and save the queen.

Catrin had been the queen's talisman, or good luck charm, ever since. That one moment had led to status at court and a glimpse of the sort of freedom that was possible if she married well.

And now she was risking it all.

She would lose everything if the queen found out she was defying her, and her stepfather would be only too delighted to take everything away and watch her beg in the streets. But she felt compelled to continue — to push onward in her quest. She did not even know how to stop.

Her fingers trembled as she reached the spot in the garden where a loose stone she had found months before had revealed the perfect hiding place in the wall behind it. The domed coffer fit inside easily, but she could not leave it there without a final look at the items she had collected from the inn. The comb, the pomander, the miniature. Catrin stroked her finger over the case, and to her surprise that light touch was enough to make the portrait fall out. She picked it up and tried to fit it back in, but something was lodged in the back of the case, making it impossible. It was stuck so firmly that she had to warm the metal in her hand before she could pry it loose.

At first, it seemed to be nothing but a lump of wax, but when she tilted it to the light she could see faint ridges and lines. A coat-of-arms, perhaps? If so, she would have to ask Lucy to identify it. Lucy knew every coat-of-arms in the realm.

Catrin set the portrait carefully inside the case and closed it all in, locking the coffer carefully and hiding the key in her skirts. Then she fitted the stone into place, scuffed out any sign of her presence on the ground, and left the gardens.

She felt safer with those precious items hidden. Knowing that no one could take them from her smoothed out the tangle of her thoughts, and suddenly she could think clearly. Which was surely why one particular question jumped into her mind at that moment — a question she should have asked before.

How had the queen known about Catrin's journey?

Catrin stopped short. Sir Nicolas — it had to be. Only he had been privy to it. Catrin did not know how he had determined her purpose, but she did not need to know. The fact remained that he had violated her trust, and his own oath of honour.

And she would tell him so, the very second that the opportunity arose.

CHAPTER ELEVEN

Catrin found Sir Nicolas on the new wharf, leaning lazily against the balustrade while he tossed scraps of bread to the seagulls. He straightened when he saw her, and a beatific smile spread over his face. "Lady Catrin, will you marry me?"

An unexpected question, but she was so angry that it did not even knock her off her stride. "I would not marry a man who breaks his vow within hours of making it."

His face went wooden. "If you were a man, I would demand satisfaction for such an insult."

"If I were a man, I would have run you through by now," Catrin snapped. "You have placed me in great danger, and thus it is I who deserves satisfaction."

"What danger?" he cried. "I have done nothing against you, my lady!"

"The queen knows of our journey," Catrin said. "She knows, and there is only one person who could have told her. You."

"Nay, indeed — there are spies everywhere at court. She could have found out from any of them."

Catrin's spine went rigid. "I notice you do not deny the charge."

"Of course I deny the charge!" He lifted his hands, palms outward. "Which is more likely, that I betrayed your trust, or that a servant saw us leave and took the opportunity to earn an extra penny or two?"

"A servant could not have known what my purpose was," Catrin said. "Only you could have learned that."

"But I did not," Sir Nicolas said hotly. "Upon my honour, I still do not know."

"You dare speak of honour to me?" Catrin turned her back on him. "I was right not to trust you. Leave me now, and do not speak to me again."

Sir Nicolas stormed away without another word, and Catrin crossed to the balustrade and stared out over the Thames, the wind whipping the silk of her hood around her face. She heard familiar footsteps and knew Lucy was approaching, but was too angry to greet her. Lucy seemed to pick up on her mood, for she stopped a few paces away and was silent for several minutes.

Finally, she spoke. "You have been a hard person to find this morning."

Catrin's fingers clenched around the balustrade. "So you too know my secret. Is there nothing sacred in this cursed place?"

"I know no secrets of yours," Lucy said stiffly. "But I have managed to discover that Sir William Cecil's man hasn't been anywhere near Amy Dudley."

Catrin sent her a flat stare. "I don't know what you're talking about."

"The missing secretary; the one Sir Nicolas mentioned. Christopher is his name. He was injured in late summer; that is why he is not at court."

Catrin passed a hand over her forehead. "I see."

"He has been home in Hampshire, which is nowhere near Cumnor."

A well-planned excuse, no doubt. "And how do you know this?"

"Another of Sir William's secretaries told me."

Catrin turned to face her. "Has he *seen* the injured man?"

"No… Sir William told him what had happened when he arrived at court."

Of course he did. "I see."

Lucy flushed. "Sir William wouldn't tell a falsehood, Catrin."

Catrin pursed her lips. "Lucy, dearling, if he was as truthful as you claim, he would not have retained his lands during the reign of Catholic Mary. Nor would he have the position at court he now holds."

Tears sprung to Lucy's eyes and she hid her face in her hands. "It wasn't him, Catrin. It *wasn't*."

Catrin's anger vanished in the face of her friend's distress. "Dearling, do not weep. I merely meant —"

"Do not say any more."

Catrin clasped her hands together, fingers entwined so tightly they hurt. "Prithee, do not be angry. I did not mean to upset you."

"*I'm not upset.*" Lucy's shout startled a gull, which took flight with a screech.

Catrin raised her eyebrow. "Oh, my, you are right. I was mistook. 'Tis clear now that you are all sunshine and sugar cones."

"Do not mock me," Lucy said, but there was no sting to the words. Indeed, a faint smile was already peeking through. "You are a very difficult person to stay angry with, Catrin Surovell."

"Not all would agree with you, but I appreciate the sentiment." Catrin took a step toward her. "And I appreciate your loyalty to Sir William — I do. I just think that he, too, has a reason to kill Amy Dudley."

Lucy's face darkened once again. "I'm sure he wouldn't — I'm sure he didn't —"

"Yes, I know. But I wonder what makes you so sure." Catrin folded her hands in front of her. "I hope you know, dearling, that I am neither judge nor jury. If you have anything you'd like to tell me, remember that I keep the secrets of my friends as if they were my own."

"Oh, I am aware." It was Lucy's turn to watch the waters of the Thames roll and heave. "You have many secrets to keep … including a mysterious journey away from court."

"So you do know my — ah, I see now. That is why you were upset." A strand of Catrin's hair loosened and fluttered in the wind. She thrust it behind her ear. "Dearest, I didn't tell you for your own protection."

Lucy's lip trembled. "I would rather not be protected if it means Sir Nicolas becomes your boon companion instead of me."

Catrin scowled. "Sir Nicolas is not my boon companion and never will be."

"Then why did you choose to journey with him?"

"I didn't — he insisted on coming with me." Catrin sighed. "I will tell you if you wish — but be warned, the queen is not happy with what I have done."

That gave Lucy pause. "Does it have to do with your mother?"

"Aye. I was told where she went after she left Ashbourne Manor two years ago, and I went there to find out more. She was not there, but I learned more about what happened and an innkeeper gave me some of her things."

"That was a journey well taken, then," Lucy said. "Do you know where she went next?"

"Perhaps. And I also found something which may tell me who went with her." Catrin drew the piece of wax from her purse. "It was in a case behind a miniature of my father."

"It's sealing wax," Lucy said, and examined the marks on it with a critical eye. "With a partial imprint of a coat-of-arms. Do you know whose family it belongs to?"

"I had hoped it was the crest of Sir William Paulet, Marquess of Winchester. It seems he may be connected to my mother."

"No, it is not. I am familiar with that crest, and I have not seen this one before." Lucy sent Catrin a tentative smile. "But I can find out whose family it is, if you like."

"I do like." Catrin took a breath and surrendered the precious seal to her friend. "Thank you."

When Catrin and Lucy arrived back in the royal apartments, the bedchamber was full of ladies sewing, brushing clothes, pinning ribbons and counting pearls. Mistress Ashley immediately started scolding Lucy for the tangled state of the pillowcase she was supposed to be embroidering, and then turned on Catrin. "And you!" she said indignantly. "Did I not give you one of Her Majesty's nightgowns to hem?"

"Yes, Mistress," Catrin said meekly. "I left it in a coffer in the privy chamber to keep it safe until I could return to it."

"Fetch it now, then."

Catrin hurried to obey, but a few steps into the chamber she stopped as if she had run into a wall. The Earl of Shrewsbury was looking out the window, loneliness etched on every line of his face. And Sir William Paulet was nodding off by the fire.

Either man was far more important than the queen's newest nightgown. The earl could be Catrin's future: she was sure it would not take much to convince him he needed a wife, and then she would have the money and freedom she craved. But the marquess … he could tell her of her past. He could tell her about the dark-haired lady living in his country home.

And if she asked, she was ignoring the queen's wishes. Could she risk it?

The question was answered before it fully formed in her mind. Her feet were already moving toward Sir William Paulet. She settled on a low cushion beside him and he sat up, peering at her suspiciously. "Lady Catrin," he said, and drew his robe more tightly around him. "What do you need?"

Catrin smiled. "Why must I need something to come and sit with you, my good lord?"

"Youth and beauty seek not old age," the marquess said dryly.

"But they do seek wisdom," Catrin said solemnly.

He laughed a thin laugh that ended on a cough. "Only if they are already wise."

Catrin leaned forward. "Or longing for answers."

The marquess' old eyes sharpened. "What answers, prithee?"

Catrin laced her fingers together over her knee. "I'm looking for my mother."

He leaned forward and rested his dry, wrinkled hand on hers. "You are a young, bright, fair maiden, Lady Catrin. There is no need to taint these precious years by worrying about —"

"I cannot just forget her, my lord. It would be like abandoning her."

He sighed. "Sometimes it is best to forget, child."

Catrin closed her eyes for a moment, gathering her courage. "I recently discovered that she was sent to West Drayton, where you have your country seat. Did you ever see her there?"

He gazed at her for a long moment. "I cannot answer that without the queen's permission," he said, and looked up sharply when the Duke of Norfolk approached them.

Norfolk bowed low. "Apologies for interrupting your discourse," he said. "I must speak to Lady Catrin."

Catrin rose to her feet and let the duke draw her away. "Does something ail thee, your grace?"

He spread his hands wide. "Some would say so, some would say not."

"Some would say cold, some would say hot," Catrin responded dryly. "What would *you* say?"

"It is what Her Majesty says that matters." He rested a hand on the pommel of his sword. "She wishes us to go to Cumnor Place after all."

Thwarted again. "I thought she wanted to wait for the coroner's report?"

"The royal mind has changed," the duke said wryly, and seemed about to add something else when he noticed the Earl of Shrewsbury approaching rapidly from across the room. "Can we help you, your lordship?"

"I wish a word with her ladyship, your grace." He did not give the duke much of an option, taking Catrin's arm and escorting her to a cosy corner behind a massive cupboard. His urgency was really quite satisfying, and an opportunity not to be missed.

She sent him a winsome smile. "It is such an unexpected pleasure to be alone with you, Sir Francis."

For a moment he looked pleased and flattered, but his face quickly fell back into serious lines. "Is it true you have been tasked to return to Cumnor?"

"As I have just discovered myself, yes it is."

That troubled him. He paced out a quick circle and then returned to her side. "I need to tell you something in confidence."

She gazed up at him through her lashes, as if all she wanted to do in the world was listen. "Of course, your lordship."

"I recently discovered that the queen knew Lady Dudley was ill before anyone else — even Lord Robert himself."

"Ah, but Her Majesty sees all and knows all," Catrin said mischievously. "That is what she tells her ladies, at least."

The earl responded with a grim smile. "And perhaps it is true. The question remains how she knew so soon, and why it interested her so much that her favourite's wife seemed on death's door."

It was almost like he was suggesting that the queen knew in advance that Amy Dudley was going to die, and that was a dangerous suggestion indeed. Catrin straightened. "Are you saying...?"

"Nay, indeed. To say such a thing would be treason." He took her hand, holding it lightly in both of his. "I just want to ensure you are aware that it may be best to fail in this task the queen has set for you."

For a moment she just stared at him, speechless. "How?"

He squeezed her hand. "That I must leave to you," he said, and took his leave of her. Catrin retreated further behind the cupboard so she had a moment to think. The queen had talked about Lady Amy's illness several times — she had even mentioned it to the Spanish ambassador during her birthday celebrations. Most people had interpreted that as concern for a favourite's wife, but what if she had wanted to prepare everyone for news of her death? What if she had hoped it would make people less suspicious? And when Bowes had come with the news, the queen's first question had been whether Lady Amy had died in her bed. She had not been surprised by the death, but by the manner of it. That, too, suggested that she knew Lady Amy would die.

But no — it did not make sense. Why would she send Catrin to investigate Amy Dudley's death if she already knew who killed her? It would be better to do nothing and let the incident fade from everyone's memory. The queen was clever enough to know that. Perhaps she really did think that Catrin wouldn't find anything, and report as much. That would stop speculation at court, and Lord Robert would finally be at peace. Or, perhaps she was sending Catrin because she believed her to be loyal enough to destroy anything that would incriminate the crown.

Another possibility occurred to Catrin then, one which made prickles run up and down her spine. Perhaps it was all a ruse, to get her away from the court and in a suitably lonely and isolated place. Perhaps the intention was that she — and her questions about her mother — would never return from Cumnor.

A hand landed on her shoulder. "Lady Catrin."

Catrin jumped and spun around, to find the duke standing there wearing a puzzled expression. "Are you ready, my lady?" he asked. "We must leave at once."

"Almost, your grace," Catrin said, and swallowed hard. "I'll just go and … gather what I need."

CHAPTER TWELVE

The afternoon light was deeply golden when Catrin and the Duke of Norfolk left Windsor. They cantered steadily past fields rich with grain and bordered by shrubs, while ahead and behind them rode two of the duke's men, almost invisible in their black livery.

Catrin was glad she had changed into the thicker of her two travelling-costumes; the dark blue velvet offered good protection against the crisp autumn chill. She suspected that the duke wished he had made a similar choice; he seemed distinctly uncomfortable in his thin woollen cloak and satin doublet.

"Are you all right, your grace?" she asked, when he tugged at his collar for the tenth time.

"Aye; it is a new doublet and I find it somewhat stiff, that is all," he said, and sent her a sideways glance. "You have a good riding-seat, my lady."

"Thank you."

"I rather expected you to be reluctant to make this journey again."

So had she. She was as surprised as anyone that she had not made a more vigorous effort to fob this task onto someone else. Had she been manipulated? "I live to serve the queen."

Norfolk laughed at that. "I doubt you're that idealistic."

"Perhaps not." She considered, but decided against striking up a flirtation. After all, he was newly wed and — worse still — there were rumours that his family clung to the old queen's religious beliefs. "But then again, perhaps I am. This whole journey has been quite fascinating."

"It is a waste of time," Norfolk said. "'Tis obvious who arranged this death, but only I seem able to see it."

"By that, I assume you mean that you do not think Lord Robert killed her?"

"Nay, indeed. The man is far too intent on his religion and as greedy as a child, but he is not unintelligent. He would know that a scandal such as this would make it less likely that he will become king, not more."

"So whom do you suspect?"

Norfolk sent Catrin a wary look and she laughed.

"Fear not, your grace, I am not so unwise as to tell tales at court."

He hesitated, but finally lowered his voice so low she could barely hear it over the squeaking of the saddles. "Sir William Cecil."

Interesting. "Because the scandal reduces Lord Robert's influence over the queen and increases his own?"

"And could well ensure that Robert Dudley is never king of England." Norfolk shrugged. "If the woman had died a natural death, there would be far less resistance to the marriage. Still some, but less."

"Including your own?"

"A queen should not marry her horse-keeper," Norfolk said with a curl to his lip. "Do you not agree?"

Catrin knew better than to answer. "Perhaps we will find evidence to prove your theory at Cumnor Place."

"God willing." Their path turned to the west and the sun lit his face in an orange-yellow glow. "Tell me, my lady, do *you* think Lord Robert killed his wife?"

She knew better than to answer that, too. "The most likely explanation is that it was an accident."

Norfolk snorted. "And do you think that anyone is likely to accept that explanation?"

Catrin stroked her horse's glossy black mane with one gloved hand. "Perhaps, if the evidence is compelling."

"The evidence against it is the more compelling. The queen told me that there were two deep dints in Lady Dudley's head! That information must be hidden for anyone to believe it was an accident."

"I do not believe in hiding information, my lord."

"Do you not? How very noble of you." He chuckled. "I admire you greatly, Lady Catrin."

She decided a little flirtation wouldn't hurt and sent him a coy glance over her shoulder. "And I you, your grace."

Their arrival at Cumnor Place caused a stir. A man carrying a sheaf of paper saw them coming and ran into the great hall, waving the paper like a flag above his head. Grooms appeared from the stables to take their horses, and Gryse took charge of the saddlebags, grinning with delight when Catrin waved at him.

Master Forster dashed out of the great hall a moment later, hurrying to greet them. "Welcome, your grace — and my lady," he said, but shifted his feet restlessly as if he would prefer to be anywhere else. "May I offer you food and drink?"

"Yes," Norfolk said, and offered Catrin his arm before he started toward the hall. Master Forster had to break into a trot to keep up with them. "Did you receive the queen's message?"

"Yes, your grace," Master Forster said breathlessly. "Though I do not believe there is anything here that would shed light on this tragic event. Why, even the coroner has ruled it an accident."

Norfolk stopped walking. "The verdict has been handed down?"

"Aye. I sent a messenger to the queen about an hour ago."

"She will receive it tomorrow morning, then, I wager. And that means that Robert Dudley will be re-installed at court before we have even finished our search," Norfolk said grimly. "As I told my lady Catrin — this journey was a waste of time."

Master Forster brightened. "So will you abandon your plans and return to court?"

"Nay, indeed — we must obey the queen's request until she tells us otherwise," Norfolk said, then turned to Catrin. "After we dine, my lady, I will begin by talking to the servants. Will you investigate Lady Dudley's chamber for any signs of distress that could have led to suicide, or any threat that could have resulted in murder?"

"Yes, your grace," Catrin said, although she had every intention of doing far more than that.

"Excellent." Norfolk clapped Master Forster on the back, releasing a rather embarrassing amount of dust. "And now to the wine."

Without Picto's grief to distract her this time, it was far easier for Catrin to examine Lady Dudley's chamber. Catrin stood in the doorway and let her gaze travel, searching for anything that seemed odd or out of place. The room was a large one, and appointed in a way that befitted a lady of Amy Dudley's status.

On the left, a fireplace without a surround, made of grey stones too large and heavy to create convenient hiding-nooks in either hearth or chimney. Directly before her, a window with a deep sill piled with cushions, next to the shelves where Catrin had found the coded book. To the right, a canopied bed with thick curtains, and a satin screen behind which Lady Dudley had changed her clothes.

Several chests sat in the far corner, and Catrin went to them first. The first contained Lady Dudley's clean linens, lying in crisp readiness. The second contained various sleeves, shawls and scarves, wrapped up in bundles of lavender. The third contained quills, ink bottles, paper and books such as *The Properties of Herbs*, *Many Excellent Remedies Against Diverse Diseases*, and *The Book of Common Prayer*. The last and smallest contained only a small silver rattle and a baby's linen smock, embroidered with silken thread around the neck and hem. The linen was old and yellowed, and the stitching obviously done by a youthful hand. It was the remnant of a dream, long treasured, and long lost.

Catrin closed the chest with a twinge of regret for opening it, and moved on to the bookshelves. Unfortunately, they yielded nothing new, and the windowsill was attached firmly to the stone wall beneath it, yielding no hidden spaces.

Next she laid down on the floor and slid under the bed. The mattress was pristine, the ropes suspending it lying in neat undisturbed rows. The wooden planks of the floor were solid, too; there were no creaks that spoke of a hollow core.

Catrin slid out again, annoyed that she had gotten covered in dust for no reason, and brushed off her gown before she went to investigate the headboard. It was made of square panels of ash, set out in neat rows. Each panel had the Dudley crest in the middle, with its bear and ragged staff. They were not the most skilled carvings Catrin had ever seen, but the bears did have an air of realism. She slid her finger over the closest waving paw, and to her surprise the whole bear moved.

Of course! A perfect place to hide treasures. Catrin slid her fingers gently behind the bear and tugged, and the whole panel slid out from the headboard so that she found herself holding a wooden box with a lid. There was no lock; she could lift the lid free with just a tug.

"My lady!"

The voice made her jump upright. Gryse was peeking at her from the doorway, something white dangling from his fingers. "God's heart, child, you startled me."

"Sorry, my lady." He tiptoed into the room. "I found something."

"What is it?"

He held out a ragged paper, charred at the edges with holes burned into it so that some of the words were gone. She let it rest on the tips of her fingers so she could read it.

destroy Lord Robert's wife.
she was not ill at all
I suppose they would send me to the Tower
before they would let me go
Dudley would be better in paradise than here

Catrin took a deep steadying breath. "Where did you find this?"

"In the fireplace, my lady. In the great hall."

"Did you see anyone put it there?"

"No, my lady." His eyes rounded with anxiety. "Should I have left it?"

"No, Gryse, you did exactly the right thing," Catrin said. "We shall have to show it to his grace."

"Yes." Gryse tilted his head, listening. "I think he is coming now, my lady."

He was right; Norfolk himself stepped into the room moments later, and he did not look pleased. "The servants know nothing and there is no evidence of any wrongdoing," he said. "This has been a useless exercise."

"Take heart, your grace." Catrin hefted the wooden box on one hand. "Both Gryse and I have had better luck."

"So you have." His sharp gaze rested on the space she had left in the headboard and then on the box in her hand. "I suggest you open it, my lady."

"Certainly," Catrin said, and set the box down on the bed so she could remove the lid. The scent of primroses floated up around her, released by a small vial of oil tucked in one corner. In the opposite corner lay a cloth bag filled with coins, and in the middle were five sheets of blank paper.

"An odd collection," Norfolk said. "Perhaps Lady Dudley was of a strange mind after all."

"These things certainly don't seem worth hiding," Catrin murmured, and trailed a finger over the thick, rough paper. She wondered why Lady Dudley hadn't hidden the coded book instead, but didn't think it wise to voice such a thought aloud. Instead she closed the box and slid it back into place in the headboard. "But it does not matter, your grace. Gryse has found something that will prove far more helpful."

Gryse picked up the paper with delicate fingers and carried it over to the duke.

Norfolk took one glance and asked, "Do you recognize the script? It is the hand of Sir William Cecil."

"Then your suspicions were correct."

Norfolk tugged on his collar. "So it would seem."

CHAPTER THIRTEEN

Lucy knew some of the clerks, and they were used to her coming in to look at the records that were stored in their writing-room. As always, they were sitting on benches on both sides of the long, pitted table in the centre of the room, hunched over their papers. Their sleeping-rolls were lined up neatly against every wall but one, where giant cupboards held leather-bound volumes and massive scrolls. There were even some loose sheaves of paper, tied with ribbon and stacked all the way to the broad wooden beams of the roof.

The only sound was the scratching of their quills and the guttering of the candles in the draught. The room was icy cold despite the fire, for they kept the windows open to let as much light in as possible, and Lucy shivered as she took down a familiar volume from a middle shelf. It was a collection of information about the peers of the realm, including their family histories, colours and coats-of-arms. Sir William Cecil had shown it to her weeks ago, during one of their discussions about the great houses.

She carried it over to the fire, sat down on a low stool and carefully drew the broken seal from the purse on her belt. It was a shame that the fragment was so small, because it had to be important or Catrin's mother would not have hidden it so carefully. It had to mean something.

Seals were always simpler than the coat-of-arms they represented, simply because it was hard to etch an entire coat-of-arms into the stamp. They were also small, making it hard to see the finer details, so all she could make out was part of a shield and what looked like wavy lines, next to an animal's head. She searched through the pages, trying to find a match, but nothing quite fitted. After an hour, during which the clerks seemed to grow less and less content with her presence, she gave up and returned the volume to its shelf. Sir William, she knew, had much more detailed records; she would have to ask for his help.

The very thought pleased her, so she was smiling as she returned to the royal apartments. But then a page approached her with a letter, intricately folded and sealed with wax. The imprint was simple; just 'CS' in flowing script.

Immediately Lucy knew something was wrong. She thanked the boy and hurried to a window-seat so that she could see better. It was fortunate that she did, for when she opened the letter a key fell out; a key so tiny she was sure it would have been lost between the floorboards had she opened it while standing. As it was, she had a moment's panic trying to find it within the folds of her skirts.

With the key safely secured in her pomander, she turned her attention to the letter.

Lucy,

I am off to Cumnor after all, and in truth, I am afeared.

I need to know that someone will continue to look for my poor mother if anything should happen to me. I want you to know that I have hidden all the information and clues that I have found, so you can use them to keep looking. If I do not return from Cumnor, find our favourite lady. She will point to where I have hidden them.

Prithee burn this letter once you have read it; it will be safer for both of us.

Catrin

Lucy read the letter again, tears prickling her eyelids. Then she slid slowly down from the window-seat, walked into the privy chamber and directly to the fire. She cast the paper in and watched it blacken and crinkle, ignoring the curious looks from those around her.

Hours later, Lucy still could not forget about the letter. It occupied her thoughts so completely that her embroidery lay on her lap, the needle still stuck in the fabric and her hands at her sides. She heard some of the ladies muttering about her idleness, but she did not care. Catrin seemed to think that she might not return from Cumnor, and that made Lucy worry.

The queen rose from her chair and wandered over to the window, her skirts trailing behind her. She stared out, twisting her coronation ring around and around her little finger, and everyone could see that she was deep in thought and did not wish to be disturbed.

Well, almost everyone. Katherine Grey piped up then, breaking the silence. "Would you like me to make you a posset, Your Majesty?"

"No."

"Perhaps some wine? Candied fruit?"

The queen sent her a withering glance. "No."

Katherine subsided, looking strangely pleased with herself until her sister rolled her eyes in exasperation. She could not read the mood in the room for all the gold in the Tower.

The door to the privy chamber swung open with a bang, and they all jumped. A guard leapt into the opening, just in time to block the entrance of a figure in a familiar scarlet doublet. "No admittance. The queen wishes to be alone."

The figure collapsed over the guard's arm. "Your Majesty, in your mercy, grant me an audience! I beg of thee!"

The voice was as familiar as the doublet. The queen sighed. "So granted. Come in, Sir Nicolas."

Sir Nicolas pushed past the guard and dropped to his knees before the queen. "Your Majesty, I beg you to allow me to leave the court."

The queen sat down in her chair by the fire and leaned a weary head on her hand. "Why do you wish to leave?"

"I must find Lady Catrin. I must help her."

"She has help from the Duke of Norfolk, Swann. What need has she of you?"

His face crumpled. "I fear for her, out in the wilds…"

"…of an English village?" The queen laughed. "She will be safe enough."

"She believes that I betrayed her — I cannot bear to think that I might never have a chance to prove that I did not — would not —"

"As I have said, she will be safe enough. She will return."

"But what if Lord Robert finds out about her mission? He might —"

The queen's eyes sparked in sudden fury. "Young fool, do not tempt too far a prince's patience."

"But Your Majesty —"

"*We have spoken.*"

The words actually echoed, making the ladies shiver, and even Sir Nicolas had the sense to know he had gone too far.

"Yes, Your Majesty," he murmured, and rose to his feet. He backed so hastily out of the room that he stumbled more than once, and the queen sighed.

"We must prepare for the evening meal," she said. "And once it is over, may blessed sleep grant us all oblivion."

Sir William Cecil came to dine in the queen's chambers that evening, and Lucy was grateful. She wasn't sure she would have had the courage to go to his rooms. As it was, once the ceremony was over and the plates finally emptied, people started moving about and it was easy to rise from her place and cross the room toward him — or would have been, had her knees not weakened beneath her when he smiled.

"Lady Lucretia. Are you well?"

"Yes, your lordship. And I have a question for you about the history of the great houses."

He was immediately interested; she could tell because his grey eyes gleamed silver. "Indeed, my lady? I hope I can answer it."

She drew a rubbing of the coat-of-arms from the purse at her belt, having hidden the wax seal away … just in case. "Do you know to which family this belongs?"

He took the paper and squinted at it, then held it so close to a candelabra she feared it would catch fire. "It is not a shield I recognize," he said thoughtfully. "Partly because it is incomplete. What would you say these shapes would be, were they whole?"

"Sunbursts?" she suggested tentatively. "Those wavering lines could be rays."

"Aye, and that shape there might be a boar's head … I believe I see crude tusks. Forsooth, that tells us nothing. There are neither sunbursts nor boars on any crests I know."

"Nor I," she said. "Could it be a former crest, for a family which has adopted a new one?"

"That seems most likely." He tilted it again. "May I keep this, my lady? If so, I will consult my records."

"Certainly," she said, and winced when Lady Mary Grey called her name from across the room. The woman's strident tone always cut through the chatter like a knife through flesh.

Sir William chuckled. "What does she want of you?"

"A fourth for a game of cards, or another lady to complete the dancing," she said, and pulled a face at the thought.

"Are you obliged to answer?"

"Not if you rescue me," she said hopefully, and he laughed again.

"Then I have immediate need of a partner for chess," he said. "Do have a seat, my lady."

It was no use; Lucy could not sleep. Sir William had been so merry over their game … and it wasn't difficult to guess the reason. With Lord Robert removed from court, the queen was once again listening to him. He was rarely out of her sight, in fact. And as much as it pained her, Lucy had to wonder: had he orchestrated this tragedy, or was he merely clever enough to know how to benefit from it?

With all her heart, she hoped it was the latter.

Lady Mary Sidney, on the pallet next to her, rolled over abruptly and her hand fell against Lucy's chest, knocking the wind from her lungs. She sat up, gasping, and heard a hiss from across the room, warning her to be quiet.

That tipped the scale. Enough was enough. She got up, slipped into her dressing-gown and slippers, and left the queen's bedchamber. Two of the esquires, charged with the security of the queen's rooms at night, stood up when they saw her and settled down again just as quickly. She pointed to the door and they nodded sleepily and let her go.

It was not like her to wander the corridors at night, but she could not stop herself. She walked for what felt like hours, listening to the creaks and groans of the ancient walls and the scampering of small creatures. Finally she found herself overlooking the moonlit upper court and the newly finished fountain. Water splashed merrily over its slender columns, falling from the delicate dome at the top to the hexagonal basin at the bottom. She leaned against the stone to watch the water play in the silvery light, and at long last felt her shoulders relax.

Then a shadow moved below. She watched idly as a man in a long, dark cloak moved from the edges of the court to the pool of moonlight around the fountain. He stood still, waiting, his head obscured by his hood, until another figure emerged from the shadows. This one was small and slight, and Lucy fancied it was a woman although she could not truly tell. She, too, wore a heavy cloak with a hood.

They faced each other, and began to speak most intently — or so she guessed from their gestures. She wondered idly if they were lovers, but then they parted as quickly as they had met and merged back into the shadows. Not lovers, then — lovers would have left together. But who else would meet in secret and at night?

The obvious answer was unsettling, and Lucy quickly decided that it was best she return to her pallet. Some facets of the truth were far too perilous to see.

CHAPTER FOURTEEN

Catrin lay on her back in her bed, staring into darkness. The scent of primroses hung in the air, as if Amy Dudley herself was standing in the room, and that faint presence made Catrin unable to stop thinking about the meagre contents of the hidden box. The Duke of Norfolk considered the search over and the answer found, but she wasn't so sure. Why would anyone hide blank paper?

There was nothing for it; she had to look more closely. She pulled on her riding boots and dressing-gown, strapped the sheath of her *stiletto* to her arm, then lit a candle and carried it out into the courtyard. Even with the protection of four tall stone walls, the air was cold enough to make her shiver, and the crescent moon gave barely enough light to make the cobblestones glow. She thought she saw light flare in one of the upper rooms, but darkness returned so quickly she decided she was imagining it.

She tiptoed to the top of the stairs where Lady Dudley had met her end, holding tight to the balustrade just in case, and slipped into the lady's chamber. There was nothing there but a still stronger scent of primroses, and the cold ash of a long-dead fire. Catrin lit another candle and retrieved the box from its hiding-place in the headboard, spreading out its contents on the bed.

A shadow moved in the doorway. "My lady?"

Catrin jumped, making the papers on the bed crinkle sharply. "Gryse! You scared me. Why aren't you asleep?"

"My pallet is in the great hall, my lady. I saw you go by. Do you need help?"

Catrin fingered the bag with the coins in, making them clink, but kept her eye on the paper. "Can you think of any reason why someone would hide that?"

Gryse crept closer to the light. "No, my lady."

Perhaps it was another pinprick code. Catrin held each sheet up to the light, but saw only the twisting fibres. Which reminded her of something her mother had once done. She held the paper over the candle, so close that Gryse drew in a breath.

"Lady, beware!"

"I will be careful, Gryse."

He stared as she held it closer still. "What are you doing?"

"There may be a sort of ink on this page that reacts to heat." She waited until her fingers tingled from their proximity to the flame, but nothing showed. She tried again with the second page. And then the third.

"My lady!"

"Yes, I see it," Catrin murmured. Spidery lines were turning dark brown against the creamy paper; she shifted it around until all corners had felt the heat and two line drawings gradually emerged. A field spread across the top half of the page, with a single tree on the left and an alder grove to the right. On the bottom was the outline of a man holding a spear.

Gryse's eyes went round with awe. "How pretty."

"Yes, they're well done. And well hidden," Catrin said, and peered closer at the drawing of the single tree. A tiny drawing that seemed to be hovering beside it revealed itself to be a hand, with the index finger pointing at the tree's largest branch. And that, too, reminded her of something — not her mother, but Lord Robert and what he had said of his early memories of his wife. "Gryse, is there an apple tree here?"

"Three, my lady. In the garden."

"Could you show me, please?"

He glanced outside at the looming dark, swallowed hard and nodded. Catrin didn't give him a chance to change his mind, but led the way out of the room and down the stairs. Her heels thudded on the stone, and once again instinct made her hold tight to the balustrade.

For the second time that night she picked her way across the courtyard in the half-dark, although this time Gryse's small sturdy figure carried a second candle at her side. He protected the flame with his hand as they slipped through the south entrance and the wind suddenly picked up, making the light dance and flicker against the tree trunks. The moon's light was strong, enough for them to move along the paths without stumbling, and for some late-blooming flowers to show dull yellow against the grey-green foliage beneath them.

Gryse led her to a trio of wide-reaching gnarled trees that hung heavy with fruit. The nearest one had a thick branch that started nearly at the ground and extended far out, easily the strongest of any of them. Two-thirds of the way along it, a dark patch spoke of a possible hollow. Just what she had been hoping for.

She handed her candle to Gryse. "Hold it up as high as you can," she said, and stepped up onto the branch.

He stretched himself high enough for the candles to light the entire branch, and watched as she slid her way toward the hollow. The voluminous linen of her nightclothes hindered her progress somewhat, and the heavy fabric of her dressing-gown made her slower than she had been when she had climbed trees as a child, but finally she made it.

She peered into the hollow and saw nothing to concern her, so she reached in a hand and felt around in the crevice until her fingers touched oiled leather. She tugged it out and found herself holding a fair-sized satchel, complete with a very useful strap. She slung it over her shoulder to hold the satchel steady, and reversed her slow crawl back to the ground.

"What is it, my lady?"

Something flickered at the edge of her vision. She looked up just as a pale fluttering figure slipped behind a large cotton lavender bush. The grey-white branches waved as if in protest, but though she strained her ears she couldn't hear retreating footsteps. It unsettled her. "I don't know yet," she said. "Take me back to Lady Dudley's chamber, please."

"Yes, my lady." Gryse led the way at a fast pace, as if he too sensed something in the air. Fresh gusts of wind made the flowers twist and bend and the leaves rustle restlessly, and the ground crunched under their feet. It felt like the garden was full, somehow, even though she could not see another soul.

She was grateful to be back inside, and even the twisting staircase didn't hold so many terrors. But at the doorway of Lady Dudley's chamber, Catrin stopped short. Something was different. Something made the hairs stand up on the back of her neck. It only took a second to determine what it was.

The scent of primroses was gone.

For a full minute, Catrin couldn't move. Gryse slipped around her and into the room, holding out a hand as if to help. "What's wrong, my lady?"

Catrin shook her head. "It's cold, that's all. Prithee light a fire, and then you can return to your bed — or stay here, if that would be more comfortable."

"I will stay here, my lady. With you."

"Very well."

Gryse busied himself at the fireplace, and Catrin lit fresh candles off the stubs of the ones they had brought. Then she sat down on the bed again and opened the satchel. It was full of papers, more crinkled than those in the box. She drew out the first and found what looked like a draft letter, unsigned and without any salutation at the top. The ink was blotched and the writing hard to read, but one part stood out clearly.

I desire you to take pains to discover whether the queen has taken my beloved Husband from me. If so she is no sovereign of mine

Catrin stared at the words. Was Amy Dudley so foolish as to commit such thoughts to paper? Perhaps foolish wasn't the word — perhaps this was the 'desperation' Picto had mentioned. Catrin glanced at Gryse, now lying prone before the dancing flames of the fire, and slid the paper out of sight beneath the coverlet, just in case.

The second paper, also a letter, described Lady Dudley's fears of poison and blamed the queen for putting her in such danger. The third was written by a different hand, in large and heavy strokes that made Catrin think the author was a man.

Leave the knife under the Cross in Cheap and he will collect it. She will pass the Standard and trumpets will sound; that will be his cue. When she passes the little conduit he will spring forward like God's justice and dispatch her back to hell. Thus will the coronation procession be the royal bastard's beginning and her end.

Catrin pressed her hand to her mouth, memories flooding her mind. This was exactly what had happened on the day when she had first come to the queen's attention. The man had appeared out of nowhere as they passed the little conduit, and she could still see the hatred in his eyes as he raised the knife above his head. This was proof that someone had sent him. Someone had been conspiring against the queen.

But who? Catrin sorted through the rest of the pile. There was a printed tract filled with horrible vitriol about the queen's lineage and behaviour, and a piece of music with lyrics scrawled underneath. Finally, there was a page written in a strange spidery scrawl, using thick black ink that had bled through the paper. It was a string of symbols, letters and numbers that looked much like the secret messages her mother had designed. Would this be as difficult to decipher?

Catrin chose a blank piece of paper and sharpened a quill, and a yawn surprised her just as she filled it with ink. She forced herself to start methodically tracking patterns in the words, but soon the markings on the page began to waver and float before her eyes. She set aside the ink bottle before she spilled it and decided to take a little rest. Not long — just enough to refresh her for the work ahead. Just a little rest…

She leaned back, and was asleep before her head settled on the pillow.

"Lady! Lady!"

Catrin awoke with a start. The air was thick with smoke, and great clouds of it billowed underneath the closed door. She was propped up against the pillows, and a heavy drowsiness weighted down her limbs. "Gryse?"

"Here, my lady!" The boy stumbled toward her, coughing terribly. "We must go — quick, my lady. We must go."

"One moment." Catrin forced herself upright, her lungs burning with every breath, and snatched up the papers, including the one she had hidden under the coverlet. At the last second she pulled the papers out of the hidden box in the headboard as well, and stuffed them all into the leather pouch. She threw the strap over her shoulder just as Gryse headed toward the door.

"Not there!" Catrin cried, but it was too late. Gryse opened the door and the space was suddenly filled with flame. He threw up his arms to protect his face and screamed as the blaze licked at his skin.

Catrin leapt to push the door shut, feeling her palms sear against the hot wood, and flung the boy to the ground, using her dressing-gown to smother the fire consuming his tunic. He whimpered and went limp.

"We'll get you some help — soothing balm — it will be fine, Gryse. Just be strong. Try to stay awake," Catrin said, and tore the hangings down from around the bed. Four quick knots and she had a rope; a second later and she had it secured to the bedpost. She opened the window and the flames outside the door roared. New billows of thick smoke swirled into the room, burying Gryse in their hot, dry folds. She hurried over to him, pulling him to his feet.

He moaned.

Catrin choked on smoke and sobs and shook him gently. "Stay awake, my pet, it will hurt far worse if we do not move. Can you climb?" He looked at the makeshift rope and nodded vaguely. "Very good. You go first, and I'll steady the rope for you."

He managed to rouse himself to climb up on the sill and then rested one foot on a knot. Catrin held the rope and waited anxiously as he started down; it seemed an age before his head disappeared over the sill. The door was smouldering; she could smell the burning wood, and some of the walls on either side had burned through, leaving only bright jagged circles of flame.

Suddenly Gryse screamed and the rope jerked in her hands. She leaned out of the window and saw a small figure lying on the moonlit grass, limbs bent at unnatural angles. Her heart came up in her throat and she jumped onto the rope, heedless of how it swayed and spun as she descended as quickly as she could.

"Gryse! Gryse!" She dropped to her knees beside him, just as flame burst out of the window above and lit up his small round face.

His eyelids fluttered open. "Goodbye, my lady," he murmured.

Tears rose in Catrin's eyes and fell in rivulets when she tried to blink them away. "Gryse, please don't. Please ... stay with me."

His eyes went round, staring at something over her right shoulder, then he gave a long sigh. His head fell to the side and the light faded from his eyes.

Catrin gave a sob and closed them with her fingers. Behind her, shouts and the ringing of bells told her that people had finally noticed the fire. She considered going to help — every hand was needed at the buckets if they had any hope of saving the building — but she couldn't make herself move. And then she heard a long thin whoosh and a sudden twang as an arrow landed inches from her hand.

She stared at it in disbelief as she scrambled to her feet. Men were pouring out of the building in all directions, and fully half a dozen of them had longbows. They planted their feet with their backs to the blaze and drew arrows from their quivers, and Catrin turned and fled. She wanted to demand answers — to find out why the response to a fire was a flight of archers — to determine who had set that fire and killed a young boy — but the arrows were on the string and they were all aimed at her.

So she ran. Around the corner of the building, into the gardens. An arrow whistled past her ear and she ducked, darting around a rose bush. If she could only make it to the forest that edged the deer park, she could hide. If only —

Footsteps thudded behind her and another arrow shot past her. All she could do was keep running, further from the burning building where Amy Dudley had died, further from Gryse's broken body, further from Norfolk's theories and Forster's secrets.

Blessed darkness surrounded her, and she pulled the fabric of her dressing-gown tightly around her to hide the white linen of her nightgown that could give the archers a target. Finally she left the path for the meadow, and the grass muffled her footsteps. Sounds of pursuit faded, and she paused at the edge of the forest to look back and wonder.

Far across the fields she could see the hulking mass of Cumnor Place, but the curling, rising smoke and running shadows outlined against the flame told her nothing. So she moved onward, letting the trees swallow her up.

The darkness was deeper in the forest; she stumbled around for what felt like hours before she found the shallow hollow where the oak-trees grew. There she noticed a friendly-looking niche at the base of a trinity of branches, and climbed up there to hide. Her legs burned, nearly as badly as the red and shiny patches on her palms, but at the same time she was shaking with cold.

Worse still, her mind refused to function. She could not determine what course of action to take. Should she go back to Cumnor Place? It seemed both the safest and most dangerous option: it would give her Norfolk's protection — assuming he was alive — but it would also put her back in the path of the archers. Why did Master Forster have six archers defending his home? Why did they assume she was an enemy?

Perhaps she should run for Windsor, and take refuge with the queen. Unless her suspicions were correct, and the queen had never intended her to return from Cumnor. Could the archers have been carrying out her orders? No, that made no sense … Catrin had found nothing to incriminate the queen at Cumnor. It was more likely that Sir William Cecil was to blame. He had cause to hate Lord Robert, the note Gryse found in the fireplace of the great hall incriminated him, and he knew that Catrin and the Duke of Norfolk had gone to Cumnor. He also had the power to send archers to kill her. But the queen was still more powerful, so it was with her that Catrin would be safe. And that meant that she had to get back to Windsor.

But how? She did not even have her clothing, let alone the money or jewels that could buy her passage. Windsor was only thirty miles hence, but it may as well have been a thousand.

She straightened her shoulders and dismissed the thought. Her lot was dire, yes, but she still had her health, her wits and the documents that would surely explain why Amy Dudley had to die. She would get to Windsor somehow … starting in the morning. For now, she had to rest.

Twaaannngg.

An arrow hit her arm with enough force to tumble her out of the tree. She landed hard on the ground and heard a familiar laugh. "This is the penalty for betraying me, Catrin."

She staggered to her feet. The arrow had grazed her right arm, and blood was freely flowing. She clasped the wound with her hand, staring in astonishment as her stepfather stepped down into the hollow. "What are you doing here? Why — ?"

He was already fitting another arrow to the string. "You had me humiliated before the entire court, Catrin, and banished by the queen. This is the price you pay."

"But how —" Once again her desire for answers abruptly vanished in the realisation of danger. She turned and ran, dodging between the trees. Another arrow hissed over her head and she held in a shriek that would have betrayed her position. A stitch in her side made her breathless and her legs cramped, but still she didn't slow down. Not until she found herself at the edge of the forest.

Before her stretched a great wide field without any cover, and she gazed at it in dismay until a glimmer of light at the far side gave her hope that she would soon find people — help — protection. She ducked down and ran between the rows of wheat, trying not to disturb the heads of grain hanging heavy and still in the fading moonlight.

Finally she reached the edge of the field. To her right was a long low barn, and directly in front of her was a cottage made of broad wooden beams and mud brick. She started toward the cottage, but something made her pause. What if they too were in league with her stepfather and Master Forster? What if they handed her over without a second thought? Better to wait and see what they were like.

She tiptoed to the barn and opened the latch. The rough pine door, held carelessly together with a single nailed board, swung open with a soft creak and the warm scent of hay and animals rose around her. She found enough strength to climb the ladder to the loft, where she found haystacks aplenty, and — even better — a ragged blanket. So she formed a nook in the corner furthest from the door, crawled in, and pulled the blanket over her.

Before the wool had settled, she was asleep.

CHAPTER FIFTEEN

Hay tickled her nose, but she held in the giggles. She could hear her father's footsteps at the edge of the loft, but just barely. He knew how to walk without making a sound, and he knew how to hunt.

Suddenly everything went silent, and she held her breath. A second later, he swooped in and lifted her up from the hay. "What, ho! Look what I have found!"

She shrieked in surprise and delight. "How did you find me?"

He laughed, holding her close in his arms. "Blue kirtles show up well in golden hay, my kitten. If you are going to hide, you need to blend in."

"Next time I'll wear wool like a sheep," she said, and made him laugh again.

"Next time, don't hide," he said. "It's best to keep moving."

Catrin heard her father's voice as clearly as if he was standing by her side, and it brought her fully awake in an instant. She waited for a second, listening for any sign that someone knew she was there, then crawled over to the shuttered window and peered out through the slats. It was a bright day, and the sun was already high. She could see laundry drying on the grass next to a rapidly flowing river, and a steady trickle of people walking toward the cottage. It must be time for the mid-morning meal for the farmer's family and workers, and that meant it was her only chance to get away without being seen.

But she was still in her nightclothes … and she feared serious damage to her throbbing arm. Her dressing-gown was caked with dried blood, and she could see a large gash in the fabric. Her wound needed to be washed and bound. Did she dare ask the farmer for help?

The sound of hoofbeats made her heart race. She peered out again and saw three men ride by, longbows strung over their shoulders and full quivers of arrows strapped to their backs. Were they looking for her?

She was not going to wait to find out. She jumped up and climbed down the ladder as quickly as she could, then darted across the farmyard to the grass. There were no gowns or linens for a woman, but she found a boy's shirt, tunic and breeches, and snatched them up before speeding back to the barn.

There she ripped a piece of linen from the hem of her nightgown and dipped it in a bucket of water left there to fill the animals' troughs, before she went back up to the hayloft to change. It was painful to pull the gown and linen away from her arm; breaking the seal of the caked blood made it start bleeding again. She washed it as best she could, tore more linen free and wrapped it tightly around the wound. Then she wrapped more torn linen around her chest, flattening her enough to fit into the shirt and tunic, and checked that her *stiletto* was still safely in place. Finally, she pulled on the breeches and added her riding-boots, now scuffed and muddied almost beyond recognition.

She hid her ruined clothes and the bloodied linen in a shadowy corner of the hayloft, slung the leather pouch into place at her side, and descended back down the ladder. Another careful glance around, to ensure that everyone was safely occupied by their food, and she ran back into the safe embrace of the forest.

In her stolen dun-coloured clothing, she blended in far better than she had in her embroidered dressing-gown. It was unlikely she would be taken for a boy, though, with her hair loose and uncovered. Alas — all she could do about that was tuck it under the collar of the borrowed shirt and hope no one looked too closely.

She set off through the woods, aiming for the east because that was the general direction of Windsor. Hopefully she would soon find a road, and better yet someone travelling the same way who was willing to let her join them.

The forest thickened, but she moved between the branches and bushes with ease. It reminded her of her dream, and the days spent with her father learning to hunt and track. He had taught her to move silently, watch carefully, and listen for any snap or rustle that spoke of animal or bird.

Just as the thought passed through her mind, she heard a loud crunch to her right that made her stop short. Only a large animal could have made that sound, and she knew of only one animal careless enough to do so. She crouched down and moved silently sideways, until she was hidden behind a large tree, and then leaned slowly out and around. Before her was a small clearing, well-blanketed in fallen leaves, and — as expected — a man, settling amongst them with his back to a tree. He had taken off his flat cap and unslung his bow, and he seemed to be preparing for a nap.

She had come very close to crossing paths with one of the very men she had to avoid.

Catrin held her breath as she backed away, but at the last second she hesitated. He was an enemy, yes, but perhaps he could be useful too. So she crept around the edge of the clearing, until she was directly behind the man. There she waited, until his heavy breathing turned to soft snores. And then she reached out a delicate hand and picked up the flat cap. The man didn't move.

Catrin retreated, moving silently away until she could no longer hear the snoring. Then she tucked her hair up under the cap, pulled it firmly down over her forehead, and melted into the forest.

The rich scent of sun-warmed apples drew Catrin out of the safety of the trees, even though the orchard bordered a large field where a dozen men were swinging scythes. Her stomach cramping with hunger, she climbed the nearest tree and lay flat amongst the branches before she grabbed the largest and reddest apple she could see and devoured it in a few famished bites. She had eaten two more before the sound of a core falling to earth alerted one of the men at the edge of the field. "You there! Boy!"

Catrin froze, but the branches of apple trees are neither high nor thick enough to hide a person. The man found her easily, and prodded her foot with the handle of his scythe. "Get down from there, sirrah, or I will use the other end."

Catrin slid down and landed with a thud at his feet. She kept her gaze down, but could not help but notice that the man had a very crooked nose. "Yes, sir?"

"There is no room for wastrels at harvest-time," he said. "Take the water-bucket around to the men."

Catrin shuffled her feet. "Um — sir — I cannot. My master has charged me to go to London."

Crooked-nose snorted. "If you had a master, you wouldn't be stealing apples for food. Now obey me, or I'll report you to the sheriff as a vagrant."

What little she knew of the laws against vagrants — people who left their own parish to try to get work — made her want to avoid falling foul of them, so she followed the man over to the field and picked up the heavy wooden bucket, while he went back to swinging the scythe. She considered running away, but it seemed simpler to do as she was told until he had forgotten her, then slip back into the forest.

She trudged around the edge of the field first, and found that a dirt track cut it in half at the far end. She couldn't help but stare down it, wondering.

A man with a bush of curly hair let his scythe fall and leaned on the handle, breathing hard. "Nothing but trouble down there, lad."

Catrin took the bucket over to him. "Where does it go?"

"Hell." He took a tin cup from a swinging hook on the side and dipped it into the water, then drank deep. "That stinking cesspit that is London."

"Oh," Catrin said, and nearly made a run for it there and then. The man shook his head sorrowfully.

"You'd do better to go home to your mother," he said, and dropped the cup back into place.

Catrin moved on, her skin tingling. She had a road and she knew the direction. If she timed it properly, she would be able to jump onto one of the carts travelling by, and be back in Windsor by the following morning.

As if her thought had called them, she suddenly heard the faint thunder of hoofbeats approaching. Catrin's heart leapt in a matching pattern and she set down the bucket, ready to go. Then three men appeared, a cloud of dust in their wake, and she froze. At the front was her stepfather, his hat drawn low over his right ear to hide the missing lobe and a scowl on his face. He reined in and called out to Crooked-nose. "What, ho!"

Crooked-nose hurried over, eyes bright with excitement. "Yes, my lord?"

"Have you seen a girl in the forest? She is wearing nightclothes and may tell a wild tale of house fires and murders." Lord Ashbourne gave his version of a fatherly smile, which had always made Catrin's skin crawl. "Poor girl, she is not right in her mind. I need to get her home safe."

"No girls have wandered through here, my lord." Crooked-nose paused, and Catrin could practically hear the click as he put it together. "There was a young boy, though."

Lord Ashbourne narrowed his eyes. "Are you sure?"

"Yes, my lord. I set him to carrying the water-bucket; he should still be here somewhere."

"Find her!" Lord Ashbourne roared, and the two men jumped from their horses to obey. Catrin retreated back into the tall stalks of grain, her eyes fixed on the two men advancing steadily before her. Then the curly-haired man moved in front of her, hiding her from their sight.

"You are not defeated yet, child," he whispered. "Run!"

Catrin stumbled through the darkening forest, avoiding the thickest brush and sidestepping poacher's traps. The sun slid slowly down in the sky, making the air cold enough for her to see her breath. She longed to stop, longed to rest, but fear of her stepfather and his men kept her moving.

Then the ground suddenly dipped, and Catrin's weak and trembling legs could not react quickly enough to keep her upright. She slid down, down, down, clutching the leather pouch at her side, and landed with a thump at the bottom of what seemed an insurmountable cliff. There she lay limp, watching grey clouds skidding across the blue-black sky, unable to force herself to rise.

"Are you hurt?"

Catrin jumped, but even the shock of another human voice could not rouse her to action. It was a young girl, no more than eight, picking her way across the dirt and leaves toward her. She wore the simple skirt and cap of a poor child, but she was clean and well-cared for. "I saw you fall," she said. "Did you break anything?"

Catrin shifted painfully and discovered that all her limbs did still work. "It seems not. Thank you for asking."

"What's your name?"

"Ca — oh." She hadn't thought of that. "Ah … James. You can call me James."

"I'm Grisel." She crouched down by Catrin's side, her hands on her knees. "Are you hungry?"

The question awoke the tearing emptiness inside that Catrin had tried for hours to ignore, and she could not stop the tears that filled her eyes. She did manage not to cry aloud, and merely nodded instead. "Very hungry, I'm afraid."

"Come then." Grisel popped to her feet and held out a hand. "My Mama will feed you."

CHAPTER SIXTEEN

"The Duke of Norfolk craves an audience, Your Highness."

Lucy looked up at the words, just as the queen rose abruptly from her writing-desk. "He has returned from Cumnor so soon?"

The yeoman bowed low before her. "Aye, Your Highness. He says he has news of great import."

"Grant him access." The queen waved her hand at the assorted ladies gathered in her privy chamber. "And all of you depart, bar Lucy."

Katherine Grey shot Lucy an irritated glance from the midst of the knot of ladies as they left, but Lucy was not concerned. Her only thought was why the duke had returned so soon and on his own. Perhaps Catrin was ill. Perhaps she had found the murderer and he had hurt her. Perhaps —

The duke strode in wearing a dusty doublet and muddy boots, his travelling-cloak still slung over his shoulder. There was a dark smudge on his cheek, and he smelled unpleasantly of sweat and smoke. Hardly how one usually presented oneself to the queen.

"You must have travelled quickly, Norfolk," the queen said coolly. "To return so soon ... and in such a state."

Norfolk dropped to his knee. "My humblest apologies to present myself thus, Your Majesty, but this cannot wait. I must tell you what I have discovered ... and with that, tell you of a great tragedy."

Lucy's embroidery fell from her fingers. She had no right to speak, she knew that, but she could not stop herself. "Where is Lady Catrin?"

The queen didn't comment on her impertinence. "Yes, begin there," she said. "Has she not returned with you?"

Norfolk pressed a fist against his heart. "There was a fire at Cumnor Place last night. It consumed the eastern portion of the manor, including Lady Amy's chamber."

The queen swayed. "Surely no one was sleeping in that chamber."

"No one was supposed to be, Your Highness, but some of the servants saw Lady Catrin go to that chamber with Lady Amy's boy late in the evening. We think she intended to collect some items that we had found earlier in the day." He hung his head. "After the fire, the boy was found dead outside the window. We have sadly assumed that her ladyship —"

Someone started screaming. "No! No! It is a falsehood — an evil lie — no —"

"Lucy," the queen said sharply, and that was when Lucy realised that she was the person screaming. She bit her lip hard, and the screams turned to whimpers. "This is a foul tale indeed, Norfolk."

"Aye, Your Majesty, and I fear it grows worse." He pulled a rolled piece of parchment from the purse at his belt and handed it to her. Lucy could not see what it said and at that moment she did not care, but she saw the queen's face grow white before she leaned heavily against the arm of her chair.

"I cannot believe this."

Norfolk nodded solemnly. "'Tis truly a betrayal one could never comprehend."

"It must be false — forged —"

"Perhaps," Norfolk said, though his face said otherwise. "But if not, we must find out to whom Sir William Cecil sent this missive to kill Lady Amy."

"Sir William?" Lucy cried. "Surely not!"

The queen held out the parchment, and Lucy read the words in horrified disbelief. Sir William had ordered Lady Amy's death, and suggested killing Lord Robert as well — just as Catrin had suspected. Was this what she had died to find? Had Sir William killed Lucy's dearest companion to save himself?

Norfolk cleared his throat, delicately. "If you wish, Your Majesty, I will continue to search for the person to whom Sir William sent this letter. He is the person at whose hand Lady Amy died, so he may well have the proof we need."

"Yes." The parchment rattled in the queen's hand. "No. Perhaps — nay. I cannot wade in such deep waters with such a shallow wit. Leave me now so I may think."

Norfolk bowed low, and the movement brought the faint scent of charred wood into the room. Then he left them.

Lady Mary Sidney slipped into the room and quietly led the queen to her cushions by the fire, then guided Lucy to her chair in the corner. Lucy bent forward and let the tears come, and Lady Mary smoothed her hand over her back in soothing strokes. "Remind me, child, what does Catrin say about truth?"

"It has many f-facets, like a jewel," Lucy sobbed.

"Ah, yes." Lady Mary slid her arm around Lucy's shoulders and held on tight. "So, a different light may reflect a different truth. Hold on to that."

The queen raged, throwing paperweights and ink pots at the walls. Then she wept. Then she screamed in a fury so fierce that all her attendants but Mistress Ashley fled her chambers. Then she dissolved into tears again, incoherent, and was struck down by a violent pain in her head. She collapsed, exhausted, and let Mistress Ashley tuck her into bed.

Lucy heard it all from the garden, where she had retreated to let loose her own grief. She plodded through the empty gravel paths between the railed beds, where the summer flowers had long since withered and died. The breeze was brisk and she did not have her cloak, but she did not feel the cold. Indeed, she felt wrapped in heat — much as poor Catrin had been — and prayed it would take her too.

Eventually she found herself at the edge of the garden, in a private corner where clipped hedges surrounded a stone sundial with brass fittings worn thin by weather. Catrin had once found out that the pointing part of a sundial was often called a gnomon and for some reason that had kept them in giggles throughout the afternoon. This gnomon looked strangely like a reclining lady — something that may or may not have been deliberate — and they had found that funny too. Since the day they discovered her, they had often come to visit their favourite lady, and rest in the silence of this neglected corner.

Lucy had known that this was the lady Catrin had meant when she first read her letter — *find our favourite lady* — but now, with her head in a fog, she could not quite remember what else the letter had said. Was the lady hiding Catrin's treasures?

Lucy walked up to the sundial, and looked down at the gnomon.

"Show me, lady," she murmured, and immediately felt foolish. What could a worn piece of brass tell her? She bent down and looked around the base instead, and found nothing but sticks and fallen leaves. The base was far too heavy to move, so Catrin could not have hidden anything under there. Lucy straightened, annoyed with herself, and noticed that the gnomon pointed directly to the garden wall. That was it! *She will point to where I have hidden them.* Catrin had said the lady would point to the hiding place.

She went to the stone directly in line with the gnomon and quickly discovered that it was loose. A bit of effort, and it fell out in her hand. Behind it was a space bigger than the stone, half-filled with a domed coffer. She retrieved the key from her pomander and opened it, only to find another box within. Its latch lifted easily, and there she found the miniature that had hidden the wax seal, a letter from a youthful Catrin, a tarnished silver pomander, and a lot of paper. One was a copy of the secret message from Catrin's mother that Lucy had known about for years, and there were several sheets full of mysterious grids of letters and numbers that seemed to be Catrin's attempts at deciphering it. The one on top used 'Robert' as the code key, but it was not correct.

Looking at it all, Lucy could easily understand what Catrin wanted her to do, but how could she ever do it? If Catrin, who had learned all the methods for creating secret messages in her cradle, could not understand what her mother had written, what hope had she? Alone, she was doomed to failure, and there was no one to help. The only person she knew who had any knowledge of such things was Sir William Cecil, and she could not go to him. It was bad enough that he knew of the wax seal.

Lucy bundled everything back into the coffer and slid the stone into place. "I'm sorry, Catrin," she whispered, and kissed the key before she hid it amongst the rose petals in her pomander. "I'm so sorry."

Lucy helped the queen into her riding costume while Lady Mary stood outside in the privy chamber telling everyone the queen was indisposed and could not be disturbed. The queen herself added a hat that hid her red-gold hair and came with a thick veil, and then they slipped down a passage Lucy had never seen before, and out through a small door Lucy could have sworn did not exist. Two horses waited there, and the queen mounted a slim grey mare with practised ease. Lucy pulled herself onto her own white mare with rather less grace.

"Tush," the queen hissed, and Lucy went very still. Two men had moved into view between them and their path to escape. She recognized the heavy gold chain over the black doublet of the taller of the two; it was the Duke of Norfolk. He was half-carrying another man who seemed unable to stand on his own.

"Dudley killed her," the man wailed, slurring every word. "My beautiful dove, my Catrin —"

"Hold your drunken tongue, Swann," Norfolk said. "You're making a fool of yourself."

"I need to see her — I need to — I'm goin' to go find her —"

"That's enough," Norfolk snapped. "You're going nowhere but to your bed."

Sir Nicolas started to cry, and the duke let loose a string of oaths which Lucy would once have found shocking. Now, it just seemed like the most suitable response to the entire situation.

They watched until the two men moved out of sight, and then the queen urged her horse forward. Lucy followed her, and a single yeoman fell into place behind them as they rode swiftly and silently out of the castle and toward London. The horses were fresh and anxious for exercise, so Lucy had to pay close attention to her mount just to stay in the saddle. It became an exercise in endurance as they rode on, mile after mile, hooves thudding in the dirt and the cold wind whipping around their ears.

At long last they arrived at Kew House. The queen jumped off her horse on her own, but Lucy's legs had become so stiff that the yeoman had to help her.

Lord Robert knew of their arrival by the time she was on the ground. He met them in a room hung with thick tapestries and boasting several padded chairs, in one of which Lucy was grateful to rest. "You look chilled to the bone," he said, and called for the servants to bring mulled wine. "What has happened?"

"There was a fire." The queen's voice broke and she clung to his hand. "Amy's chamber is destroyed and Catrin is among the ashes."

Something dark and angry kindled in Lord Robert's eyes. "It must have been deliberate."

"Of course it was."

"Do we know who did it?"

"I can only assume it was Lady Amy's murderer, trying to prevent discovery."

Lord Robert folded his arms over his chest. "What else?"

The queen turned abruptly away and walked to the fire, holding out her hands before it. "Norfolk brought a document suggesting that Sir William Cecil is responsible."

Lord Robert's lip twisted. "I have told you many times that he hates me with a passion."

"I know, but still I cannot believe it. Sir William Cecil — a man who, like you, helped me survive the years of my sister's reign. How could he be a murderer?"

"Any man will kill to survive," Lord Robert said. "And he considers me a threat."

The queen could not deny that. "Perhaps I should take him from his place at once — before he can harm anyone else."

"That would be wise, Your Majesty."

The queen considered, and a shudder went through her whole body. "No, it would be a betrayal. He cannot have done this, and he is loyal to me. I know he is."

"Are you sure?" Lord Robert asked mildly.

"Yes," the queen said stubbornly. "He would not stage a scandal that could so easily push me from the throne. And he would not kill an innocent like Catrin."

Lord Robert knew better than to challenge her. Instead he started to pace back and forth, his boots thudding against the wooden floor, and took another tack. "Whomever is responsible — be it Sir William or no — certainly did not do the murder himself, nor did he personally set the fire," he said. "We need to find the man whose hand was the instrument of this destruction."

"Norfolk said the same; he is looking for him now."

Lord Robert did not seem to find that reassuring. "In such circumstances it may prove useful to send more than one hunter after the prey."

The queen tilted her head to the side. "What do you suggest?"

"By Your Majesty's leave, I will go to Cumnor. First I will look for Catrin — until I see her, I will not believe that she is dead."

Lucy's heart leapt. "I will go with you, my lord."

Lord Robert caught the queen's gaze and gave a great sigh. "Alas, I am confined to my house."

"Nay, you are recalled to court," the queen said. "The coroner has ruled the death accidental, and so we must behave accordingly."

Lord Robert's face lit up and he bowed low before her, kissing her hand. "My beautiful and gracious queen, you have granted my dearest wish. I want nothing more than to bask in your presence."

She cupped his cheek in her hand. "Then come home to Windsor, Robin, and we will stand together."

"To Windsor, Your Majesty?" Lucy asked. "Not to Cumnor?"

"Yes, to Windsor," the queen said. Lucy's disappointment must have shown in her face, for she reached out a soothing hand. "But I will consider allowing you to go to Cumnor in a day or two."

"Consider?" Lucy said. "But, Your Majesty —"

Lord Robert held up a hand to stop Lucy's protest, though she saw in his eyes that he agreed with her. "Yes, Your Majesty. We are at your service."

Before Lucy, a caudle of mussels bathed in almond milk, vinegar and verjuice sat in a silver bowl. A goose dish with a sauce of sage and parsley steamed beside it. Baskets of soft white mancet bread were scattered all over the table, between dishes of mutton stew made with wine and onions.

Lucy could not eat a bite.

None of the other ladies seemed to have the same trouble. They ate quickly, washing down each morsel with wine. The queen was not there; she had retired to eat in her bedchamber after the usual ceremony. Lord Robert had been wise enough not to join her; he was eating with several others in the presence chamber. Sir Nicolas was not one of them. Norfolk had told everyone that he was still sleeping it off.

A man Lucy did not recognize spoke to the guards at the door, and they let him in. To her surprise, he crossed directly to her and took a knee. "Good e'en, Lady Lucretia," he said. "I am Christopher, one of Sir William's secretaries."

Christopher? Surely not. "I thought you were ill in Hampshire."

"I was, your ladyship, but I have just returned to court."

So he could have been in Cumnor in time to kill Lady Dudley after all. Suddenly Lucy felt sick. "I see."

"His lordship has sent me with a message. He asks that you join him for a game of chess this evening. He says he has curious tidings for you."

She pushed herself to her feet so quickly that her stool tipped over and clattered to the floor. "I — he — nay, I cannot. Please tell his lordship that I am ill and I must go and lie down."

"Yes, my lady," he said, and his eyes betrayed his surprise.

"Thank you," she said, and fled.

CHAPTER SEVENTEEN

Grisel lived in a one-room cottage with a packed-earth floor. There was a long wooden table at one end and a bed at the other, tucked under a large loft. In the middle was a second smaller table, in front of a hearth, with a fire that crackled merrily and a column of smoke that rose sedately up the chimney. Pots and pans were attached with nails to the beams in the wall, and a cupboard to the right of the chimney held tin cups, plates and cutlery.

As Grisel led Catrin through the door, a woman was setting a basket of dark brown bread on the table by the fire. "You're nearly too late, child," she said, and then glanced up and sighed. "Grisel, what have you done?"

"This is James," Grisel said cheerfully, and skipped over to hold out her hands to the fire. "He's hungry."

"Oh, is he?" The woman eyed Catrin up and down, and Catrin had the uncomfortable feeling that her disguise wasn't working. "And I wager he needs a place to sleep, too."

Catrin glanced out the window at the darkening sky and shivered. "Yes, I do."

"You shall have one, then. I am Mistress Drury. We will give you a meal and a space to sleep in the attic loft, and as payment you shall help me tomorrow."

Catrin bit her lip. It would delay her return to Windsor, but what choice did she have? "As you wish, Mistress Drury."

"Very well. Bring the dishes over like a good child, Grisel, and we shall eat before it's cold."

Her legs ached and the gash on her arm itched, keeping Catrin from the blessed sleep she craved. She tossed and turned in the loft, hemmed in by chests and bundles of cloth, the precious leather pouch carefully hidden under her pallet of straw.

She gave up after what seemed like an eternity, and took the pouch out. She drew out the one letter that was not in plain English and a piece of the paper that she had taken from Lady Dudley's room. Then she descended the ladder as quietly as she could and tiptoed over to the fire.

Mistress Drury was fast asleep in her bed, with little Grisel on a tiny mattress on the floor by her side. Neither of them stirred when Catrin spread out the papers on the stone hearth. The embers of the fire gave her just enough light to examine the strings of letters and determine how to read them, and it did not take her long to decipher it. Compared to her mother's methods, this one was easy, but even when actual words emerged they made little sense.

At the feast with the branch
Cut back the bastard stock to purify
How once foiled
Under the canopy
The promised gold
Before the silver shard
7th day 9th month

Catrin read it over and over until she had memorised it, then threw her scribblings into the fire and returned to her pallet to think. Lady Dudley had definitely been involved with something that she did not want her hosts, fellow-guests or husband to know. As Lord Robert had said, she had not mentioned messages or gifts in her letters to him, and the obvious explanation of a lover did not fit with the documents Catrin had found.

It seemed more likely that Lady Dudley, an abandoned and disgruntled wife, was working against the queen who had taken her husband. And that finally disproved any chance that her death was an accident. No, someone had discovered her and executed their own justice on a traitor. But who? Not Lord Robert — she was sure of that. Nor the queen — she would have punished Lady Dudley with a trial and a violent public execution, just as the old king would have done. Sir William still seemed the most likely, but who had been his instrument? Surely someone at Cumnor. Master Forster? Richard Verney?

Catrin sighed. Speculation served no purpose. She needed to return to court and lay out the whole matter before the queen. Should she leave right there and then? No, she couldn't do that. She had given her word, and it was a matter of honour to keep it.

No matter how much trouble it would cause.

"Woman! Where is my food?"

The shout jolted Catrin out of a deep sleep. She immediately checked that the leather pouch was safely out of sight, then slid cautiously to the edge of the loft and peered down.

Mistress Drury pushed herself out of bed, yawning. "And what time do you call this, John?"

A man not quite as tall as Mistress Drury reeled across the floor, scuffling up dust. "You've no call to tell me when I can come back to my own house, woman. Now get me a plate."

Mistress Drury muttered as she turned to the fire, where she spooned pottage from the cauldron sitting in the embers into a wooden bowl. He flopped down at the table, and she set the bowl down in front of him with a thump. "Now keep your voice down, you'll wake Grisel."

The very first beam of sunlight that morning fell across her eyes, forcing Catrin awake. No one else had woken at the same time — not Mistress Drury, not Grisel, not even the foul-tempered Master Drury. But the birds outside were twittering madly, and their enthusiasm meant that there was no way that Catrin could get back to sleep.

Catrin climbed down the ladder, tiptoed across the room and went outside into the crisp morning air. The light was better there, and she could finally escape from Master Drury's snores.

Inevitably, her hand found its way into the leather pouch. She pulled out a sheet at random, and found herself looking at the sheet of music. The musical notations were scribbled hastily, but the words were neat and clear.

To reach for but an empty claim
Bent fortune takes the chance away
Royal grace, please now grant me strength
So he may go and she may stay

What was Amy reaching for? Her husband, most likely, and it was not hard to imagine that she found her own claim to him empty in comparison to the queen's. The loss of her chance seemed also to cast blame on the queen, especially when considered in light of the other documents Catrin had read, but the next line seemed to plead with the queen to grant her strength. And who was the 'she' that Amy wanted to stay? It was a jumbled message at best.

"What do you have there, James?"

The paper was plucked from her hand, and Catrin leapt to her feet with her heart in her throat. "Please! Give that back!"

Mistress Drury chuckled and retreated two or three steps. "But I do so love a secret, and I can tell that you're full of them," she said. "Why, 'tis a song!"

"Yes, now please give it back."

Mistress Drury's eyes twinkled with glee. "I know this tune," she said, and hummed a few bars. "Aye, of course. It's 'Greensleeves'."

Catrin went still, unable to believe she hadn't noticed that. "Is it?"

"Don't you know? Didn't you write the words for it here?"

"No, I did not," Catrin said, and snatched the paper from the woman's hands, storing it safely away.

"Full of secrets, and no more a boy than I am," Mistress Drury murmured. Catrin looked at her in alarm, and she laughed. "Do not fret, I will not betray you. This is the most excitement I've had since Grisel was born, and I do not mind paying for it with silence."

Catrin lowered her gaze. "Thank you."

"No need to thank me." She grinned and started rolling up her sleeves. "Now let's get to work."

Vile work it was, too. Mistress Drury melted animal fat over the fire while Catrin cut reeds for wicks. Then Mistress Drury brought the smoking, stinking cauldron to the table and set it on a linen pad to save scorching the wood, and the two of them dipped reeds into the liquid fat over and over, trying not to burn their wrists on the hot steel or their fingers in the bubbling fat. Every now and then a scum formed around the edges, and Mistress Drury took the cauldron back to the fire to melt the fat again.

After several hours, Catrin was hot and sweaty and had developed a new fondness for the gentler tasks assigned to her by the queen. She would have given anything to be making possets or pomanders, with the scent of roses and cinnamon around her. "May I have a moment, Mistress Drury?"

Mistress Drury put the pot back on the fire. "Just as long as this needs."

"Yes, ma'am." Catrin went outside, checked that the pouch was still safe at her side, and took a deep breath of cool clean air with great relief. Then she stretched her aching legs with a stroll around the Drury farm. It was set up in a horseshoe, with the outbuildings nestled close together on one end and the open lane at the other. They had a buttery, a malthouse and a dairy, and both a barn and a stable. The stable sat opposite the house at the open end of the horseshoe, with hay stacked against one side of the door and a cart in need of repair on the other.

Master Drury was sitting in it, repairing a bridle, and Catrin slipped silently past him and into the stable. There were three horses in there, a beautiful bay mare and two geldings. Catrin found some apples in a corner and fed them, so they let her stroke their velvet-soft noses.

So absorbed was she in the glossy coat of the mare that she didn't register the clattering of hooves outside until it was too late. "What-ho, goodman!"

Her stepfather's voice. Catrin spun around and watched him walk up to Master Drury, who was just taking a sneaky drink from a leather bottle. He hid the bottle in the cart before he staggered to his feet. "Yesh, m'lord?"

"I'm looking for a young boy who has run from my estate," Lord Ashbourne said, with all the glib ease of a habitual liar.

"He is not right in the head and needs to be brought back to safety."

"We got a boy," Master Drury said, and waved vaguely toward the house. "He's helpin' the wife."

Lord Ashbourne sat up straighter in his saddle, while his two henchmen jumped down from theirs. "Are you sure?"

"Aye," Master Drury said.

The two men went into the house, and Master Drury smiled a bleary smile and held out his hand. Lord Ashbourne scowled, but he reached for his purse. And Catrin's nerve broke. She swung open the stall door, leapt onto the mare's back, and urged her out the stable door at top speed. Fortunately, the mare was well fed and well rested; she leapt forward with seeming delight, tearing up the road with long powerful strides.

Behind her, Master Drury started to swear and Lord Ashbourne shouted for his henchmen. Catrin bent over the mare's neck and the wind whipped the cap from her head. Her hair streamed out behind her, and she had a sudden terrible feeling that it wasn't only her disguise that had met its end.

She gave the mare her head and they flew down the country lane and past another farm. Angry shouts came to her on the wind, telling her the men working the harvest recognized the mare and knew she wasn't supposed to have it. She veered off the main road into the woods, thundering along a grassy path. It was only when she didn't hear any hoofbeats behind her that she reined the mare in and jumped down, taking the reins so she could lead the mare deeper into the trees.

Catrin shuddered at the thought of what could happen if they caught her and tugged the mare on faster. The horse went reluctantly when the trees grew thicker, whinnying so loudly that it made sweat stand out on Catrin's forehead. She soothed the mare with petting, and that was when she noticed the remnants of a stone cottage behind a thick clump of young aspen trees. Two slabs of rock leaned against each other on the ground in the centre, framing a small round stone, and Catrin hastened to scrape at the crumbling mortar around it and pry it loose. The space behind was just big enough to hide the leather pouch, and she was able to quickly replace the stone and secure it in place with some dirt. Then she used a branch to wipe out her footprints and went back to the mare.

Did she hear hoofbeats, or was that just her imagination? And were they coming from ahead of her or behind? No matter — she jumped up onto the mare's back and urged her along the path. She had no choice but forward.

CHAPTER EIGHTEEN

Lucy went back to the sundial the next morning. Nothing had been disturbed, so at least she had not failed Catrin completely. She thought of opening the box again, but knew there was no purpose to it. The task was impossible.

"Lady Lucretia."

She froze. That was Sir William Cecil's voice. God help her, she had led him straight to Catrin's treasures, and there was nowhere in that corner of the garden to hide. Not a tree, not a bush. She had to turn and face him. "Yes, my lord?"

He paused a few paces away, his velvet robe rippling in the breeze. "I saw you leave the castle and wanted to ask if you have recovered from your illness."

His face was taut with concern. It made her heart ache, but at the same time it made her angry. "As much as I can be, my lord. But my friend is still dead."

"Yes … it is truly a tragedy to lose such a bright, beautiful maiden so young," he said. His voice was rough with obvious distress, and for some reason that gave Lucy hope. Could he have had her killed, and still be so disturbed?

"Someone killed her, and she knew it was going to happen."

The words were said before Lucy could stop them, and tears followed. Sir William hesitated, then came close enough to rest his hands on her shoulders. "Weep not, my lady. I will do all I can to find the villain, and punish him."

The kind words burst the dam within her. This was the Sir William she knew — this was the Sir William she dared to love. "So it wasn't you?" Tears turned to sobs, and she took tight hold of his forearms, desperate to know for certain. "Say it wasn't you — p-please, Sir William, t-tell me —"

"Calm yourself, my lady," he said sharply, and took a step away from her. "Only a man without honour would burn a woman in her bed, without recourse to any process of law. Do you think so little of me?"

"No!"

"Then cast the thought out of your mind."

She took deep, shuddering breaths, trying to get control of herself. "What about Lady Amy Dudley?"

His eyes narrowed. "What of her?"

"The Duke of Norfolk brought proof —" Horrified, Lucy pressed both hands to her mouth. "God forgive me, I wasn't supposed to —!"

"You have started now, so continue," Sir William said woodenly. "What so-called proof has the duke brought?"

"A letter in your hand, found at Cumnor," she said miserably. "It says to destroy Lord Robert's wife."

Sir William stumbled backwards. "That is why the queen says she is ill," he whispered. "That is why she will not see me."

Fresh tears ran down her cheeks. "Is it real? Did you write it?"

"Yes — no —" He passed a hand over his forehead. "It is not what it seems. I must go to the queen."

A new horror. "Oh, my lord, if you do she will know I told you!"

"And if I do not, I may well find myself dining in the Tower!"

Lucy's knees gave way; she sank to the ground and found herself at eye-level with the gnomon. He was right — there was no other way. "Then you must go to her and explain."

"I must. Yes, I must." He turned and started away on legs that did not seem steady. At the edge of the garden he turned, breathing hard. "I will protect you if I can, my lady."

He would not be able to, and well she knew it. "Thank you, my lord."

Lucy was walking on the wharf, looking out at the restless grey waters of the Thames, when the summons came. One of the maids of honour — a tall girl with an arrogant twist to her lip — brought the message. She did not speak as Lucy followed her back to the royal chambers.

The queen was ensconced in furs before the fire, her face pale and drawn with pain. Her tone, when she spoke, was frosty, and she used the royal 'we' with devastating effect. "Lucy, Sir William has requested an audience, which we have granted," she said. "And he begs us to have mercy on you both, which we have not."

Lucy sank to her knees in dread. "Your Majesty —"

"The very request made us wonder why a child such as yourself needed mercy." Her gaze on Lucy seemed to burn. "Explain yourself."

Catrin had often said that Lucy needed to learn to dissemble if she were to succeed at court, but she could not — even when the consequences were dire. "I told Sir William about the letter, Your Majesty."

The queen rose up slowly, magnificently, like a phoenix from the ashes. "You did *what?*"

"I did not intend to — it just came out —"

"Will you never learn to hold your tongue?" the queen shouted, and collapsed back amongst the furs, a hand to her head. "We should send you to the Tower; they have instruments there that will hold it for you."

Lucy very nearly lost control of her water. "Oh, no, Your Majesty, please! I did not —"

"Your Majesty." The interruption came from Sir William himself, who was rushing through the door toward them. "Please do not be angry with the child — I used all my methods to learn the truth."

That wasn't true. Lucy opened her mouth to say so, and Sir William sent her a look that told her very clearly not to speak. Then he knelt before the queen. "I beg you, Your Majesty, do not punish Lady Lucy," he said. "She had no choice in the matter."

"You are very skilled at extracting information, that is true. Very well, Lady Lucy, you are forgiven," the queen said quietly, and then turned to Sir William. The fury in her dark gaze was spent; all that was left was a deep well of hurt. "Now tell me the truth. Have you betrayed me, William?"

The royal 'we' was gone; in that moment, the queen was merely a young woman facing something that was breaking her heart. "No," he said simply, and his hands shook as he held them out to her. "You are my avowed sovereign and my beloved friend, and I have never done anything against your interests."

The queen drew the charred letter from amongst the furs and held it out. "Explain this, then. It was found in the great hall at Cumnor Place."

He took the parchment, and flakes fell from it like blackened rain. "These are my notes, Your Majesty. Notes — not a letter, not an order."

A faint smile brought colour to the queen's cheeks. "You were ever one for making notes."

"Aye, and I was frustrated and sad when I wrote them." His voice went low, as if the words were hard to say. "I considered resigning, Your Majesty, and these were my reasons."

The colour vanished. "You would leave me?"

"Because I felt you no longer needed me," Sir William explained hastily. "Lord Robert had your ear, and the journey to Edinburgh broke me financially and in health. I thought I could not continue."

The queen stared at him, trembling. "Do you still think this way?"

"You have needed me, this week," Sir William said diplomatically. "While you need me, Your Majesty, I will not leave you."

The queen reached out and took his hands in a tight grip. "I shall always have need of you, Sir Spirit," she said intently. "You must remain by my side."

He bowed low and kissed her hand. "Yes, Your Majesty."

"Good. My hearty thanks to you," the queen murmured, and drew her hands away. "Now tell me; what do you believe I should do about the death of Lady Amy?"

Sir William looked up at her, but remained on his knees. "Further investigation would be beneficial, Your Majesty. I do not know how my notes came to be in Cumnor Place, but surely Lady Amy's servants would have insight. I believe it would be helpful to send Lord Robert to Cumnor to speak to them, as he is their rightful lord."

The queen tilted her head, considering. A flare of hope lit inside Lucy, and was dashed just as quickly when she shrugged her shoulders. "Thank you, my lord. I will consider it."

CHAPTER NINETEEN

For some reason, Catrin could not stop thinking of the Earl of Arran. His visit to court the summer before had been planned by Sir William Cecil, who wanted to convince the queen to marry him. Lord Robert had done all he could to ensure that the match did not happen, and she, Catrin, had helped him. It had only taken a bit of flirting to discover that the earl was going mad, and easily triggered into hallucinations that set him raving. Lord Robert ensured that the queen was aware of this, and the earl's visit came to a discreet end.

Sir William had not been pleased.

It made Catrin wonder whether Sir William had nursed a grudge against her since that time. He was determined to the point of ruthlessness, she knew that, and he was also one to leap at any opportunity that might arise. He could well be walking around Windsor now, delighted with how she had fallen into the trap. Perhaps Lady Mary Sidney was his ally, and that was why she had suddenly shared that information about Catrin's mother, after two years of silence.

Around her, the leaves rustled in a sudden breeze and she shivered. The poor mare was plodding now, pushing past stray branches and rocky outcroppings with her head hung low. Catrin's heart ached for her, but all she could do was stroke her neck in sympathy. "I understand you're tired, sweet girl, but — what's that?"

The mare's head came up and she whinnied as if answering. It was a spring, bubbling and splashing out of a rock into a large black pool, and beside it was a soft expanse of long green grass. Gratefully Catrin jumped down and led the mare over to it, and they both drank deep. Then Catrin let the mare feast on the grass, and sat down with her legs outstretched. She ached from her head to her toes, and she was certainly not used to riding bareback. She also felt painfully naked without that leather pouch, and worried every second that someone had found it.

The mare's head came up and she sniffed the air, just as the smell of sour sweat reached Catrin's nostrils. She scrambled to get back on the mare's back, but it was too late. A half-dozen men burst from the trees around her and dragged her back to the ground. She fought with all she had, hitting and kicking, but she had no chance against so many. In no time she was flat on the ground, rope around her wrists and ankles and the men standing above her in a circle.

"Why, it's not a boy at all!" one said breathlessly. "We've got ourselves a wench!"

"She's a horse-thief," growled another. "Drury's practically mad with worry about his mare."

"He's mad with drink," snorted a third, then grabbed Catrin under the arms and hoisted her to her feet. "Let's take her to the parish constable."

A fourth man pushed his face so close to Catrin's that his beard scraped her chin. "It'll be branding for you, lass. We don't take kindly to horse-thieves around here."

She snapped at him and nearly caught his nose between her teeth. The men laughed at this feeble attempt at resistance and swung her headfirst across the mare's back, tying her hands and feet together under the horse's belly so that she could not move. It stretched her arms painfully forward and the pressure in her head was unbearable. "No — please — let me go. Please—"

The first man laughed. "No chance of that, duckling."

Catrin strained her head backward, trying to see him. "Then let me ride. I promise not to try to escape."

"We don't take the promises of horse-thieves," growled the man. "Now be quiet, or it will be the worse for you. Understand?"

She understood, but she was trussed so tight she could barely breathe. "Please — I can't —"

The man with the beard grabbed a stick from the ground and hit her hard across the back. "Not another word, do you hear?"

She couldn't speak if she wanted to; the blow had taken what little air remained in her lungs. She let her head hang down and concentrated on breathing, and the men led the horse forward. The mossy ground of the forest soon gave way to rough dirt, telling her that she had been painfully close to the freedom of the road. The men had horses there, meaning that their pace increased tenfold. Catrin was soon choking on dust, while pebbles peppered her face and arms with small stinging cuts and bruises.

The tears came; she couldn't stop them. By the time the horse stopped, the dust on her face had turned to mud, and the world kept fading to black before a jolt on her strained shoulders brought her abruptly back to reality.

"What, ho! Constable!"

The shout came close to her ear, and then there was a scrape of a knife as the ropes tying her to the horse were cut. She slid down into a heap on the ground, unable to stop herself. There was a glimpse of a small huddle of buildings and a stone church, and then she was on her back and looking up at the darkening sky.

She heard the patter of feet from a distance and knew that everyone in the village was coming out to see what was happening. Then a heavier tread came closer, and a man loomed over her. Out of all the men surrounding her, he was the only one whose hat boasted a feather. "What's this?" he asked.

"We got a horse-thief, Constable," growled the bearded man. "And a cheeky one at that — look at her clothes! It's indecent. Unnatural."

The other men grunted assent. Catrin managed to draw a breath. "Good sir, I am not a thief. I am working for Her Majesty the queen on urgent business and —"

A roar of laughter drew more men into the circle. "Oh, an agent for the queen!" the constable said with a grin. "Welcome to Chiswell, your ladyship!"

"It's true!" Catrin said, and pushed herself into a sitting position. "I was under threat so I borrowed the horse to escape. I would have returned it once the queen —"

"She's telling lies about our sovereign!" a man shouted. "Have her whipped!"

"Branded!" came a woman's voice.

The bearded man aimed a kick at Catrin's knee. "Put her in the pillory!"

The constable gazed thoughtfully at Catrin and finally nodded. "The pillory it shall be," he said, and glanced up at the growing dark. "Until tomorrow, when she shall be branded."

"Branded?" Catrin cried, and struggled to her feet. It was the worst thing she could imagine: a 'T'-shaped scar on her cheek would ruin her for the marriage-market and ensure that she would never be free of her stepfather. The queen would have nothing further to do with her. "You cannot do that to me! Send messengers to Windsor Castle — people know me there. They will explain!"

The constable just laughed and waved a hand at three men, who came forward with all eagerness. They seized her and dragged her to a tall wooden frame covered with foul-smelling stains.

She screamed and twisted her body from side to side, trying desperately to throw them off, but to no avail. One of the men cut the ropes around her wrists and the others forced her hands and head into the holes of the pillory. The constable himself slammed down the upper half and locked it.

Catrin struggled, but the rough wood bit into her skin and forced her to be still. "Mercy," Catrin sobbed. "Please, have mercy."

The constable reached out and took a fistful of Catrin's hair, letting it flow through his fingers. A smirk spread across his face. "This is mercy."

"Thief!"

An apple sailed through the darkness and hit Catrin's injured knee with a thump. She jolted in pain and heard a boy's cackle before the top of her vision caught his running feet leaving the square. That left her alone — painfully, horribly alone. She remembered her frustration at the crowds at court, her boredom with the dozens of ladies talking fashion and food. Now, she longed with all her heart to be there again. She wanted to see Lucy waving her hands about as she tried to teach Catrin Spanish, and tell the queen the stories of ancient Wales, and flirt with the courtiers. She wanted to be where she belonged.

Strange, that. When she had left Ashbourne for court she had never thought that she would find a home there. Indeed, she had never intended to find a home. A home came with obligations and loyalties, and she wanted to be free. She had intended to work only for herself, and feel no affection or loyalty to anyone.

Lucy had begun to change that, offering her friendship with a wholehearted innocence. And then the queen's favour had drawn her into a circle of people she found fascinating. Vain, demanding and erratic they certainly were, but they were also loyal, brave, and intelligent. Against her own will, Catrin had grown to admire them.

And that had brought her here.

Did she regret it? Her knees weakened, causing extra strain on her arms and neck as they were pulled more tightly against the boards. She could have been comfortably asleep in the queen's bedchamber right now, had she not accepted Lady Mary's terms. And did it really matter how or why Amy Dudley died? Catrin was about to suffer a fate worse than death for trying to answer that question, and it made no difference at all. No one would ever know what had happened.

A breeze sprung up, and Catrin's clothes flapped damply against her skin. Her hair stirred, bringing up the scent of the horse dung an old man had dumped over her head. Tears rose up in her eyes and trailed down her cheeks, and she caught her breath on a sob. Again, what did it matter? It was useless. Whoever had killed Amy Dudley had won. She could not fight them anymore.

The acrid scent of burning coal roused Catrin from a stupor. She opened her eyes to a flood of light and tried to crane her neck back to see what was going on, but she had stiffened in the chill of the night and every movement was agony. All she could do was listen to the shuffling of the gathering crowd and the faint buzz of excited conversation. Then heavy footsteps approached her.

"Take my hospitality, then take my horse, will you?" The voice was a hiss and came on a breath heavily laced with ale. "Damn you to hell, whoever you are."

"I had no choice, Master Drury," Catrin said. "That man —"

Drury clapped his hands over her ears hard enough to make them ring, and the whole world tilted madly from side to side. Someone cheered, encouraging Drury to backhand her across the face. Tears burst from Catrin's eyes at the blow but she bit back the cry, determined not to give him the satisfaction. So he grabbed her wrist and twisted, and the agony that shot through her made a red mist descend before her eyes.

"Enough."

It was the constable's voice, and Drury let her go at once. He stepped off the platform, and the constable stepped up. Another man followed, and set down a cast-iron trough full of glowing coals at the constable's side. A branding iron sat within it, and Catrin screamed. "No — no — I beg you, don't —"

"Tush," the constable said, but Catrin paid no attention. She screamed again, twisting her hands in their wooden prisons and frantically pulling her head backward. "Someone hold her still," the constable said, and two more men mounted the platform. Catrin could see only their feet, but their hands wrapped around her neck with enough pressure to make her gasp for air.

A woman's voice rose above the murmuring of the crowd in a desperate shriek. "Stop! Stop!"

The constable sighed. "What is it, Mistress Drury?"

A pattering of footsteps on the edge of the platform. "I gave him — her — permission to take the horse," she panted. "She didn't steal it at all."

"That's a lie!" Master Drury shouted. "And what's more, it's my horse, not hers."

"I'm the one what feeds it and mucks it out," Mistress Drury retorted. "When was the last time you pulled yourself from the drink to —"

"Tush, Mistress Drury, or it'll be the scold's bridle for you," the constable said wearily, and lifted the brand out of the coals, bringing the glowing red 'T' close to Catrin's face. Mistress Drury screamed a protest while Catrin was held fast, struggling for air.

"Stop in the name of the queen!"

The shout rang out over all the noise, and a second later horses thundered into the square. The constable jumped and the branding-iron clattered onto the platform, scorching the wood. Catrin stared at the smouldering black patch, the world fading in and out, as more men shouted and horses stomped and men's boots clattered all around her. She couldn't hear what they were saying; it was like a fog had descended over her, muffling everything. Then the pressure on her neck was gone, and the board holding her down was lifted away with a rattle. She slid backward as her knees gave out, and landed hard against a solid chest.

"Catrin … my own heart's root … Catrin, my beautiful dove — what have they done to you?"

The gentle voice was somehow stronger than the shouting, and Catrin opened her eyes to see Sir Nicolas bending over her.

"Lost home in the forest. At the centre of the trinity," Catrin murmured, and fainted.

CHAPTER TWENTY

In the frozen garden, a red rose bloomed. Her mother sat beside it, stroking the soft petals with one pale hand. The child Catrin walked toward her, her little boots making the frosty grass crunch beneath her feet. "Mama?"

Her mother's waist-length black hair slid forward and covered her face. "Yes, my sweeting?"

"I have not forgotten you. I will find you."

"No, sweeting. I do not want you to come to where I am."

"Are you with Papa?"

"Whenever I think of him."

Catrin nudged a piece of earth with her toe. "I want to be with you."

Her mother raised her head and her blue eyes were warm enough to melt the frost. "Not yet, sweeting. You have a task to complete."

A voice called to Catrin and the garden started to fade. She cried out and her mother raised her hand as if in blessing. "Go now, child," she said. "Go and finish it."

Catrin was tightly wrapped in something, so tight she could not move, and yet she was being jostled unmercifully. Her head kept hitting something hard enough that she could feel the bruise rising beneath the skin. She opened her eyes and saw only the polished metal of a breastplate. If she turned her head, she saw the glossy head and flowing mane of a dappled grey stallion. Neither of which made any sense.

"Who —? What —?"

"Catrin!" The voice above her was familiar; it was Sir Nicolas, riding like fury with her wrapped in his arms. He slowed the horse and stopped under the spreading branches of an oak tree that still held most of its leaves. "I worried you would never wake."

Catrin struggled to free her arms, and he jumped down from his horse and set her gently on her feet before he freed her from the folds of his cloak. "Thank you," she said, and carefully stretched aching limbs. "What happened?"

He lifted his chest with pride, and even his wispy blond hair stood at attention. "Some of my men and I scattered those damned peasants and whisked you away," he said. "I sent my men in three different directions to confound the villains and made for Windsor."

Windsor? It was both all she wanted and the worst thing to happen. "Oh, no — have we come far?"

"Ten miles at least." He saw the dismay on her face and his own fell. "Do you still think that I betrayed you to the queen? Do you not trust me, my lady?"

"Nay, Sir Nicolas, that is not my worry," Catrin said. She shuddered at the thought of what he had prevented and impulsively wrapped her arms around him in gratitude. "You appeared just in time to save me from my own hell on earth."

He pressed his face to her hair. "I would fight the queen herself for you, my lady."

She almost laughed; it was a ridiculous image, for all it was a sweet sentiment. "Thank you, good sir. I am in your debt."

"There is no debt, my lady." He held out his hand. "Now, let us return to Windsor before the queen notices my absence."

Catrin blinked. "She did not ask you to come?"

"Nay, my dove ... she thinks you dead. As do they all." A shadow crossed his face. "As did I, in truth. I was riding to Cumnor to seek my revenge when I heard a boy talking about the branding of a horse-thief who claimed to know the queen."

They thought her dead. She had been truly alone, for not a soul had been looking for her. How close she had come! "Someone certainly wants me dead, and has tried more than once to end me," she said. "I have gained knowledge that was supposed to remain hidden, and I have to deliver it to the queen."

"What knowledge?"

"It is too complicated to explain. But I must return to Chiswell before I go to Windsor, Sir Nicolas. Truly, it is a matter of life and death."

"We ride directly into danger if we go back into that town," Sir Nicolas said. "My men killed one of the blackguards, and injured another. The peasants were crying for weapons when we escaped."

"We do not need to go into the town, but the forest surrounding it. And we must go before they search too thoroughly," Catrin said. Still he hesitated, so she clasped her hands together. "I beg thee, Sir Nicolas. Trust me, I would not ask if it were not vital."

"I trust thee, Lady Catrin." He offered his hand to help her mount. "Let us to horse."

Lucy woke early, and left her pallet on the floor to cross to the window. Clouds were skidding across the sky, grey smudges against the pink sunrise. Catrin had loved the sunrise … she always said her father used to carry her up to the rooftops to watch the sky turn from purple to pink to blue.

In a way, Lucy hoped she was dead. If it was as Lord Robert and Sir William suspected, that she had survived and was still somewhere in Cumnor, Lucy could not bear it. To think of her alone and frightened, without help, without friends — possibly injured or ill — the very thought made her cry.

"Oh, by God's heart."

The cross words made her jump. She spun around and saw the queen standing beside her bed, gown and hair sleep-rumpled. Lucy hastily wiped her eyes dry and put on a smile. "Your Majesty — good morrow — fare you well?"

"No. There is a lady drooping around in my presence like a mournful puppy," the queen retorted. "Dress yourself and go to my Lord Robert. Tell him to make plans for you both to go to Cumnor."

It felt like the sun had suddenly appeared. "Truly, Your Majesty?"

"Aye; I can live no longer with a mournful child." The queen said it with amusement rather than anger, and Lucy came very close to breaking all protocol and embracing her. At the last moment she stopped herself, rushing to her chest instead so she could retrieve her clothes.

"Thank you, Your Majesty!"

It had proven difficult to find Lord Robert, and more difficult still to collect the men and supplies Lord Robert was sure they needed. Half of the day had gone by the time they could go to the stable yards and collect the horses, and they lost more time still when one of the horses threw a shoe only a mile from the palace and they had to return. But finally, they were ready. Lucy pulled on her riding-gloves while she waited for the stableboy to lead the horse to a mounting-block, her insides fluttering with nerves. It was less than half a day's journey to Cumnor, but still it seemed too far. Was there any chance that they would find Catrin alive?

There was a sudden commotion at the gate, and three stableboys flew past them and joined in. Lucy couldn't tell what was happening until she had mounted her horse, but from that vantage point she could see that the chaos had been caused by the Duke of Norfolk and his men returning from the hunt. The duke saw Lord Robert there as he dismounted, then deliberately chose a path that forced Lord Robert to step out of his way.

Lord Robert's eyes turned icy cold. "I beg your pardon, your grace."

"There is no pardon," Norfolk said. "Not for a base-born son of a traitor."

Lord Robert clenched his fists but said nothing, and Norfolk smirked as he bowed before Lucy with exaggerated courtesy. "My lady."

Lucy frowned at him. "That was unnecessary, your grace."

Norfolk pretended he had not heard her, and resumed his journey to the castle. Lord Robert swung up onto his horse and passed a weary hand over his eyes. "But, alas, it is true."

"You are noble born," she reminded him. "And behave with far more nobility than the duke has just behaved, I would add."

He chuckled. "Thank you, my lady," he said, and gazed at her for so long that his mount skittered with impatience. "Are you afraid of me?"

That was a disturbing question. "Not if the queen has confidence in you."

He inclined his head in thanks. "And do you think I had my wife murdered?"

"I did," she said, and then sighed. "I don't know what to think any more."

"Nor does anyone," Lord Robert said sadly. "But I promise you, my lady, you are safe with me. I did not kill my wife, nor did I have any quarrel with Lady Catrin."

He seemed sincere, and that was comforting. "Then to what did you refer when you said it was life or death in more way than one when talking with your servant?"

"My…? Oh, you mean Laneham. He forgot to secure the queen's New Year gift. It is both very delicate and very costly, and I did not want it lost." He smiled a sad smile. "Since Amy died, such things have seemed less important."

Lucy rested a comforting hand on his. "It will all come back into balance eventually, my lord, and you will look forward to New Year again."

He smiled and urged his horse to a trot. "Thank you, my lady."

The scent of manure alerted Catrin that they were close to a farm, and she asked Sir Nicolas to draw closer, hoping it would give her some reference as to where they were in the trackless forest. The trees thinned, showing a rutted dirt lane and, on the far side of it, a familiar group of buildings in the shape of a horseshoe.

Catrin slid down from the horse. "It's the Drury farm."

"Beware," Sir Nicolas murmured, and she drew back under cover of the trees just in time. The door to the cottage opened, and Mistress Drury emerged, holding Grisel by one hand and carrying a bucket in the other. They walked together toward the stable, swinging their joined hands between them as they sang 'Scarborough Fair'. The sweet melody drifted to Catrin on a breeze, and gave her an idea.

"Sir Nicolas, do you have any money?"

"Some, but we may need it to buy supplies."

"There is nowhere we would be safe to buy supplies, and our need right now is the greater."

"I can't deny that." He removed the purse from his belt and handed it to her. "What are you going to do?"

She smiled. "Buy a horse."

Catrin decided to re-name the mare Ariadne, because she was helping them escape just as Ariadne had helped Theseus escape the labyrinth. Sir Nicolas approved of that, but he approved of the oat-cakes Mistress Drury had provided far more.

Somewhat revived, they pressed on through the forest, with Catrin leading. She found the pond first, and they stopped to let the horses drink deep and eat what they could get of the grass beside it. Sir Nicolas drank too, and lay down in evident exhaustion. Catrin too was weary, but the pressure inside her to find that satchel overruled all else. She waited until Sir Nicolas drifted off to sleep, and then got up silently and glided through the trees. It was certainly easier to move in a boy's tunic and breeches, but by this point they were stained with all manner of unpleasant things, and thick with dust. Discomfort had become greater than convenience.

She pushed through the undergrowth, searching for the crumbling wall, and finally — finally — caught sight of its pale stone in the shadows cast by the overhanging trees. She dropped to her knees before the triangle of stones and began to dig, and to her delight her fingers soon rested on the smooth, well-worn leather.

She pulled the satchel out and quickly glanced inside. There was no evidence of water damage and it seemed that none of the forest creatures building nests for winter had torn away any of the paper. But was it all there? She was about to look more carefully when Sir Nicolas' voice made her jump. "Is that our prize?"

She rose to her feet and tucked the satchel safely into place at her side. "Yes, it is." Sir Nicolas' face lit up with mingled relief and pleasure, and she smiled at him. "Now we can go to Windsor."

They travelled more than half the distance before the early-setting autumn sun rendered them blind and vulnerable. In silence, Sir Nicolas lit a fire while Catrin foraged for food. The result was a few damsons and some barberries; hardly a feast.

Sir Nicolas ate silently too, his gaze cast to the ground so that the firelight caught his red-gold eyelashes and set them glittering. Catrin stretched out her legs before the heat and tried to rub the stiffness from her knee with her good arm.

"How fare thee, my lady?" Sir Nicolas asked sullenly. "Not in too much pain, I hope?"

"Compared to the pain I might be feeling right now, all is well," Catrin said, and offered a smile. He just cast his eyes down again and started scratching in the dirt with a stick. It was annoying. "Sir Nicolas, I thought you of all people would understand my position."

He shot her an irritated glance. "All I understand is that you do not trust me enough to see the documents we have fought and bled for."

"It is not a matter of trust," Catrin insisted. "Those small pieces of paper represent all the queen asked me to accomplish. I am duty-bound to take them to her unopened."

He sent her a sour look. "Have *you* opened them?"

"I collected them together and put them all in the satchel," Catrin said, and felt it wiser not to expand. "Can you not understand?"

He wrestled with it — she saw the effort it took — but finally nodded. "Thank you," she said, and offered another smile. "And to show my good faith, I will share a different secret."

He looked intrigued, and all the more so when she slid her hand under the linen that bound her breast. She pulled out a copy of her mother's letter and handed it to him, and he frowned at the random strings of characters.

"Where did you find this?"

"My mother sent it to me, which makes it my secret and not the queen's," she said. "Thus, I feel that I can share it with you."

"All is out of order; it means naught but chaos," he said.

"It is a secret message that needs to be deciphered." She sent him a smile, determined to make him forget about the documents she had carefully hidden. "I hoped that you could help me."

CHAPTER TWENTY-ONE

The morning dawned cold, and Catrin's limbs were painfully stiff. She rubbed life into them as best she could while Sir Nicolas doused the embers of the fire, but still had to bite back a cry of pain when he helped her onto Ariadne's back.

Sir Nicolas was silent again, but she suspected that this time it was due to shame. He had had no more luck finding the key to her mother's letter than she had, and he seemed to be far more bothered by failure than she had expected.

She had had enough of trying to cajole him into good humour, so they set off without speaking, moving slowly along the dirt road to save the horses. Her stomach pinched with hunger, but it was no worse than the days of her youth when her stepfather chose to punish her by taking away her meals. So she rode on, into the rising sun, wondering how exactly she was going to explain all this to the queen. And that drew her mind back to Lady Dudley's strange message written in symbols. *The promised gold ... the silver shard.*

Suddenly Sir Nicolas tensed in his saddle. She nodded when he glanced at her; she had heard it too. A horse and cart, approaching with speed.

"We should hide," Catrin said. "Let him pass."

Sir Nicolas nodded and they both dismounted, but they had no time to leave the road before the cart and horse swung around a bend in front of them, wooden wheels rattling. They had to leap out of its way, and the driver twisted in his seat as he passed, staring at him. When he was almost out of sight, they heard him give a loud shout.

"God's teeth," Sir Nicolas swore. "He recognized us."

"He will raise the hue and cry the moment he sees another soul," Catrin said, and jumped back up on Ariadne's back. "We need to get away as fast as we can."

Clouds were gathering over the sun when Lucy and Lord Robert left the inn and pressed onward toward Cumnor. Lucy was glad that Lord Robert set a faster pace than he had the day before; they had barely gone any distance before the darkness had made travel impossible. However, the new day didn't seem much brighter; Lucy had to pull up the hood of her cloak to keep the chill from her neck. Lord Robert noticed the gesture and glanced up. "We'll have a storm before night," he said. "But we'll be in Cumnor by then, and my man is securing rooms for us in the inn."

"Thank God for that," Lucy said. "How far do we have to go?"

He didn't answer; something on the horizon had caught his eye. Before them, the road rose upward, the hard-packed earth flanked on either side by thick tree cover and undergrowth. At the crest of the hill, two horses appeared, riding hard. It looked like two men riding — a gentleman and a page in rough breeches — but Lucy recognized the page. The riding-seat, the way he held the reins, the dark uncovered hair tucked into the tunic's neckline. "That's Catrin!"

Lord Robert squinted dubiously at the two riders. "Ah ... perhaps you see what you wish to see, my lady."

"No, by my heart's root I swear — it's Catrin!" Lucy spurred on her horse and galloped up the hill, her heart bursting with hope and joy — and, yes, fear that she was wrong. To be so close — so sure that she had survived — and then for that hope to be crushed — she was not sure her heart could weather such a blow. "Catrin!"

The page gave a cry but she could not hear the words; the wind whipping around her ears snatched them away. And then the riders were gone. Lucy reached the crest of the hill and found it empty, but for the echo of hooves.

Lucy pulled up her horse and looked around in dismay. Had she imagined it all? Was Lord Robert right, and she had seen merely what she wanted to see?

Lord Robert himself reached the top of the hill and pulled up, and Lucy blinked away tears. "I am sorry, my lord, I thought —"

"They went that way," Lord Robert said, and pointed ahead of him, into the undergrowth. "The question is, why did they run from you?"

Lucy looked down at the marks on the edges of the road that clearly indicated that horses had passed through and was grateful. "I don't —"

"There are more riders approaching." Lord Robert set his hand on his sword, just as a band of men leapt into view.

The next few minutes were all confusion — the men shouted, brandishing clubs and axes — Lord Robert and his men drew their weapons — the horses whinnied and reared up — Lucy's mare tried to bolt and it was all she could do to keep her under control. By the time she had brought the horse back to the crest of the hill, all that was left of the band of men was an abandoned felt cap and the sound of rapid retreat.

Lord Robert spat on the ground. "Miscreants," he said. "I wager they were chasing our two riders, and realised too late that we were not they."

"So the riders need our help," she said.

"Aye," Lord Robert said, and sheathed his sword. "That they do."

Catrin shoved a tree branch away from her face hard enough to hear it crack. "How dare you force me off the road like that?"

Sir Nicolas glanced backward. "I know I saw Lord Robert."

"Aye, and I saw Lucy. They have clearly been sent from court to help us, and you have taken us in the opposite direction!"

"Lord Robert wasn't at court; he was at Kew," Sir Nicolas said. "The queen removed him from her presence, remember? He has no reason to be here, unless he aims to find those documents you are so carefully protecting."

That gave Catrin pause. "But Lucy was at court, and she would never leave without the queen's permission."

Sir Nicolas circled an outcropping of rock and pressed on. "Perhaps he gave her no choice. She certainly seemed eager to get away from him, did she not?"

"She was coming to me, God bless her."

"Perhaps to warn you."

Catrin huffed out a breath. "You see danger around every corner, and treachery in every face."

"Aye," Sir Nicolas said. "And I will do all I can to protect you from it, my lady."

Lucy's eyes ached from the strain of trying to see beyond the trees, and she was growing more and more anxious as the miles passed. "Surely we should have seen something by now, some sign showing where they came back out onto the road," she said, and Lord Robert agreed.

"I can think only that they remained in the forest for some reason — a foolish choice, for I have seen signs of wild boar and possibly wolves in the area." He glanced up at the black clouds rolling about in the sky above them. "It will soon be dark; we must seek shelter at the nearest inn."

"We cannot abandon our search," Lucy protested. "They need our help."

"There is nothing we can do for them until tomorrow," Lord Robert said, and urged his horse to a trot. "Fret not, my lady. As soon as dawn breaks we will make our way into the forest."

Catrin and Sir Nicolas stopped twice when they came across a stream, to water the horses and let them rest, but aside from that they pressed onward, weaving through rough paths in the wood. By dusk, Catrin had reached the end of her endurance. She had no choice but to close her eyes and leave Ariadne to fend for herself. Random words and phrases started drifting through her mind and she fancied she could see them scrolling across her mind's eye. *The truth has many facets ... the blade must land on the right neck ... the knife ... the talisman ... promised gold —*

She bolted upright, startling Ariadne into a whinny. Sir Nicolas glanced back in concern. "How do you fare, my lady?"

"I am well," Catrin whispered, because she suddenly understood. *At the feast ... Cut back the bastard stock....* The message was about an assassination attempt. The killers had once been foiled — stopped — when they attacked the queen with a knife, and now they intended to try again. "Sir Nicolas, we have to hurry. We need to get back to Windsor. Are we close?"

"I ... I don't know." Sir Nicolas reined in his horse and his youthful face blushed red. "I confess, my lady ... I have lost the way."

She bit back recriminations, remembering that he was but a young man and an impulsive one at that, and slid down from

Ariadne's back. "Hold the horse, my lord, I will be but a moment."

She left the path, heading toward the rocky outcrop she could see peeping out between the trees. A second later she heard his footsteps behind her, and glanced back to see him following, his brow furrowed with worry. "Where are you going?"

"To find our way," Catrin said, and began to climb the rock. Once again he followed, and the wind flattened his hair to his head when they reached the top. Catrin peered through the darkness in every direction until she saw a thin brown line sneaking through the trees, off to the right. "I see the road," Catrin said, and pointed. "We need to go that way."

"No, we need to find shelter," Sir Nicolas said, as a crack of thunder sounded. "Quickly."

The rain came with a mighty roar. Lightning made Ariadne pull frantically at the reins, while Sir Nicolas' stallion snorted in displeasure and tossed his head. Catrin had hoped that the rock formation itself would yield a cave, but it was smooth all the way around. They had to press onward, regularly deafened by the roar of thunder while above them the trees tossed and moaned.

Catrin did not mind the rain; it felt cleansing after all she had gone through. She could feel the mud and filth sliding from her skin and was grateful. The cold soothed the itch on her arm and the ache of her knee, as well, and that was a blessed relief. She was almost sorry when a shape loomed before them in the dark. A flash of lightning let her see that it was a sort of hut formed by interlocking branches, and guessed it was somewhere hunters would hide, waiting for prey to pass by.

Sir Nicolas led the horses into a deep sheltered grove, where the pine needles and fallen leaves were dry underfoot, while

Catrin went into the shelter and lit a fire. By the time Sir Nicolas returned, carrying the saddles, it was relatively dry and cosy.

He arranged the saddles so they could lean against them, and settled wearily into a bed of moss. "I saw a stream nearby; when the weather settles I'll take the horses for a drink," he said, and let his head fall back.

"That is a good idea," Catrin said, and fanned out her hair in hopes that the fire would dry it. "I doubt it will last much longer; these sorts of storms quickly blow themselves out."

The words were no sooner out of her mouth than a peal of thunder crashed and the wind howled around them. Sir Nicolas smiled. "Perhaps not this one," he said, and then started to sing an ancient tune she hadn't heard in years. "Shall I go walk the wood so wild; Wand'ring, wand'ring here and there; As I was once full sore beguil'd; Alas! for love I die with woe."

He had a beautiful tenor voice; it called to Catrin like a church-bell and she had to join in. "Wearily blows the winter wind; Wand'ring, wand'ring here and there; My heart is like a stricken hind; Alas! for love I die with woe."

The sound of their voices filled the space with a serene beauty that stood in stark contrast to the rage and fury outside. Sir Nicolas reached out to take her hand. "I didn't know you were a songbird, my dove."

Catrin gently withdrew her hand. "The queen enjoys the ancient songs of Wales, so I have many opportunities to practise."

"So you sing for duty, not for love?"

She dropped her gaze and laced her fingers together in her lap. Once, she could have let him hope and felt no guilt. But now … she could not treat him so. "I cannot love, Sir Nicolas. 'Tis too dangerous."

"Ah, no, my lady. To love is to be safe in the arms of another."

The very thought was absurd, but to spare his feelings Catrin did not laugh. "No, to love is to be left alone and broken."

Lightning flashed, showing the sorrow in his eyes. "I hope to show you differently, my dove," he murmured.

"I fear 'tis I who will show you differently." Catrin said it lightly, but the concern was real. "Guard your heart, sir knight — like the storm, I will soon depart."

To her surprise, he grinned. "And I wager that, like the sunshine, you will return."

CHAPTER TWENTY-TWO

The storm was over, but water still dripped from the trees and splashed on the dead leaves below. Catrin went to the nearby stream to water the horses and wash her face, longing for a hot bath and a change of clothes. But at least they knew what direction to take now, and she would guide them. It was her own fault that they had gotten lost; she had allowed Sir Nicolas to take the lead without considering whether he had as much experience in the forest as she. A mistake she would not make twice.

A twig snapped on the other side of the stream, and on the far side of the horses she heard a sudden splash. She rose silently, leaving the horses behind, and backed into the forest, moving lightly to the shelter. Sir Nicolas was still asleep, his back propped against the saddle, and she nudged his elbow with her foot to wake him. He rose to his feet in one smooth movement, and nodded once when she warned him to be silent with one finger against her lips.

She led them out of the shelter, parallel to the path, retracing their steps toward the wall of rock they had climbed the day before. A faint shout made Sir Nicolas swear under his breath; he knew as well as she did that it meant their pursuers had found the horses.

Catrin promised herself that she would retrieve Ariadne no matter what she had to do, and kept moving. After several long minutes, she had the sensation that someone was moving along with them on their left side, just out of sight among the trees.

Sir Nicolas glanced behind them, then caught her gaze and held up two fingers. Ahead of them the trees abruptly thinned, and they found themselves at the edge of a mossy clearing. Catrin began to circle the edge, moving toward the right, holding the satchel tight against her ribs with the pressure of her arm. But then she caught sight of a flash of white through the trees and knew there were people on that side as well. To their left, to their right, directly behind … they had only one choice.

As one, she and Sir Nicolas plunged into the centre of the clearing and ran. Men brandishing homemade weapons burst from the trees, shouting with glee and triumph. Sir Nicolas let out a roar and drew his sword, swinging it in wide ferocious arcs that made them fall back with snarls of frustration. "Run, my lady," Sir Nicolas cried. "I will hold them off."

Catrin's eyes locked on the man at the edge of the trees and her whole body froze. It was the one who had kicked her, injuring her knee. And beside him was the man who had held her still with his hands around her neck. Suddenly she could feel the heat of the branding iron, hear the sizzle of the coals, and the terror of it held her fast to her place.

Sir Nicolas swung again and a wide band of blood bloomed from a man's chest. His scream jolted Catrin into action. She drew her knife from beneath her sleeve and faced off the first man who charged her, deflecting his club with her blade and slicing through his fingers. He shrieked and fell to the ground, just as another man grabbed her from behind. She swung the knife up and back, and buried it deep in his shoulder. He too fell screaming.

Sir Nicolas was fighting three men at once, his short *main gauche* blade in his left hand and his sword in his right. "What are you doing?" he shouted. "Run!"

Where did he think she could go? They were all around them, circling now like dogs at a bear baiting. The injured men were crawling away, but there were plenty left to fight. And even as she thought it, two of them darted forward. One grabbed her right hand, squeezing her wrist until she dropped the knife. The other grabbed her left, twisting it up and behind her back. She kicked at him, trying to break out of his grip, and then heard Sir Nicolas cry out.

He was down.

Three men were on top of him with clubs and knives, and Catrin had no doubt that he was dead. They were lost, and she could feel the doughy fingers of the man who held her reaching toward the pouch at her side.

"Sirrah, blackguards! Fall back, you scoundrels!"

The roar startled them all, and every face turned toward the sound. Three figures in black leapt out of the trees with swords and daggers bared, and the surprise of it loosened her captors' grip. Catrin tore herself free and dropped to her knees to retrieve her knife, then drove it into the nearest foot. The man swore and toppled, just as another reared up before her with a knife in his hand and hate in his eyes. Catrin jumped up to defend herself, and saw a small figure in pale green jump into the clearing behind him. She had a gnarled branch in her hands and brought it down on the man's head with a sickening thud.

"Lucy," Catrin gasped. "*Lucy*."

"Catrin, come!" Lucy cried, and ran back into the forest.

Catrin stumbled over to her and collapsed, unable to believe what she was seeing. In seconds the three men in black had sent four men howling into the forest. Three more lay groaning at their feet, and several hovered at the edge of the trees, unsure whether or not to flee.

"Enough!" The tallest of the three black-clad men, who was Lord Robert himself, swung his sword up in salute and his men stepped back from the fight, breathing hard. "Come and collect your wounded, you knaves. We will not attack you."

"That woman is a horse-thief, and that man has grievously wounded our constable," said the man who had kicked Catrin. "We wish to claim the queen's justice, my lord."

"These two people were engaged on a task by the queen herself, and you have obviously done all you can to stop them," Lord Robert said coolly. "Are you certain you wish to involve the queen in this matter?"

The man grunted in frustration and held up his hands in surrender before he told three of his men to collect their wounded. Meanwhile, Lord Robert's two companions had already started helping Sir Nicolas. He was hideously pale, and his forehead wet with sweat. When they lifted him up, Catrin saw that his doublet was dark with blood.

Her stomach lurched. "Is he dead?"

"No, my lady, just injured. He needs to rest," one of the men said. "We'll set up a shelter uphill from the stream and —"

"Shelter?" Catrin glanced up at the sun, which still hung high in the sky. "Would it not be better to return to Windsor?"

"I'm not sure he can ride that far," Lord Robert said.

Catrin pressed her hand against her side. "Perhaps your men could stay with him, then, and we can return."

Lucy's eyes went wide with shock. "You would leave him? After he fought for you?"

Lord Robert said nothing, but Catrin saw the disappointment in his eyes and marvelled that it bothered her so much. It had not been very long ago that the opinions of others — any others — had counted for little when weighed against her own interests. But now… "I have good reason, I swear to you both.

It is very important that we get back to Windsor as soon as possible."

Lord Robert furrowed his brow. "Does this reason have something to do with what happened at Cumnor Place?"

"Yes, it does," Catrin said. "But I cannot say more until I have spoken to the queen. Please, Lord Robert, trust me. I will reveal all when I can."

Lord Robert pondered for a moment more and then turned to his men. "Rig up a litter for Sir Nicolas and follow us when you can," he said. "We three will return to Her Majesty."

The sun shone brightly on the burnished orange and gold of the trees around them as they cantered back to the palace. They saw not a single soul on the road, which remained clear from obstacles and pitfalls all the way. In no time the trees gave way to grasses and fields, and then to small, neat dwellings between cobbled streets. They slowed to a walk as King Henry's gate reared up before them, and Catrin dared to believe that she had finally made it home.

"Wait!"

Lucy's cry made Catrin jump.

"What is it?"

"I saw something. We have to stop."

The last thing Catrin wanted to do was stop, but Lord Robert had already pulled up so she had little choice. Lucy slid down from her horse and landed hard on the ground, then scurried over to the long grass just outside the castle and reached in to retrieve something that glinted gold in the sun. Lord Robert dismounted just as she held it up to the light. "The hilt of a ballock knife," he said. "It's finely wrought — and gilded with gold."

"The blade is broken," Lucy said. "It's at a strange angle, is it not?"

Catrin slid down as well so she could see it more closely. "I think it matches the angle on the blade we found at Cumnor," she said. "And that means we must hasten all the more."

"Why?" Lucy asked.

"If the hilt is here," Lord Robert said grimly, "so is the murderer."

For all their haste, they still had to prepare themselves before they could see the queen. Catrin entrusted the documents to Lucy and took a bath, scrubbing herself clean of the muck and mire she had gathered over the long journey. It felt very good indeed to be clad in fresh linen and the soft folds of black velvet, with her hair neatly pinned up underneath a hood lined with tiny diamonds and a rope of pearls around her neck. Her aching feet were soothed by the soft cushiony comfort of court slippers, her burned hands bathed in perfumed balm, and a shawl scented with lavender draped around her shoulders for warmth. The simple pleasure of it freed her mind to focus entirely on the problem at hand.

Namely, how to tell the queen that her favourite's wife had been a traitor.

They gathered in the same hidden antechamber in which they had once met in the dead of night. Besides Lord Robert and Lucy, the only other person granted admittance was Lady Mary Sidney, who came bearing food from the evening meal they were missing.

The queen sat down in a cushioned chair of sandalwood and satin, and the rest of them settled on low cushions at her feet. There was no fire, so a draught of cool air eddied around them, making the candlelight sputter and the tapestries on the wall wave gently back and forth.

"Let us begin by thanking God that you are still alive, Catrin," the queen said. "We all mourned sincerely when we thought you had died."

"I mourned when I thought I would never return," Catrin said, and meant it. "My place is in your service, Your Majesty, and I am so grateful to be in your presence again."

The queen's eyes lit with humour. "That sounds like a prelude to a sad song."

She wasn't wrong. Catrin cleared her throat and opened the satchel, pulling out the documents and piling them neatly at the queen's feet. "I found these in Lady Dudley's hiding-place in the orchard," she said. "There are letters expressing her dissatisfaction with — ahem — Lord Robert's dedication to Your Majesty, and a defamatory tract against Your Majesty which I believe has now been printed. There is also a secret message suggesting that the lady was involved in the attempt on Your Majesty's life during the coronation. Most importantly —"

"No," Lord Robert broke in harshly, breathing hard. "This is not true. How dare you impugn the honour of my wife! How dare you suggest that she was — she was —"

"A traitor," the queen said calmly.

Lord Robert's face turned deeply red. "She was no such thing, Your Majesty. I swear to you, she understood that my position required me to be at court. She was not angry to remain in the country; that was where she preferred to be." His voice quivered with fury, and Catrin had to admire his control. He simply said, with quiet intensity, "There was no reason for her to take part in treason."

"Yes, there was," the queen said quietly. "It was upon my request."

Lord Robert jumped to his feet and backed away until he hit the wall with a thump. "You ... you..." He cleared his throat forcefully and tried again. "Your Majesty, I beg your pardon, but I thought I heard you say —"

"I did," the queen said, and Catrin noticed that while her voice was calm, her hand was shaking. "Soon after my sister died, Sir William Paulet, the Marquess of Winchester, came to me. He said that he had heard of a conspiracy against my claim to the throne, but did not know who was involved. At first I did not believe him, but after the ... incident ... at the coronation procession took place, I realised that the threat was real. The marquess and I tried to discover more, but every attempt was thwarted."

"So you decided to force the conspirators to reveal themselves by placing someone amongst them," Lord Robert said woodenly.

"Yes."

"It is a good strategy." He clenched his fists so tightly the knuckles cracked. "But Amy ... why Amy? She was so shy, so innocent ... how could you ask this of her?"

"She had every cause to be disgruntled, so they believed quickly in her loyalty to their cause. She and I told everyone that she was ill, to make them believe that she had nothing to lose. And then, later, her supposed bad health — which some speculate was poison — gave her an excuse to move to Cumnor when she grew suspicious of Richard Verney."

"But Amy was not up to such a task," Lord Robert said. "She was such a simple girl..."

"It was difficult for her, yes, but for both your sake and mine she was willing to do as I asked," the queen said. "She was so passionately determined to discover the conspirators, Robert — so very determined."

"Picto told us she heard Lady Amy asking God to deliver her from desperation," Catrin said quietly. "Perhaps it was not the desperation of despair, but the overwhelming desire to succeed in her mission."

"I truly think it was." A faint plea crept into the queen's tone. "She did good work, Robin. She told us about the publishers of the tract, and we were able to find and stop them before its printed poison could be spread throughout the realm. She reported the involvement of Lord Ashbourne and the suspected involvement of Richard Verney. And it was she who found the proof that the conspirators were responsible for the attack at my coronation."

Silently Catrin retrieved that paper and handed it to Lord Robert. He read it, his throat working. "Churls and blackguards, cowards and slaves," he muttered violently, and handed it back. "What could my Amy do against such dangerous foes?"

"Gather information. Specifically, we needed to know who was at the heart of this conspiracy," the queen said. "We left Ashbourne and Verney alone despite our knowledge of their guilt, because we knew that the person we needed to find was their master. They are but foot-soldiers; we need to know who gives them their orders."

"But if she found out their master's name — and she may well have done — that master had cause to kill her," Lord Robert said hoarsely. "And that means that … all this time … you have known that my wife was murdered, and why."

"I suspected. I did not know," the queen corrected him gently. "And that is why I did not accept the coroner's verdict, and why I listened with such interest to the discoveries that suggested that someone was with Amy on that last day, even though she sent everyone away."

"I understand your reasoning, Your Majesty, but the fact remains that my wife is dead." Tears glittered in Lord Robert's eyes. "She is dead, and her death was in vain."

"That is not true. We know far more than we did when Amy first started to gather information. This move to Cumnor Place was most advantageous; we believe that Amy may have discovered who the master was. She hinted as much in the last letter she sent to the marquess of Winchester."

"But she died before she could confirm her suspicions," Lord Robert said.

"Yes — after she managed to hide all of her notes and proofs. And now, thanks to God's good guidance and Catrin's courage, we have those notes and proofs. We have a chance to learn what she knew."

Lord Robert's eyes lit on the papers with the first hint of real interest. He and the queen started sifting through the documents, and he paused for a moment at the page with the musical notes. "My songbird," he murmured, and set it delicately aside.

The queen passed quickly through the letters, and stopped on the page of drawings. "Hmmm."

"They were drawn with invisible ink, which takes great skill," Catrin said. "And hidden within a stack of blank paper."

A streak of red burned across the queen's cheeks, revealing an excitement her tone did not. "This tells us much."

Lucy leaned closer, a faint line appearing between her brows. "But it is naught but a drawing of a field with trees, Your Majesty. With a soldier at the bottom."

"A spearman. The name 'Roger' means 'spearman' — and the Earl of Ashbourne's first name is Roger," the queen said. "Also, the printer's name was Field."

Lucy's eyes went wide. "She was naming the conspirators as she discovered them!"

"I believe so." The queen pointed to the drawing of the clutch of trees. "Those are alders, and the name 'Verney' means alder grove. So she had finally confirmed Verney's involvement. That is three conspirators named — Roger Surovell, Richard Verney, and John Field. I do not know what that little hand means — it seems to be pointing at the branch of the tree."

"And that leads us to the most important of these documents, Your Majesty," Catrin said, and started sifting through the pile. "It is why I needed to see you so urgently. I believe another attack is imminent."

Lord Robert's shock immediately gave way to anger. "They intend to try again?"

"It seems so," Catrin said, and a chill ran down her back as she reached the bottom of the pile. She searched through once more, paper rustling as she grew more and more frantic, and finally she had to sit back on her heels and face the truth. "It's gone."

The queen frowned. "What is gone?"

"The letter written in symbols," Catrin said. "I-I translated it, but burned my notes. And now the original is gone."

Lord Robert knelt before her, his shoulders tense beneath his grey doublet. "Do you remember what it said?"

"Of course, but —" She put a hand to her head in an attempt to stop it spinning. "I can't believe — how could it possibly be missing?"

"Catrin," Lucy said. "Please — don't distress yourself —"

"I — I never let the documents out of my sight after — but did I retrieve it from the forest? I can't remember — I can't say when I saw it last — when did I —?"

So much effort — so much time and discomfort — and she had failed. That most important letter, that vital proof, was gone. "I'm so sorry, Your Majesty."

"Calm yourself, child," the queen said. "What did the letter say?"

It took Catrin a moment to clear the fog in her mind, and in that time Lucy quietly readied a quill and paper. "*At the feast with the branch, cut back the bastard stock to purify, how once foiled, under the canopy, the promised gold, before the silver shard.*"

Lucy wrote it down and tilted her head to the side, reading it. "Um … are you sure this is about an attack? Oh, wait, I see. The bastard stock is the queen." She froze, horrified. "I mean — I do apologise, Your Majesty — I just meant —"

"I know what you meant," the queen said with a chuckle. "But do not repeat it."

"Yes, Your Majesty," Lucy said meekly, and squirmed. "I mean, no, Your Majesty."

"Promised gold," Lord Robert murmured. "That could be payment … due when?"

"Before the silver shard. I thought that might mean the new moon," Catrin said. "That is why I thought it an imminent problem — the new moon will first show itself two days hence."

"But the moon waxes and wanes each month," Lord Robert said. "We have no way of knowing when the letter was sent."

"It was dated the seventh of September," Catrin said.

"The same day as Amy wrote her last note to the marquess," the queen said thoughtfully. "Something in that letter of symbols must have told her who the master conspirator was."

"And she died the day after." Lord Robert rose to his feet again and turned away from them all. "My poor Amy."

"Could we perhaps keep our minds on our current task?" the queen said coolly. "It does seem that my death is at hand, after all."

"Perhaps you can avoid it simply by not attending feasts," Lucy said.

"I must attend feasts," the queen said impatiently. "They are held in my honour, or to honour important guests whom I cannot slight."

"So we must discover what — or who — this 'branch' could be," Catrin said. "And as quickly as possible."

Lord Robert quirked one eyebrow. "Lady Catrin, your tone suggests that you already have an idea of how to do so."

"I think we must continue Lady Dudley's work," Catrin said. "Using what she has discovered, we must find out who is behind this conspiracy."

"A fine idea, but I fear the action will prove more difficult than the planning," Lord Robert said wryly. "Where could you even begin?"

"With my stepfather, Lord Ashbourne," Catrin said. "If you were to recall him to court, Your Majesty, and I convinced him that your forgiveness was my doing…"

The queen shook her head. "A man as experienced in deception as he would not give up the name so easily."

"I agree, Your Majesty," Catrin said. "That is why I would not ask for the name — I would ask to become a conspirator."

Lucy gasped. "Oh, Catrin, no! That is too dangerous."

"It is necessary," Catrin said, and turned to the queen. "Please, Your Majesty. Let me finish what Lady Amy began. It is the only way to find out who killed her, and prevent another attempt on your life."

"I admire your courage, my talisman," the queen said quietly. "I will consider it."

The queen did not need them in her chamber that night, and Catrin was grateful. The effort of hiding her injuries was nearly as painful as the injuries themselves, and she was exhausted.

Lucy knew — she always knew — but she didn't say so out loud. Instead, she turned away from their usual path to the ladies' bedchamber and took the shortest way, which cut across the kitchen court. They pushed open the arched wooden door that led outside, and a damp wind scented with impending rain fought them ferociously, whipping around their faces and snatching the door from their hands. It thumped shut, leaving them penned in a deeply shadowed square of stone, where their every footstep echoed and the darkness was absolute. They linked arms without thinking and started forward, only to freeze when a mighty sound — a long keening roar — ripped the air above their heads.

A horror remembered since childhood snatched the strength from Catrin's limbs. "'Tis the *Cyhyraeth*," she whispered. "The black-clad spectre who weeps and wails for the Welsh who die far from home."

"Oh, don't," Lucy cried. The sound came again and she tugged hard on Catrin's arm. "We need to hurry — get inside — quickly, Catrin, please!"

Catrin forced herself onward, but as they emerged from the shelter of the gallery above, she cast a haunted glance upward and a cry tore from her lips. A great black hulk was hurtling towards them, whistling and flapping like an enormous bat. Catrin pushed Lucy out of its path and dived in the opposite direction. The thing landed between them and they both scrambled further away, breathing hard.

"Lucy," Catrin whispered. "Are you all right?"

Lucy rose shakily to her feet and wiped her hands on her skirt. "I-I think I am. Are you?"

"Aye, well enough."

Lucy sidestepped the thing with her eyes averted and returned to Catrin's side, taking her arm in a grip so tight it pinched. "What is it?"

Catrin led Lucy away, stepping carefully around a dark puddle that was spreading around the thing with sickening speed. "It is a man, dearling. No, do not look. It is a sight you should not see."

Lucy's voice came out as a squeak. "A man! Is he dead?"

"Most certainly."

The wind rippled the surface of the puddle, raising a sickly sweet metallic scent, and Lucy covered her nose. "What should we do?"

"Get far away from here," Catrin said. "And then send for Lord Robert."

CHAPTER TWENTY-THREE

After the horrors of the night, it seemed strange for Catrin to start the day as she always did, walking in the gardens with the queen and talking of light-hearted, meaningless things. It also proved too difficult to take up her hemming when they returned to the castle; she simply could not settle down. Finally she gave up trying, and asked for permission to leave the queen's presence. She said that she wanted to go see how Sir Nicolas had fared on the long journey home, but that was only part of the reason.

The queen agreed readily, and allowed Lucy to accompany her on the long walk from the royal chambers to Sir Nicolas' lodgings. When they arrived, they found a young man sitting on the floor outside, legs crossed, busily repairing a tear in a pair of red hose. He leapt to his feet when he saw them, and bent low. "My ladies, God give you good morrow," he said in a voice decidedly tinged with Cornwall. "How can I help you?"

"We wish to see Sir Nicolas," Catrin said. "How fares he?"

"He is still sleeping, my ladies. The physician came several times yesterday, and it has exhausted him."

Lucy bit her lip. "Is he in mortal danger?"

The servant glanced back at the door. "I do not think so, but if the wound grows infected…"

"We understand," Catrin said. "When he wakes, please tell him we came."

The servant bowed low again. "Of course, your ladyship."

"Thank you," Catrin said, and turned to go back the way they came. The echo of their footsteps against the flagstones brought the events of the night before vividly back to mind, and reminded her of the other reason she had wanted to leave the royal chambers. "Dearling, what do you remember about last night?"

Lucy shivered. "I'm trying hard not to remember anything."

"I understand, but it may be important. Do you recall if there was anyone in the gallery above us?"

"No … I saw only that mass of black. I thought you were right and that wailing spectre had come for us both."

"It was certainly a strange sound," Catrin murmured. "Like a man … and yet also like an animal."

"Yes, and I hope I never hear it again," Lucy said fervently. "Did you see anyone?"

"Not a person, no … more like… like a moving shadow. I could not identify it. Forsooth, I wonder now if I truly saw it at all." Catrin sighed and passed one hand over the satin of her hood. "We have turned full circle. Once again I find myself asking if a death was murder, accident or suicide."

"But it is not our task to find out," Lucy said. "It has nothing to do with Lady Dudley."

"We cannot know that for certain. Perhaps the man was part of the conspiracy, and the master conspirator had him killed." Catrin straightened, and started moving with purpose down the corridor. "We must go to the gallery."

Lucy raised both hands before her, as if to fend off the thought. "Oh — no — I do not wish to see that spot again."

Catrin understood. Nor did she, in truth. "Fair enough, dearling. I will meet you back in the queen's chambers, then."

She turned to the right, expecting to hear Lucy's footsteps take the alternate path. When she heard nothing, she paused and looked back. Lucy was fingering the pomander at her waist. "Wait," she said, and hurried to catch up. "I cannot let you go alone."

Catrin smiled at her. "Thank you."

They went not to the kitchen court, but to the gallery above, and leaned out between the stone arches to look down. In the morning light the flagstones seemed to glow golden-yellow, but for one spot in the middle which was stained dark brown. Lucy could not tear her eyes from it. "I hear the sound of the fall," she murmured. "The rush of wind, that sickening thud —"

A quiet sob interrupted her. It was one of the maids of honour, a slip of a girl in a white gown with fur-lined sleeves. She stood just a few feet away, fat tears rolling down her thin cheeks. Her chest heaved with the effort of keeping them in check.

Lucy went over to her, offering the handkerchief she kept in her sleeve. "Prithee do not weep, little pet. Can we be of any help?"

"Only if you can wake the dead," the girl said, and wiped her eyes with such vigour her cheeks turned red. "Oh, Richard, to think you died for me!"

Catrin stroked her fingertips over the stone balustrade. "You knew the man who died here?"

"I wanted to marry him, but my father refused," the girl sobbed. "He betrothed me to a greasy lump of a baron instead … and when I told Richard he was so upset. He left me there and then. I-I returned to my chamber alone, and this morning I heard … I heard…" She let out a wail and cast herself into Lucy's arms.

Lucy soothed and petted her as best she could, but Catrin walked away. It did not seem likely that this Richard had thrown himself over the balcony just because his wooing had failed. However, until she found reason to believe otherwise, it was just as possible as any other scenario.

It did not take long to find reason to believe otherwise. And to make sure the girl did not see it, Catrin turned so quickly her long full sleeves caught the wind and billowed outward. "You poor creature," she said. "I think you should go to the great hall for some wine, and then take a good long sleep."

The girl seemed to think that was a good idea. Lucy offered to go with her, but she said she could make her own way and tottered off down the gallery.

Lucy looked at Catrin with suspicion. "That was a good suggestion, and yet I suspect you did not even listen to her troubles."

Catrin shrugged. "Wine and a nap are always a good suggestion," she said. "And I needed her gone so I could show you this."

She retrieved her proof from the crack in the stone beneath her skirts, and a gleam of metal made Lucy's jaw drop. "It is the same button as we found at Cumnor Place!"

"Not literally the same, for I imagine that particular button is at the bottom of a well somewhere. But it is certainly its twin. I found it here."

Lucy frowned, and peered not at the spot but at the balustrade above it. Long, angry marks scored the stone, showing nearly white against the moss and lichen. "Are those the marks of a knife?"

"Or a dagger," Catrin said. "It makes me wonder if that man — Richard, if we believe our heartbroken lass — was stabbed here and then thrown over the balcony."

"He was not."

The quiet voice made them both turn. Lord Robert was standing in the stone arch, holding the door open with his hand. He let it fall and came forward to inspect the marks. "I just came from the coroner. The man died when his head hit the flagstones below."

"How horrible," Lucy whispered, and murmured a prayer under her breath.

"So there were no wounds on his body?" Catrin asked.

"None. Which suggests either that the blade missed several times before his attacker finally resorted to pushing him — which calls his skill into question — or the marks and button have nothing to do with this death."

"Who was he?" Catrin asked. "Did anyone have reason to kill him?"

Lord Robert lowered his voice. "He was one of the queen's esquires of the body."

"They're the men who guard the queen's chambers at night," Lucy said. "Catrin, we may well have known him!"

"Perhaps," Lord Robert said. "He was not on duty last night, which is why he was not wearing his livery. His fellows do not know why he left the barracks to go wandering around here."

"We might know that," Catrin said, and summarised what the crying girl had told them. "But I'm afraid we didn't get her name, so it may be difficult to question her further."

Far to their right, another arched door swung open and a man stepped out onto the gallery. He was clad in black robes, with a great chain around his neck, and the sight of him made Lucy's face light up. "Sir William!"

He squinted over at them, and then his face relaxed into a smile. "Lady Lucretia! Just the person I was looking for. May I have a word with you?"

"Of course, my lord," she said, and scurried toward him. He started toward her at the same time, so they met nearly in the middle. He drew a piece of paper from the leather case he carried, and her face turned pink with excitement. "Catrin, come see!"

Catrin took her leave of a highly amused Lord Robert and joined them. "Good morrow, my lord."

"Good morrow," Sir William said, and handed her a rubbing of the wax seal she had found in the miniature. "I have found the family attached to this seal."

"My hearty thanks, Sir William," Catrin said. "Whose is it?"

"It belonged to the Swann family, before they took the title of Viscount D'Alloway."

Catrin's fingers clenched tight around the paper. "*Swann*?"

"Yes. One would have thought that birds would feature in a Swann family crest, but apparently … are you quite well, my lady?"

"I am, thank you," Catrin said, though her heart was pounding. "Please do excuse me, my lord, I must speak to someone about this."

"Of course," he said, but the crease on his forehead told of his concern.

"I will come with you," Lucy said, and curtsied quickly to Sir William before they went back into the castle. "I don't understand, Catrin — it seems you're angry that Sir William found the owners."

"Nay, I am angry at Sir Nicolas for saying nothing about his family's connection to my mother," Catrin said, and picked up her skirts with one hand so she could move all the more rapidly through the corridors. "For days we travelled together. I even let him see my mother's last letter. And he never gave any indication that they had met."

Lucy almost had to run to keep up. "Perhaps they didn't," she panted. "Perhaps he didn't know she had the seal."

"We'll soon find out," Catrin said grimly, and then said nothing more until they reached Sir Nicolas' lodgings. The young servant jumped up again, ready to stop them, but she swept by him and pushed open the door.

They entered a small room, close and stuffy, thick with the smell of turpentine and rose oil which the physician must have used to cleanse the wound. Sir Nicolas lay on a bed without a canopy, his eyes closed and his forehead damp with sweat. "Sir Nicolas," Catrin said, in a voice like winter frost. "Wake up."

The servant darted into the room, his needle and hose abandoned. "He cannot be disturbed, my lady. Please, can you not return when he is better?"

Catrin sent him a look that froze him in his tracks. "No."

Sir Nicolas moaned, and his eyes fluttered open. "My dove," he said hoarsely, and held out reddened hands. "I knew you would come."

"I have come once in friendship and once in anger," Catrin said. "What do you know of my mother's disappearance?"

He moaned again and his eyes fell closed. Catrin said his name again, but there was no response. Short of shaking him awake, which would have been an indignity for them all, they could not rouse him.

Catrin finally gave up, striding out of the room in renewed anger. "It seems like they all want to keep me from the truth," she muttered. "Why?"

"I do not know," Lucy said sadly. "Indeed, I do not even know how to find out."

Catrin pressed a hand to her forehead. "Nor do I."

The queen sat down abruptly in the nearest chair, as if her knees had given way. "One of my own esquires?"

"Yes, Your Highness," Lord Robert said. "A good, God-fearing man by all accounts."

"And he was murdered?"

Yes, Catrin thought. To her, there was little doubt of it, and it was maddening that Lord Robert was not willing to make that leap.

"'Tis hard to say for certain, Your Highness," he said. "But there is certainly evidence that someone else was there on the balcony."

"Someone associated with the death of Lady Amy," Catrin added, since it seemed unlikely that Lord Robert would. Lucy glanced up at her, eyes wide, and then prudently returned her gaze to her embroidery.

The queen sagged back in her chair. "God's heart, will this never end?"

Lord Robert sent Catrin a warning glance. "It is possible that the two deaths are not related, Your Highness."

"Not really," Catrin said, and folded her hands together in front of her. "After all, how likely is it that we have two murderers at large at the same time, my lord?"

His answering smile was the kind that showed all his teeth. "More likely than you might think, my lady."

"No, she is correct," the queen said faintly. "This must be connected to Amy's death, especially as we have not yet identified all the conspirators."

"Something we need to do soon, if we are ever again to eat at a feast without fear," Catrin murmured.

"Yes." The queen's eyes narrowed. "Lucy, have you yet made any sense of that last document, the song lyrics?"

Lucy shook her head and Lord Robert shrugged. "Amy wrote music all the time, Your Highness. I doubt it is at all significant."

"But it was hidden with the other documents. That suggests that it *is* significant," Catrin said.

Lord Robert threw up his hands in frustration. "My lady, you are very contrary today. I believe that if I suggested the sky was blue, you would argue it was —"

Catrin nodded toward the clouds sliding past the window and dared to smile. "Grey."

The queen actually laughed, and even Lord Robert managed a rueful smile. "So it is," he said. "I surrender, my lady — you have won."

"Nay, my victory will only come when our queen is safe," Catrin said. "Please, Your Majesty, let me take on Amy's task, and so finally end this conspiracy and bring her killers before you."

"No!" Lucy cried. "Catrin, we already almost lost you. What if —"

"This time I will remain at court," Catrin said. "So help will be near at hand — I hope."

Lord Robert inclined his head. "I am at your service, my lady, should the queen wish it."

The queen was quiet for a few minutes, and finally nodded once. "So it shall be," she said. "We will recall that blackguard stepfather of yours to court tomorrow."

Catrin sunk into a deep curtsy. "Thank you, Your Majesty."

CHAPTER TWENTY-FOUR

She was still being dissuaded from visiting Sir Nicolas, so Catrin stole an hour in the afternoon to look for the marquess, Sir William Paulet. He proved difficult to find — everywhere she went he had just left or had not yet arrived. She had long started to suspect that he was avoiding her when she found one of his men in the great hall, drinking deep of some ale that had been left behind from the midmorning meal.

"Good day, Master Weatherby," Catrin said, and stepped quickly to the right to block his retreat. "You move quickly, goodman. Can you not stay and talk?"

"Not if I want to keep my position." He drained his cup. "Do excuse me, my lady."

"I'm afraid I cannot. I need to know about the guests in your lord's manor house."

The man looked at her in surprise. "What guests?"

He looked genuinely confused, and a twinge of unease rippled along her skin. "I was told there is a lady with long dark hair who walks the parapet."

"I have never seen such a lady at the manor."

"And how long have you served the marquess?"

"Nearly a year."

"Have you ever heard of a lady living there? Have any of your fellow-servants mentioned it?"

"We are told not to discuss who comes to the manor and when."

"But people do come. And do they stay?"

He shifted his weight uneasily from foot to foot. "Sometimes."

"Are they all free to leave when they wish?"

"Of course. There are no locked doors or dungeons."

Catrin pondered that. It seemed her source of information may have been mistaken. "Have you ever seen an old man deliver flour there?"

He grinned. "Oh, yes. Mad old Master Walter. He has a tale to tell for anyone who drops him a coin."

"I see." The disappointment was like a stab to the heart, taking her breath away for a second. "Thank you, Master Weatherby."

Relief loosened his shoulders. "Is that really all you wanted to know?"

She narrowed her eyes. "What else *should* I want to know?"

"I expected you to ask about the riverbank. The marquess said —" He froze in horror and his cup dropped from nerveless fingers.

Catrin rose up on her tiptoes to bring her face close to his and lowered her voice to a breathy whisper. It was a method that had worked for her many times before. "I would be so happy to hear about the riverbank, Master Weatherby. Prithee, what did the marquess say?"

"Nothing," he said hastily, and beat a hasty retreat. Indeed, he was moving so quickly the tapestries fluttered on his way past.

Catrin stared after him, frustration rising like bile inside her. Once again, new information brought only new questions. Would she never learn what she so desperately wanted to know?

A hand landed on her arm and tightened painfully, dragging her around until she faced the Earl of Shrewsbury's son. "Do release me, Lord Talbot," she said icily. "I have injured that arm and you are hurting me."

His lips contracted away from his teeth, making him look like an angry animal. "Are you here in search of my father?"

"No. I have not seen him since I returned to court," Catrin said. "But if your father chooses to spend time with me, I would be pleased to have his company."

He pushed in, standing so close she could see each stitch in the lace lining the neckline of his shirt. "You want his money and status, not his company," he hissed. "And you have nothing to offer in return. You are nothing but the daughter of one of Wyatt's rebels, and that makes you no better than a traitor."

"A rebel's daughter I may be," she said, and deliberately let her eyes travel from his nose to his toes. "And yet I am still better than some."

His hand tightened and pain shot down into her fingers. "You base-born wench, you dare say such a thing to me?"

"Release her. Now."

The voice had the rumble of authority and Lord Talbot let her go at once. They both looked up to find the Earl of Shrewsbury himself advancing toward them. "Father," Lord Talbot said stiffly. "I was merely —"

"Interfering," the earl snapped. "Leave my presence."

Lord Talbot opened his mouth to speak, but thought better of it and walked away with a face like thunder. Catrin rubbed at the throbbing wound on her arm and hoped it was not bleeding again. "Thank you, my lord. I do hope I have not caused any trouble."

"I'm afraid you have, my lady." A twinkle lit in the earl's dark eyes. "But do not fret. It is part of your charm."

"Why thank you, my lord." She fluttered her lashes at him. "Shall we take a turn around the garden?"

He offered his arm. "I should like nothing better."

The evening meal came too soon. Catrin could not help but worry that something would happen to the queen, even though there were no branches in sight and it wasn't really a feast. Lord Robert was worried as well; he broke protocol completely and hovered near the queen while the ladies of the bedchamber set the table with gleaming silver and the finest linen. He retreated somewhat when the ceremony began, but only out of necessity; there was not much space for him when the ladies took up their positions.

Catrin and Lucy were on duty, so they stood ready on either side of the queen until a flare of trumpets announced the arrival of the gentlemen ushers with a dozen platters of food. Lucy quickly rubbed the gilt plates with bread and salt, while Mistress Ashley went to the first usher, cut a piece of fish from the dish he held, and fed it to him. Then she took the dish and carried it to the queen's table. She set it down and curtsied to the queen, who looked at the dish and shook her head. Mistress Ashley curtsied again, then took the dish out to the presence chamber for the ladies.

Lucy was next. She fed a piece of chicken from the second dish to the usher, and then carried the dish to the table. The queen nodded, so Lucy cut more of the chicken and transferred it to the queen's plate just as the queen sent Lord Robert a sharp glance. "You are behaving as if you expect an attacker at any moment, Robin," she said, so suddenly that Lucy jumped. "Do stop it."

"Yes, Your Majesty," he said with a sweeping bow, but did not relax.

Lucy carried the rest of the dish out of the room, and then it was Catrin's turn. She collected a dish of veal in an orange sauce, fed some to the usher, and carried it to the queen, who nodded her acceptance. "I have heard tales today, Catrin. They tell me that you have not heeded my request."

Catrin set the platter down so she could cut the meat for her. "Like Lord Robert, I cannot help but be concerned for you, Your Majesty."

"Not that," the queen said impatiently. "I refer to my advice to let the past lie."

Catrin lowered her gaze to the table between them and transferred the food to the queen's plate. "I am truly sorry, Your Majesty. I tried, but my mother's fate continues to haunt me."

The queen regarded her for a long moment, her eyes hooded like a falcon's at rest. "Perhaps it is best to tell you, then," she murmured, and Catrin's eyes widened with surprise.

"Tell me what, Your Majesty?"

The queen hesitated a moment more, but finally said, "Your mother was aware of the conspiracy that we are still fighting against."

The serving-knife fell from Catrin's fingers and landed against the platter with a dull clang. "Because of my stepfather?"

"Perhaps; that has never been clear. She came and spoke to Sir William Paulet, who offered protection but did not tell me until after I started to take the danger seriously. Then, on my request, Paulet rode to the inn in West Drayton to fetch her. She was already gone."

"Do you know who came for her, Your Majesty?"

"No. A serving-maid told Paulet that the man said he came at my request, but that was a lie."

Catrin ducked her head and drew in a deep breath to hold back tears. "Why did you not tell me this before?"

"I do not have to explain my decisions to you, Catrin."

"I know that, Your Majesty. But I also know that you don't do anything without a reason."

The queen sighed. "Paulet and I believe that the man who took her from the inn was the master of this conspiracy. Until you knew of the conspiracy, there was no purpose in telling you about its leader."

"I understand. Thank you, Your Majesty." Catrin picked up the dish, her fingers holding tight to its edge. "That gives me all the more cause to find him."

"There is more, and it may well be difficult to hear," the queen said. Mistress Ashley offered a platter full of pestelles of pork, and the queen accepted with a nod. "Paulet found blood pooled on a nearby street, near the river Colne. We have cause to suspect it was there that your mother met her end."

Catrin felt the blood drain from her face. "Her … end?"

The queen's voice grew both gentler and firmer at the same time. "Yes, child, her end. So I say again: let the past lie and look to your future. This time, however, I must insist that you obey me."

"I understand, Your Majesty," Catrin whispered, and set the platter down again. "May I be excused?"

The queen inclined her head. "Of course."

On the new wharf, the candles and torches shining through the castle windows gave no light at all, and there was no moon. Catrin stood in a pool of quivering light that beamed from the lantern at her feet and stared down at the shifting lines of white foam that swirled about in the water below.

She heard Lucy approaching, but did not look up until her friend set her lantern on the balustrade with a clatter.

"I grow weary of this, Catrin."

It was not the sympathy she had hoped for, but it was no more than she had expected. Catrin bowed her head nearly low enough to meet her hands, which lay clenched tight on the balustrade. "So you too wish me to believe that my mother is dead."

"Nay, indeed. It is this conspiracy that wearies me," Lucy said tartly. "A master conspirator we cannot name, a group of underlings who bob in and out of sight like fish coming to the surface to scavenge food. Half-truths and plain lies, secret messages, meetings in the middle of the night ... enough is enough. I would like to put every courtier in the great hall and make them talk. I would squeeze them like oranges until the pips squeak."

That surprised Catrin into a laugh. "If only we could."

"And then all would be explained and the evildoers sent to the Tower. Life at court would return to its natural order, when we used to spend our days laughing at the peers playing politics."

Catrin took a deep breath. "It seemed boring then ... now, it is more like a dream that fades when you wake."

"It is a dream that will return," Lucy promised, and picked up her lantern. "Now, come with me. Hopefully there will be some mutton stew left for us."

CHAPTER TWENTY-FIVE

Catrin slowly paced the long gallery, waiting for the man she had hoped never to see again: her stepfather, Lord Ashbourne. She could not remember a time when she had not despised him, even though he had been one of her father's oldest friends. And then came the worst day — the day she would never forget — when she had gone from despising him to hating him.

She had been eight years old. Lord Ashbourne had come early to their home in London and demanded that both she and her mother accompany him to Tower Hill. To show their loyalty to Queen Mary, he had said.

At first, she had thought it a merry outing. And then the guards had dragged her father into the yard and shouted that he was a traitor, a rebel, an enemy of the queen. They had forced him to his knees and twisted his head until his neck lay taut across the wooden block.

Then the axe rose up in an arc — the blade flashing in the sun — before it fell —

Catrin pushed the memory away. If she did not, she would not be able to play her part. It was difficult enough to pretend to ally with her stepfather; if she dwelled on all the reasons she hated him, she would be more likely to push him over the balustrade.

She and Lucy had chosen the long gallery because it contained several curtained alcoves. They had planned that Lucy could hide safely in one of those, listen to Catrin's conversation with her stepfather, and report what she heard to the queen. But first Catrin had to convince him to say something worth reporting.

She saw her stepfather approaching from a distance and continued pacing, exaggerating her limp and wincing every now and then. He climbed the uneven wooden stairs and strode towards her until she could easily see the satisfied gleam in his pale eyes.

"This pain is only what you deserve," he said in his grating voice. "You have made yourself a spectacle, Catrin. And what benefits did you reap?"

"None. I have been given nothing to make up for all this pain and discomfort, and that is why I'm here," Catrin said. "Or rather, that is why *you* are here. The queen only allowed your return to court because I persuaded her, you know."

He sent her a skeptical glance. "And why did you want me recalled to court?"

"Because I know you have plans to topple that woman from her throne, and I want to be part of it."

Lord Ashbourne laughed. "From passionate loyalty to treason in only a few days? How very ... unexpected."

"There was no passionate loyalty," Catrin said scornfully. "You know full well that I fight only for myself. And now I see that my own advancement will not come through Queen Elizabeth."

"And you think it will come through me?"

"Not at all. You are but a conduit." Catrin slanted him a cool, appraising look. "I think it will come through the man whose orders you take."

Lord Ashbourne stepped back, his face suddenly as blank as the paper masks they wore for court revels. "I take orders from no one," he said, but his eyes darted back and forth as if he feared the walls had ears. "How dare you say —"

"Let's pretend I didn't say, if it frightens you so," Catrin said. "You can just act terribly offended and walk away, as long as you choose another time to speak to me about the benefits I can offer."

"Benefits? From a disobedient, headstrong, wilful —"

"— lady of the bedchamber," Catrin said. "Do not forget, my lord, I still have the ear of this vain child-queen. She thinks I am still content to sit in her shadow."

That made him pause. "But what if it is not the queen's ear we need our associate to have?"

Catrin smiled a siren's smile. "Then what do you need? I'm sure I can —"

"Nay, it's something *you* do not have," Lord Ashbourne taunted. "It is as I have always told you! You have fostered the confidence of the wrong ladies."

"Wrong ladies?" Catrin repeated. "What do you mean?"

Something flew past her ear with a faint whistle, making a nearby curtain quiver. Then there was a thud, and her stepfather dropped to the ground with an arrow in his chest.

Aghast, Catrin fell to her knees by his side. His eyes fixed on hers and his mouth worked for a few seconds before he managed to form words. "This...this should have been you," he whispered, and went limp. His head rolled to the side, displaying that mutilated ear to the world.

A scream tore out from behind a nearby curtain. "Dead! Murdered! Help! Help!"

"Lucy," Catrin gasped, and ran over to the alcove, tearing aside the curtain. Lucy was crouched down on the ground, eyes screwed tight shut, still screaming. "Calm down, petal, this will help neither of us."

Lucy gulped down air. "But someone — someone killed him!"

"Undoubtedly the man whose existence he denied," Catrin said, and looked up and around. "If he is wise, he is no longer here now that you have raised the hue and cry."

She certainly had. The gallery was filling with yeomen of the guard and bored courtiers and ladies consumed with curiosity. The queen, of course, did not come. Lord Robert did, and he came straight to Catrin.

"I wager you are the one best suited to explain this," he said grimly.

"Nay, my lord," Catrin said, and managed to smile. "That would be the man with the bow."

"We will explain nothing," Lucy said, and Catrin was surprised by the firmness in her voice. "We will have no more to do with this, Lord Robert. Enough is enough."

He chuckled. "I think you'll find that the decision to stop is not yours, Lady Lucretia. But by all means, let us make that suggestion to the queen."

This should have been you.

Catrin lay on her bed in the ladies' chamber, listening to the rain pattering on the diamond-paned window. Her stepfather's voice kept returning to her in the darkness. *This should have been you.*

It could have been pure hate that led him to say that. Lord Ashbourne had always considered himself far better than his fellows, and he would have been outraged that such a valuable person as himself would die while a worthless person such as herself was allowed to live.

Or, he might have known that someone was hiding nearby with a bow, with the intention of killing her. He could simply have been saying that someone missed.

Neither was a particularly pleasant prospect, but the second was far more frightening. It made her wonder whether the timing of the guardsman's death was more than a whim of fate. Had he been pushed from the gallery at the exact time that they crossed the courtyard on purpose?

It did not seem possible — and surely it was a pointless gesture, for anyone could have guessed that she had already told her damaging tales, and the dangerous documents were under lock and key. So why take the trouble to kill her?

Unless it wasn't about the death of Lady Dudley, but rather her quest to find her mother.

Her mother was almost certainly dead — the queen had said so. But then, she had also pretended to know nothing of Lady Dudley's death, when she had known all along that Amy had been playing a deadly game. So could she take the queen's word, and accept that she had lost both her parents?

The very thought made her insides knot. Her father's death had ended her childhood; no longer did she look at the world with innocence and wonder. But it had also brought her and her mother closer together, and her stepfather's cruelty had drawn them closer still. When she had taken a place at court, it had been terribly hard to leave her mother. She had sworn to herself that she would bring her to court as soon as she could. But long before she could fulfil that vow, her mother was gone.

That was nearly two years ago. Perhaps it was time to forget, to press onward with her plans and secure long-lasting safety through marriage. She could not do that if she angered the queen by refusing to obey her commands, and the queen was already very loudly and openly angry with both her and Lucy. Poor sweet Lucy had boldly said they could no longer put themselves in danger, and as Lord Robert had predicted, the queen was not pleased.

So she should focus on what the queen wanted her to do. But if there was even the slightest chance that her mother was alive and in need of help — then no. She could not stop until she knew for sure what had happened to her. So she slid out of bed and took a candlestick out into the corridor with a copy of her mother's last letter. It was all a matter of breaking the code. She had to find that key.

She sat down in the empty, silent corridor and spread out papers, quill and inkpot. Inkpot. Could that be the key? Apparently not. Quill? No. Roger? Perhaps her mother had known about his perfidy even before Lady Amy … no.

She sighed and leaned against the wall, then refilled the quill and tried again. And again … and again…

This should have been you.

CHAPTER TWENTY-SIX

Catrin and Lucy had had no intention of ever returning to the gallery where Lord Ashbourne had died, but a note from Sir William Cecil before the morning meal drew them there against their will. They both stood facing away from the spot where Lord Ashbourne had lain, holding on to the edge of the balustrade as if afraid of falling. It was raining heavily, and they could hear the hiss and splatter clearly on the flagstones below.

"It's like the skies are mourning," Lucy said.

"If so, I strongly doubt that their tears are for Lord Ashbourne," Catrin responded, and knew her attempt to lighten the mood fell flat when Lucy just sent her a tragic glance.

"What if it's for the next person to die?"

Catrin did not answer, for Sir William arrived at that moment, and bowed to them both. "Lady Lucretia. Lady Catrin."

Catrin found a smile somewhere. "Good morrow, good my lord."

"Good morrow." His grey eyes peered solemnly at Lucy. "You look weary, my lady."

"I am weary," Lucy said, and her lip trembled. "There have been too many horrors."

He nodded. "Aye, and I fear this is not the end of it, if the tales Her Majesty tells me are true. Lady Catrin, did you truly find a document suggesting an attempt on the queen's life is imminent?"

Catrin drew her hand over the rough stone of a nearby column. "Aye; Lord Robert thinks that these other deaths are the work of the conspirators, laying their plans."

"At least in one matter, then, he and I agree," Sir William said dryly.

"You have been investigating the death of Lord Ashbourne, have you not?" Lucy asked. "What have you found?"

He spread his hands wide in mingled frustration and sorrow. "The arrow that killed him had no distinguishing mark; it could have come from any crossbow in the kingdom."

"How do you know it was a crossbow?"

"The arrow was short and thick — more a bolt than an arrow. Also, we know that a crossbow would be easier to hide in the crowd; a longbow is too large."

"Perhaps he hid the longbow before the crowd gathered." Lucy pointed at a nearby cupboard. "There, for instance."

"It was searched; the whole gallery was searched. No longbow."

"Oh." Lucy's shoulders slumped. "Never mind; it was a foolish notion."

"Nay, indeed, it is a good notion that is just a little late," Sir William said with his kind smile. "And I have one more piece of information: the button you found — or rather, buttons — are a distinct design, intended to echo the shape of a coat-of-arms."

That made Catrin straighten. "Do you know which one?"

"Not yet, but take heart — I have not given up trying."

Usually, the queen's temper would flare and everyone would endure the storm for an hour or two before it passed and her smile returned. This time, however, she remained cold and aloof all day. By the time the evening meal came, they were all feeling the tension. The maids of honour had stopped giggling, and even Lord Robert was subtly avoiding the privy chamber.

Catrin and Lucy were due to serve the queen at table, and Catrin was worried that Lucy would completely forget what to do. Her clumsiness always got worse when she was nervous, and the atmosphere in that room would have unnerved a knight. When the queen settled at her table, with its pristine linen tablecloth laid by Mistress Ashley, she sent a glare around the room that struck everyone silent.

The trumpet fanfare announcing the arrival of the gentlemen ushers made Lucy jump. Catrin reached for the bread and salt, but Lucy was already busy rubbing the plates. Mistress Ashley went to the first usher, cut a piece of veal from the dish he held, and fed it to him. Then she took the dish and carried it to the queen's table. She set it down and curtsied to the queen, who looked at the dish and shook her head. Mistress Ashley curtsied again, then took the dish out.

Lucy was next. She fed a piece of capon from the second dish to the usher, and then carried the dish to the table. The queen shook her head. "Wine," she said instead, and Catrin picked up the silver flagon full of the queen's special watered-down wine and took it to the table. Her hand trembled as she tilted it over the queen's cup, and wine splashed onto the tablecloth.

Several ladies gasped. Catrin set the flagon down. "Your Majesty, I do apologise —"

"Clumsy wench!" the queen shouted. "You are not fit to wait upon us!"

Lucy snatched up a linen napkin to blot at the spreading stain. "It was a mistake, Your Majesty," she said breathlessly. "Perhaps Lady Catrin is not yet fully recovered —"

"Then she is not fit at all, and neither are you," the queen retorted. "I will not have women about me who question what I say — or who cannot manage a task as simple as pouring wine. What use are either of you? Every task I give you is an utter failure."

Lucy's eyes filled with tears. "But Your Majesty —"

"Silence! Leave my presence — indeed, leave my chamber! Until you have learned your place, you shall spend your days with the maids of honour."

Catrin winced. "Your Majesty, we will serve you in any way we can, but I pray thee —"

"Speak to me no more! Go!"

Catrin and Lucy looked at each other, but there was nothing either of them could think to say. So they did what they were told, and left the queen's presence.

The maids of honour's chamber had been created from a larger chamber with partitions that did not reach much higher than the top of one's head. Outside the space were dozens of coffers and chests, storing any manner of things, and servants were constantly walking by in search of something. Inside the space, it was so full of pallets and mattresses that it seemed smaller even than that of the ladies of the bedchamber. The walls were heavily draped with ribbons and lace that fluttered in the drafty air, making the whole space feel like it was moving.

Catrin and Lucy hesitated in the doorway, for there seemed to be no space at all for two more bodies in that room. Nor did the maids seem particularly welcoming; one girl pointed openly at them, while two more giggled behind their hands.

Lady Mary Grey stood in the middle of the room, unlacing her sister's sleeves and humming a tune that Catrin knew but could not place. She looked up as they entered. "No longer the talisman, I see. What a shame."

Catrin shrugged. "Fortune's wheel has turned, that's all," she said. "It is common at court."

"True," Katherine Grey said. "Maybe we'll get to go back to being ladies of the bedchamber again now, Mary."

"Oh, hold your tongue," Mary snapped, and flung one hand toward the smallest, thinnest pallet right next to the door. "You two can sleep there."

Catrin did not like the look of the pallet, but she didn't protest. "Thank you," she said instead, and walked over to pull back the blankets. A mouse leaped out with a squeal, and the girls erupted in laughter when Lucy screamed. "Tush, dearling, it's gone now," Catrin said. "Could you help me with my bodice?"

Lucy took a breath to calm herself and started loosening the ribbons, but glanced over her shoulder at the other girls. "This is strange. I … I feel like I don't know what to do."

"Nor do I, dearling. So let us sleep," Catrin said wearily, and rubbed at her knee. "There will be time enough to make plans tomorrow."

CHAPTER TWENTY-SEVEN

Catrin and Lucy rose to a day without duties. They went to the queen's rooms with the other maids, but the bedchamber was shut to them and Lord Robert came to the door of the privy chamber to suggest they remain outside. This seemed to sadden Lucy, so Catrin took her to the castle gates to visit the peddlers. She was able to buy some new hairpins and ribbons, and — even better — one peddler was selling cheap little books of poems. Catrin doubted both their quality and their longevity, but Lucy was delighted so they were worth the penny.

One peddler had fabric of surprisingly good quality, so Catrin bought enough to make a new cloak to replace the one she had lost in the fire, and a brooch to pin it closed since her only other had been lost as well. Finally, she bought some apples, which made Lucy tilt her head in surprised curiosity.

"Why those?"

"They will either become a bribe or a weapon. I am going to speak to Sir Nicolas again." Lucy's face fell and Catrin patted her shoulder. "You don't have to come, dearling. Go find a nook and read your poems, and I will find you afterwards."

Lucy liked that idea, and trotted off toward the presence chamber when they returned to the castle. Catrin checked that her knife was in place and then started off to Sir Nicolas' chamber, swinging her basket of apples as if she did not have a care in the world. She peeked winsomely through her lashes at a group of courtiers standing idly in the corridor watching her pass, and was not surprised when the boldest of them detached himself from the group.

"Good morrow, my lady. How do you fare?"

It was actually rather enjoyable to fall into this familiar game. "Well, my lord, and you?"

He let his eyes rest on the pale flesh above her bodice. "I fear I faint from hunger."

Catrin pressed a hand to her chest in mock shock. "Why, my lord, do you have designs upon my apples?"

The courtiers hooted with laughter, and the young man grinned. "Aye, I do."

Catrin shook her head in sorrow and held out an apple from the basket. "We will say it was because you were so famished."

He laughed and took the apple. "My lady, you look like Eve — offering forbidden fruit."

"I offer only the apple," she said sternly, and when he gave a sheepish laugh she continued on her way. She heard the courtiers hooting and laughing behind her and ignored them, but paused again when she saw the Earl of Shrewsbury leaning against a windowsill. "Good my lord, fare you well?"

He looked pale and worn, and though he straightened at once when he saw her, he did not smile. "Good morrow, my lady."

She held out an apple with a smile. "May I offer you —"

"No, thank you," he said abruptly, and walked away. She stared after him, unable to contemplate such a complete change in a person's manner. He had seemed so concerned, so interested — intrigued, even. Why the change? Had the murder of her stepfather cost her the best prospect she had yet had?

It was definitely a concern, but there was nothing she could do about it right then, so she turned away and continued down the corridor. She found Sir Nicolas' door shut and no servant in sight, and was reaching for the handle when the door suddenly swung open.

One of the queen's physicians filled the space, looking at her with blatant hostility. "Why are you here, girl?"

She decided it was prudent to edit the truth. "Sir Nicolas was injured in the course of defending me. I wished to see him and bring him some —"

"No."

Catrin raised one eyebrow. "I beg your pardon?"

"He is far, far too ill to have visitors, but I will give those to him if you wish." He plucked the basket from her hands and shut the door, and she actually heard the lock turn.

She could not stop a cry of mingled anger and frustration, but she managed not to lose her dignity completely and pound on the door demanding admittance. There were other ways.

Catrin was outside Sir Nicolas' window, considering whether or not she could climb inside without ruining her skirt, when she saw Lady Mary Sidney approaching. She hastily abandoned her post and walked toward her in turn, bobbing a friendly curtsy on the way by. Lady Mary did not return the gesture; she merely gave her a cool look and flicked her hood back over her shoulder.

One flick. That meant that the queen needed her urgently. Catrin immediately abandoned her quest to speak to Sir Nicolas and took a circuitous route to the corridor where the entrance to the secret antechamber lay, to hide her intention from anyone watching. No one followed, so she could slip inside at once.

The queen was sitting in her cushioned chair, with Lord Robert on one side and Sir William himself on the other. Lucy was curled up on cushions in the corner.

Catrin curtsied before the queen and wondered why they all looked so serious. "I did not expect to hear from you so soon, Your Majesty," she said. "Is our ruse discovered?"

"No, our plans are safe as yet," Lord Robert said. "We have another matter to deal with."

There was a whimper from the centre of the floor, and Catrin realised that Mistress Rose Kene was crouched in the shadows, her arms wrapped tight around her. For one astonished moment Catrin could only stare. "What has happened?"

"I found her taking a paper from Sir William's rooms," Lucy said miserably. "One which dealt with confidential military matters."

"And she was the one who stole my notes," Sir William added. "That was how they ended up at Cumnor Place."

"Any such notes or papers would be very useful in the right hands," Lord Robert said, and glared at Mistress Rose. "So we now intend to discover whose hands would have received them."

Sir William settled onto a cushion beside the girl, and his grey eyes were kind. "Now, Rose, don't be afraid," he said in that soothing croon Catrin had heard him use with Lord Ashbourne. "You just have to tell us who you were going to give the paper to. That's all. Why you did it doesn't matter. Just tell us who else was involved."

"I will s-say nothing," Rose whispered.

"You will if we start pulling out your fingernails," Lord Robert snapped.

Rose started, and tears ran down her cheeks.

"Don't worry," Sir William said kindly. "He won't do that. Now, tell me, who wanted that document?"

Rose looked from Sir William to Lord Robert, who slowly drew his dagger. "Perhaps she'll speak if she loses a finger," he said, and Rose cried out.

"Please, no! I can't tell you, I can't!"

Sir William reached out and patted Rose's shoulder. "Well, then, if you can't tell us who, perhaps you can tell us why. Why did you take it?"

"A gentleman told me to take it — he promised me a s-s-sovereign. I heard him tell another man it was to be payment, for the gold was lost. So I told him if they were in the habit of losing gold I wouldn't do anything unless he gave me a half-sovereign right away."

A light of comprehension dawned, and Catrin leaned close to Lucy. "The promised gold in the message — I wager Amy was to provide it to the man hired to kill the queen. When she died, they had to find an alternative way to pay."

For the first time, the queen spoke, in her most formal and intimidating voice. "We charge thee, answer true. Did you know these men?"

Rose lowered her gaze to the floor. "One was the gentleman who was killed with the arrow. The one with the disfigured ear."

"And the other?" Lord Robert asked.

"I cannot say."

"Had you seen him before?" Sir William asked.

"Yes — it was he who told me to bring him any paper in your hand with the word 'Robert' or 'Dudley' on it. So I did."

"Do you know his name?"

"No. We always met out by the fountain, in the dark. I barely saw him."

"Oh — I think I saw you with him, through the window," Lucy said suddenly. "He was wearing a dark cloak with a deep hood, so I could not see his face, but he looked tall and thin."

"That man used those notes to try to convince the queen I was a traitor," Sir William said. "I very nearly lost my position, and could have lost my life. He is not an honourable man, Rose."

"Please — have mercy. I cannot say — he told me he would kill me if I said."

"We may kill you if you do not," Sir William said reasonably. "I think it best to say what you know, young Rose. Then you may go free."

Rose shook her head and closed her mouth tight. Lord Robert threatened and Sir William cajoled, but not another word came out of her.

Finally the queen lost her patience. "To the Tower with her!" she cried. "She is a traitor who deserves some time with the torturer."

Rose screamed. "No! No, please!"

The queen rose to her feet and looked down at her through narrowed eyes. "Take heed of our words," she said in a tone that was dangerously quiet. "You have brought this on yourself, but we are merciful and will delay our wrath. Two days shall you spend in the Tower. If you do not speak by then, it is the rack."

With those words ringing in the air, she knocked on the panelled wall and two guards entered the room. Rose let out a scream that made poor Lucy clap her hands over her ears, but they dragged her out despite her cries.

Catrin was unmoved. "So we know the plans are still in place," she said. "But we still don't know who will carry out this threat, or when."

The queen resumed her seat. "Has your exile among the maids told you anything?"

"I fear not," Catrin said. "But I find it hard to believe that any of them have the wit to lead — or even join — a conspiracy."

"They must have. Your stepfather said that you were in company with the wrong ladies," Lucy said. "The only other ladies to keep company with are the maids. They must be the 'right' ladies."

"And none of them has approached you, Catrin?" the queen asked.

Catrin shook her head sorrowfully. "Perhaps they have not heard what I said to my stepfather, or do not believe that my loyalty is so fluid."

"They do not like either of us," Lucy said. "Just today Lady Mary Grey was spreading tales that Catrin was going to marry Sir Nicolas, and have all the jewels she could wear within a month."

"That will not last," Lord Robert predicted. "Should you prove useful, Lady Catrin, they will soon forget all discord."

The queen nodded, but she was obviously still dissatisfied. "What have you done today, Catrin?"

"I have spent most of it trying to deliver apples to Sir Nicolas, Your Majesty," she said. "But all my wiles were in vain. Even the chamberers would not let me in to see him."

"I was told that he is very ill," the queen said. "Leave him be for now, and focus on gaining the conspirators' trust."

"Yes, Your Majesty."

"Now we must leave." The queen rose once again and settled her hood more firmly on her auburn hair. "I must prepare myself for the evening."

Catrin went to the evening meal wearing a borrowed gown, for the maids of honour wore white and that was a colour her wardrobe did not include. White did nothing for her complexion. She had made the best of it by pinning a silvery ribbon along the neckline of the too-tight bodice and wearing her French hood of blue silk, with a band that boasted a sapphire at its centre and silver embroidery.

She and Lucy went into the privy chamber with the rest of the maids of honour, and paused to survey the room. The usual entertainments were in place: musicians played in one corner for the dancing, jesters juggled and danced in another, cards and games were set up by the fire. Page boys scurried about carrying jugs of ale and cups of wine, and groups of people stood about everywhere, chattering loudly enough to drown the music.

The maids scattered to join them, and Lucy went looking for a chess partner. Catrin caught the Earl of Shrewsbury's eye. "Good evening, my lord."

"My lady."

That was all. He did not ask her to dance, he did not carry on the conversation, he did not even look at her. His son Lord Talbot smirked in vindictive pleasure, and a chill ran down her back. She was truly suffering for her seeming loss of status. Would she ever be able to recover?

"My lady, may I have this dance?"

She turned, and to her surprise saw the Duke of Norfolk standing there, his chin tilted up, his usual golden chain glittering against a new black doublet. "Of course, your grace," she said, and took his hand. Whispers followed them as they joined the other couples, and Catrin forced a smile. "You have taken a risk with me, my lord."

"Nay. It was you who took a risk, and all to serve the queen," he said, and gave a great sigh as a sprightly tune announced the beginning of an almain. "I regret that I took Forster's word about your fate at Cumnor Place, my lady."

She took her place on his right and curtsied toward the queen as he bowed. "I understand that you were obliged to alert the queen as soon as possible."

"And ensure my evidence — or what I thought was evidence — was not lost." He sighed again as they both turned to bow to each other. "As it happened, it was falsely placed."

One step forward on the heel, rise to the ball of the foot for steps two and three, point the toe for step four. Always light, always graceful. "Have you learned by whom?"

"I suspect Richard Verney."

One of the names on Lady Amy's list. "Why?"

They repeated the pattern in reverse, then turned in toward each other. Point the toe to the left with a slight bounce on the opposite foot, then the right. Arms straight at one's sides like bird's wings, half-furled. "He saw us arrive, remember? He was carrying papers, and scurried like the rat he is into the great hall, which was the only fire lit at that time of day."

She remembered the man with the papers, and was annoyed with herself that she hadn't recognized Verney at the time. "Did you question him?"

"Aye, of course, but he denied it."

"Which anyone would do, guilty or not." Catrin pondered as they went through the next series of steps. "I wish I could speak to him."

Norfolk made a disapproving sound in his throat. "It seems that your wish is his command, my lady," he said, and nodded toward the doorway. To her astonishment, Richard Verney was actually there, swaying, red-faced with drink and leering at the maids.

Her shock was such that she stumbled, but Norfolk was a skilled partner and quickly got her back in step. "I do apologise, your grace."

"Not at all, my lady."

They began a series of skipping steps that brought them closer to Verney, and Catrin couldn't help but stare. "Why is he at court?"

"Hoping for a commission, I would guess, like most minor gentlemen," Norfolk said with a curl to his lip. "If you had a trade deal or an ambassadorship to offer, you could probably convince him to bare his soul."

Verney disappeared into the crowds, and she itched to go after him. "Perhaps he was paid to put that letter in the fire."

"Or to kill Lady Amy."

"Do you really think —?"

"Aye, I do." The music came to a stop and they executed a final rise and fall on the balls of their feet. Then Norfolk bent over her hand. "Go find out."

She curtsied before him and then turned to go, but before she had taken three steps Lucy hurried up to her, laying a hand on her arm. "Catrin — look. Do you see what's on that chair?"

Catrin looked, and immediately stopped. It was a cloak of deepest green, lined with square metal buttons. "Well spotted, dearling. Watch carefully for who retrieves it."

Lucy plunked herself down in the nearest chair. "I certainly will."

Her tenacity made Catrin smile. "I must speak to Master Verney, but I will return," she said, and resumed her journey through the crowd. She finally found Verney in the presence chamber, where the music was more raucous and the air thick with the smell of alcohol and sweat. He had found some leftover platters of food and was sopping up a sweet sauce with a piece of manchet bread. "Good evening, Master Verney."

He squinted at her for a minute, but finally the fog cleared. "Surovell," he mumbled. "Angharad's daughter."

No one had said her mother's name in so long that the sound of it stole her breath. "Yes, I am."

"Alive, when you are supposed to be dead and your body nothing but ash." He drank deep from a tankard of ale. "Those who come to kill me will not fail like I did."

So, Verney had set the fire at Cumnor Place when Gryse had died. Catrin resolved that he would answer for it someday, but first his master had to fall. "Perhaps we can stop them coming."

He laughed at that, spraying crumbs and ale in all directions. "You think you can protect me?"

"I have friends who can protect you. Just tell me what you know about the document in Sir William's handwriting found at Cumnor Place."

"Don't know nothing about Sir William, or any document."

"Then tell me what you know about my mother."

He sopped up some more sauce. "On orders."

"Whose orders? What were you ordered to do?"

"Kill Angharad."

A chill like icy water drenched her from head to toe. "Did you kill her?"

"Couldn't." He gazed blearily down at the cloudy liquid in his tankard. "But I was there when she died."

Catrin fought to hold back tears. "So she is dead?"

"Aye. Killed on orders."

This time she asked the question with far more intensity. "Whose orders?"

He shuddered. "The Master."

"What is his name?"

"Can't tell you. He'd kill me."

Catrin fingered the knife hidden in her sleeve. "If you tell me, I will help you."

Verney laughed again, but the sound ended in a sigh. "You need to help yourself, little pet. Get out of here while you still can."

"My entire family is dead," Catrin said bluntly. "Where else do I have to go?"

"Find somewhere." He looked around at the laughing crowd glittering with jewels in the candlelight. "Before this whole place is bathed in blood."

CHAPTER TWENTY-EIGHT

Heavy rains delayed the queen's morning walk the next day. It was midafternoon before she ventured from the castle, and it was perhaps the later hour that inspired most of the court to come along.

With such a crowd, it was easy for Catrin and Lucy to fall back and whisper together. First Catrin told Lucy what Master Verney had said, and was very grateful when her friend's first reaction was sorrow. "Oh, poor Catrin! All this time you've been looking for your mother and she's … gone."

Catrin breathed deeply to force back her tears. "I want to find the man who did it. I want to look him in the eye and ask why."

Lucy tilted her head and a blonde curl escaped from her hood and caught the sunlight. "But don't you see — Master Verney already told you that."

"What do you mean?"

"The master of this conspiracy ordered your mother's death, so it must have been because she knew who he was. Just like Lady Dudley."

"But how would the master have known what my mother knew?" Catrin clenched her fists and answered her own question. "My stepfather must have told him. May he rot in hell."

"Or," Lucy said, and hesitated, "Sir Nicolas told him. Your mother had his seal, remember. Maybe it was meant to be proof of his involvement."

"But he would have been a lad of eighteen when my mother disappeared. What could possibly have inspired him to hate the queen enough to turn traitor?"

"Young men are easily led."

"True." Catrin considered. "He did send us on a false trail toward Sir William's secretary, and he did defy the queen to come looking for me. Despite my gratitude, it makes me call his loyalty into question. And he did get lost in the forest not five miles from the castle — or pretended to get lost. I blamed his youth, but it may have been a ploy to delay my return."

"He also may have stolen the paper of symbols," Lucy said. "I know you only noticed that it was gone when you returned, but…"

"He had opportunity, I must admit, though I kept that satchel close to my person." Suddenly, Catrin was furious with herself. "All that time! How did I not see his darker motive?"

"Because he kept it hidden," Lucy said simply, and a shadow passed over her face. "It is a situation much like myself and poor Rose."

"You did the right thing, dearling."

"I just shudder to think of her in the Tower without friends or aid. All because of me!"

"She can leave it anytime if she reveals what she knows," Catrin said. "And it is not because of you, it is because of her. She chose to play the spy — you did not force her into it."

"That is true, but still…"

"Please, dearling, do not torture yourself. You proved yourself a wise and loyal servant of the queen by what you did." Catrin squeezed her hand and lowered her voice. "Have you made any sense of the lyrics page?"

Lucy glanced around to make sure no one was listening. "I'm sorry, but I haven't been able to find any sense in it at all," she said. "I was hoping you may have had some insights."

"Very few," Catrin said gloomily, and took a piece of paper from the purse that hung from her belt. It was a copy, with the real words hidden amidst many others. She had not included the music notes, for they already knew the melody. "*To reach for but an empty claim; Bent fortune takes the chance away; Royal grace, please now grant me strength; So he may go and she may stay.*"

Lucy sighed. "If only we could determine who was 'he' and who was 'she'."

"I think I have done that much. Knowing that Lady Dudley wasn't a traitor allows us to see a different angle," Catrin said. "It may be that 'he' is the master of this conspiracy, and 'she' refers to the queen."

"But Lady Amy seems to be addressing the queen in the third line, so shouldn't the last line read 'so he may go and *you* may stay'?"

"Perhaps Lady Amy is talking about royal grace in the divine sense and asking for help from God himself in the third line."

"That makes sense." Lucy read it over again, slowly. "I wish we could determine who is reaching for an empty claim."

"That could also be the master, if he is trying to claim a throne he doesn't deserve," Catrin said.

"That's possible, but not definite." Lucy sighed. "Why couldn't Lady Amy have been clearer?"

"It was safer to be as obscure as possible," Catrin said. "Don't forget; she suspected the people she was living with."

"She did," Lucy said slowly. "You don't think … Master Forster could be the master? He did try to keep Norfolk from helping you after the fire."

Catrin's lip quirked. "That little man? I'm sorry, but I just can't see it."

Lucy chuckled. "You're right, it is absurd."

"But it does add some much-needed humour to the situation," Catrin said. "Tell me, what happened to the cloak? If you saw who collected it, I am sure Sir William could elicit a confession."

"I saw, but no confession shall we have," Lucy said ruefully. "It was but a page-boy. I followed him out of the chamber, but soon lost him in the crowd."

"What did he look like? Perhaps we can find him."

"He was rather plump and had a large purple splotch on his right cheek."

Catrin stopped short. "Are you sure he was a page? I have seen a chorister in St George's Chapel with such a mark on his face."

"But why would a chorister be collecting cloaks in the royal chambers?"

Catrin set her jaw. "I suggest we ask him."

Catrin and Lucy left the royal apartments behind and passed through the gate into the lower half of the castle. They were soon surrounded by an entirely different group of people than they were used to. Clergy were strolling by in their three-cornered caps and men in rough tunics brushed mud from the still-wet flagstones. Peddlers were plying their wares near King Henry's Gate, while laundresses criss-crossed the space, carrying baskets of linen — some soiled, some clean.

Catrin and Lucy wove their way through the crowd and entered the chapel, where the air was hushed, and heavy with the scent of beeswax. The stained glass glowed with vibrant colour in the sunlight.

They were halfway up the aisle when a voice stopped them in their tracks.

"God save him, please, do not let him go to hell…"

The voice was coming from a tiny side chapel, where a man in a plain doublet and hose was kneeling before a cross. "He did not have time to confess his sins, God — or to ask forgiveness — foully murdered — have mercy, God, have —" The man heard Lucy's step and leapt upright, his rough boots thudding on the floor. "Who's there?"

"Only me, goodman," Lucy said. "I heard weeping and came to offer aid."

"There is no aid," he said mournfully. "Richard is dead, and for me there is no aid. No life, no purpose."

"Richard? Do you mean the man who fell over the balcony?"

"He was pushed — thrown!" the man said. "I saw it happen!"

Lucy glanced back at Catrin. "Did you see who did it?"

"Damn my eyes, I did not," he said, and with a faint chinking noise drew a bottle from between the panels of his doublet. "We were off duty, and I was going home. Richard was returning from a visit with his lass, so we walked together. We saw two gentlemen on the parapet, but they were facing out so we couldn't see their faces. One was in a black rage, howling at the sky and stabbing at the stones. The other was younger, thinner, and he was trying to calm him. Richard thought he would try to help and walked up to them. I heard him say 'I'm glad you have recovered, my lord' — and then the thin man threw him over the balustrade." The tears returned, flowing free down his face. "He-he-he just grabbed him, and threw him … gave him no time to confess his sins or call for help … and I did nothing. It was like my feet were nailed to the floor. I did not move until the two gentlemen were long gone."

"That is no sin. You were frightened," Lucy said quietly. "Isn't that right, Lady Catrin?"

"Yes, of course," Catrin said, but she was no longer paying attention. Her mind was buzzing like a nest full of wasps. It sounded to her like the thin man had reacted to Richard's words, not his presence. He attacked only after Richard said 'I'm glad you have recovered, my lord'. Why would that provoke him? Who would not respond graciously to such a sentiment?

Someone who did not want people to know he had recovered.

Someone young and thin, whom everyone thought was gravely ill. A description, she could not help but notice, that fit Sir Nicolas Swann. It was further proof that Sir Nicolas was not what he pretended to be.

The man before her gulped from the bottle. "I am an esquire of the body — I have been trained to respond when someone is attacked!" he cried. "And then when Richard … a good man, my lady, a kind man — is treacherously killed — I do nothing!"

"You are doing something now," Lucy said, and withdrew far enough to get the attention of a passing deacon. He had kind eyes, and seemed to understand at once what the man needed. "And here is someone who will help you."

CHAPTER TWENTY-NINE

"You cannot go in." The yeoman of the guard was implacable. "The queen has ordered that she not be disturbed with her councillors."

Catrin took firm hold of her patience. "We are two of her ladies; I'm sure —"

"Now that is a lie, my lady." The yeoman said it sternly, but his eyes showed how much he was enjoying denying them what they wanted. "You are maids of honour now, and the maids are not permitted entry to the queen's chamber when she is conducting the affairs of the realm."

Lucy bit her lip. "Perhaps we should find Lady Mary Sidney, Catrin. She would be able to explain our urgency to the queen."

"Lady Mary Sidney, you say? She is in the chamber already, with Mistress Ashley and Mistress Blanche." The yeoman's eyes positively gleamed. "I believe they are serving the wine."

"Could you give Lady Mary a message?"

The yeoman bristled. "Certainly not. Do I look like a page boy? Off with you both! Go back to your sewing. Now!"

Catrin resisted the temptation to draw her *stiletto* by walking away. Lucy scurried after her. "We have never been stopped before from seeing the queen," she said.

"It is the consequence of our plan to join the maids of honour," Catrin said. "It has cost us much of our status."

"So, what do we do?"

"You must wait for Lady Mary to emerge," Catrin said. "I am going to go see Sir Nicolas."

Catrin approached Sir Nicolas' chamber cautiously, moving lightly so that the sound of her footsteps did not echo against the stone. The young servant was guarding the door once again, so she hid behind a pillar and waited until the sound of a distant bell announced that the evening meal was about to end. The boy immediately deserted his post, and she walked straight in.

She found Nicolas propped up in bed, his face flushed. "Sir Nicolas! At last! There are fortresses easier to penetrate than this chamber of late."

"My servants are protective of my health," Sir Nicolas said, and gave an unconvincing cough. "But it does me good to see you, my dove. With such beauty to look upon, I am sure that I will soon recover."

She made herself smile at him. "I will be glad to see you healthy again."

He tilted his head. "You do not mean that," he said, and a faint sparkle of mischief lit in his eye. "I rather think you are angry with me."

So she hadn't hidden it as well as she'd hoped. How to respond? She needed his allegiance if she was to find out what he knew — about her mother, about the Master, about the death of the poor esquire, Richard. It required a delicate balance. "Angry? Nay, not I." She spread her hands in mock innocence. "What could you have possibly done to make me angry when you have been confined to your bed for days?"

He lifted his head and gazed at her in fresh awareness. "I cannot think of anything," he said cautiously. "Can you?"

"One could argue only that you are guilty of neglect," Catrin said. "I grew accustomed to your attention in the forest, and since then I have had no one to sing to me — no one to dance with — no one to help me with that letter."

His gaze sharpened warily. "I do apologise, my lady. 'Tis shameful of me to abandon you so."

"Completely," Catrin said. "But do not disturb yourself, Sir Nicolas. I understand your reasons."

"Perhaps you do." He pushed himself upright on his pillows. "But perhaps I have shown more care for you than you know. I may have seemed far from you since we returned, but like an arrow to the target I will always come swiftly when you need me."

Like an arrow ... she understood in a single horrible second. *This should have been you.* "You killed my stepfather."

"Yes. To save your life." Sir Nicolas reached out a hand, and sadness shadowed his face. "There is something about you, Lady Catrin Surovell ... you make me long to be greater — better — than I am. I could not let you die."

Catrin swallowed her shock and forced a smile. "That is why you are my champion, sir knight. And why I have been trying so hard to see you."

"Are you sure that is why?" He captured her hand and kissed the back of it with disturbing gentleness. "I had hoped it was for love."

She forced herself to leave her hand in his. "That may come. But first, it is for loyalty."

His gaze hardened. "To the queen?"

"No. To you." She leaned in close. "I deciphered the document you stole, my lord. I know what you plan to do, and I want to be a part of it."

He sighed and lifted his gaze to meet hers. "I have corrupted you."

"You have made me see the truth."

He was silent for a moment. "How can I know you will not betray me?"

"You saved my life, my lord. Twice." She leaned over him, gazing deep into his eyes. "I will not betray you."

He looked back at her for an endless moment, and finally gave a curt nod. "Then I will tell you of our quest."

"*Our* quest?" She blinked at him innocently. "Who else is involved?"

"Many people, all led by a man of great wisdom." He pressed his hand against his heart and his eyes took on a certain dreamlike quality. "He discerned that many quests such as this one fail because they are discovered far too early. The raising of men and weapons gives the game away and spies join the camp. So, our great leader did not aim for a large-scale uprising, but small subtle changes in the governance of this realm. It has been a most effective strategy, and now our goal lies within our grasp."

"And what is the goal you speak of?"

"Our intention is to make one small change that will have great effect. First, a man called 'the Branch' will start the wheel turning. Then, our supporters will rise up in strategic places around the country and direct the watershed so it falls in our favour."

"This quest of yours sounds like a rebellion without bloodshed."

He laughed. "I would not say that, no. We have chosen a bear for the baiting, but our people, of course, will be spared."

"That is a relief." Catrin drew her fingers down over the blanket. "Can I hope to find myself in a rather more exalted position afterward?"

"Such as?"

"First lady of the bedchamber. With a salary and a pension."

"That can be arranged. You will be justly rewarded — if you are successful in your task."

A chill ran through her. "And what is my task to be?"

His voice hardened. "You do not need to know that yet."

"Perhaps not, but you have told me everything else, so why not this?"

"Not everything, my lady."

"True. For instance, you have not yet told me *when* all this will occur."

"You do not need to know that either. Not yet. Word will come to you in plenty of time. Now you must go, my dove."

She sighed. "Very well," she said, and turned away. At the last second, Sir Nicolas grabbed her arm.

"One last thing, my lady. If you speak of this to anyone, the consequences will be immediate and dire," he said. "You may well spend the rest of your life alone."

She frowned at him. "There is no need for threats, my lord."

He released his grip. "I hope that is true, for both our sakes."

Catrin left the room slowly, giving herself time to think. It was as they had thought — Sir Nicolas was involved in the conspiracy and was part of a plot that would affect the whole realm. But she did not know what the plot was — or when it would take place, or even where. Should she report to the queen at once? No, someone would certainly be watching, and the queen herself would soon be in bed, if she wasn't already. These tidings could wait until the morning, and until then Catrin could try to determine what the consequences Sir Nicolas had mentioned could be.

What did he mean about spending her life alone? He could not threaten her parents or siblings, for she had neither. Nor could he remove all of the ever-widening circle of courtiers and ladies with whom she spent her days. The only one she was close to was—

Lucy.

Catrin picked up her skirts and ran, darting down corridors and through deserted rooms, moving so fast she flew past the entrance to the royal chambers. She had to backtrack, and her eyes immediately searched the great teeming throng still enjoying the evening revels.

Lucy was not there.

CHAPTER THIRTY

The next morning, Lady Mary Sidney drew Catrin aside and instructed her to outpace the other courtiers during their ride with the queen. It was a request that suited Catrin's mood: she bent low over Ariadne's neck and rode like Cerberus himself was chasing her. The mare leapt over bushes and fallen logs as if the air were her natural element, and soon left the maids and ladies behind. The courtiers, with their more powerful steeds, were rather harder to outrun, but Catrin dodged and wove amongst the trees until she was alone. Only then did she bring the mare to a gentle stop, slide down, tie the reins to a tree, and walk so deeply into the forest that the sunlight could not penetrate.

In the darkest thicket Lady Mary Sidney stood guard, and let Catrin pass with a wave of her hand. Catrin pushed aside a branch laden with golden leaves and emerged into a small clearing, where the queen and Lord Robert stood waiting.

"Do not kneel; the grass will stain your riding costume and give us away," the queen said hastily. "Now, tell us what has happened."

Catrin opened her mouth to answer, and nothing came out. Tears burst from her eyes instead, and a great well of sobs rose up from her chest. She bit her finger to dull the sound, and the queen moved forward in a rustle of leaves and rested her hands on her shoulders. "Tush, child, this will do us no good. What has brought you to such a state?"

"Lucy did not return to the maids' chamber last night; I am sure that the conspirators have taken her." Catrin swiped at her cheeks in a futile attempt to stem the flow. "They may harm her if I do not obey them and I…I don't know what to do."

"Tell the truth," Lord Robert said quietly. "Do not forget, dear child — the truth will set you free."

But would the truth set Lucy free? Catrin needed assurances. She needed to *know* that the light would fall on the right facets. "Good my lord," she managed shakily, "I do wish to tell the truth and see this conspiracy ended, but I must first ask a great favour."

His eyes narrowed. "What favour?"

"That you will restrain yourself when you have heard what I must say, and despite all provocation remain here at Windsor."

He straightened. For a second his fingers tightened around the hilt of his sword, but then he let his hand fall. "I swear it."

"Thank you." Catrin took a deep breath, wiped her cheeks dry with the edge of her sleeve, and turned to the queen. "Your Majesty, I believe that the conspirators' target is Lord Robert."

The queen gave a small cry. "Why do you think that?"

"I spoke to a conspirator who said they had chosen a bear for the baiting," Catrin said. "I immediately thought of the symbol on Lord Robert's coat-of-arms."

The queen held out her hands to Lord Robert and he gently covered them with his. "Sweet Robin — I cannot let them take you from me — you must leave Windsor at once."

"No!" Catrin cried. "If he leaves, they will know that I have deceived them."

"And if he stays, they will kill him." The queen shook her head. "I cannot allow that."

"Wait just a moment. Let us consider," Lord Robert said, the words calm but outrage shaking in his voice. "Amy's intelligence suggested that it was the queen who was in danger, not me. Why would their goal suddenly change?"

"I don't think it has changed, my lord. The conspirator spoke of one small change having a great effect, and I dare say your loss would have a great effect on the queen."

"It certainly would," the queen said faintly.

"And who is this conspirator?" Lord Robert asked. "Do you have a name?"

To her shame, the tears nearly started again. Catrin pinched the bridge of her nose between her fingers to stem the flow and forced herself to speak. "It was Sir Nicolas Swann."

"That cannot be — he was badly wounded," the queen said. "My own physician confirmed that he has been confined to his bed."

"Perhaps we should look more closely at the physician, too, then," Lord Robert murmured.

"But it is nonsensical. Why would Sir Nicolas feign illness?" the queen asked. "What purpose could it serve?"

"It allows him to move freely about the castle, causing mischief," Lord Robert said grimly. "After all, who would suspect Sir Nicolas if the royal physician declares that he has been confined to his bed?"

"There is more to it," Catrin said. "Sir Nicolas confirmed that a man named 'the Branch' will start the wheel turning — he will carry out the initial attack."

"If that is true, the Master must have a different role for Sir Nicolas," Lord Robert said. "There may be two attacks at once."

Catrin pressed the heels of her hands to her eyes. "It seems like our task grows more difficult with each passing hour."

"Take heart, Lady Catrin," Lord Robert said. "At least we know that I am the intended target, and not the queen."

A shrill burst of laughter escaped the queen's lips. "That is small comfort to me, Robin."

He sent her a small smile. "But it is a great comfort to me."

"There should be no comfort yet, my lord: the threat continues to grow," Catrin said. "You must prepare. I think they will act soon."

"I agree. Otherwise, they would not have taken Lucy," Lord Robert said. "Do you know what they have in mind for you?"

"Not yet; I was told that word would come."

"Perhaps, then, we should take a more direct approach," he said. "I am willing to … speak … to Sir Nicolas and find out once and for all who the Master is."

"He will not tell you." Catrin was sure of that. "He thinks the Master is a man of great wisdom — a great leader. He will never betray him."

"No? Alas." Lord Robert shrugged. "We will have to find another way, then."

Something in his voice made Catrin pause. "You will not confront Sir Nicolas, will you, my lord? To do so will put Lucy in greater danger."

Lord Robert stiffened, and she knew she had been right to ask. It was a struggle for men such as he to hold back when there was a battle to fight. But then the queen rested her hand on his arm, and he let out a long sigh. "Do not fret, my lady. I will honour my vow."

After her foray into the forest, Catrin spent the remainder of the morning in the privy kitchen, helping Mistress Blanche and Lady Mary Grey make possets for the queen and some favoured ladies. It meant standing over the fire, keeping an iron cauldron of cream and eggs in constant motion while it slowly simmered and thickened. Mistress Blanche then added ground almonds, sack wine and grated biscuits, and poured the resulting mixture into pewter cups before carrying it carefully into the bedchamber.

It was certainly no worse a duty than the candle-making at the Drury farm, and smelled far better, but it was difficult to make herself stand still amidst the steam and heat, listening to Lady Mary humming a tune. All she wanted was to go and look for Lucy. Or demand answers from Sir Nicolas. Or — or — or do anything. Anything but stand and stir.

Mistress Blanche took the latest cauldron off the heat, and Catrin stepped back from the fire, wiping her steam-bathed face on her apron. A page boy appeared in the doorway and gave a nervous bow. "Message for Lady Catrin?"

"She is there," Mistress Blanche said shortly, and concentrated on pouring. Catrin reached for the paper with suddenly nerveless fingers, and nearly fumbled it.

"If I may, Mistress Blanche?"

"Go," she said, and Catrin took herself out to the privy chamber where she could stand in a window-well and see more clearly. It was a piece of paper so thick she could see the fibres, and carried a simple square seal — just like the button.

She broke it, and barely stopped a cry, for a single lock of curling blonde hair was folded inside. "Oh, Lucy," she whispered. "My poor dear Lucy."

The words were hastily written, but unmistakably in Lucy's hand.

Tonight, after the feast.

When the musicians begin to play, you must convince Lord Robert to leave the queen's side and go to the gallery by the queen's apartments. This will allow the Branch to do his pruning.

You know the consequences of failure.

Catrin stared at the words in horror. She had been right, but that was little consolation when faced with the task of putting the queen's favourite in mortal danger. In the open, empty space of the gallery, he would be at the mercy of the Branch, whoever he was.

She had only one course of action. She had to find out who the Branch was, and ensure he was captured before the musicians began to play. With any luck, the Branch would tell them where Lucy was before his co-conspirators even realised that Catrin had ignored their instructions.

Catrin refolded the note, resisting the urge to crumple it and fling it into the fire, and turned away from the window. That was when she caught sight of Katherine Grey nearby, her protuberant eyes focused on the note with undisguised distaste.

Catrin frowned. That suggested that she knew what was in it.

And then, suddenly, Catrin understood. Her stepfather *had* wanted her to forge a relationship with the maids of honour — or one of them, at least. One who had cause to resent the queen; one whose birth brought her close to the throne, but not close enough. Katherine Grey had no hope of succession unless Elizabeth died.

To reach for but an empty claim. Lady Amy's lyrics had revealed another conspirator: Lady Katherine Grey.

Did Lady Katherine know where Lucy was? Would she know the Master's name? Catrin had to find out, and for that she had to speak to the girl alone. So she pressed the back of her hand to her forehead and took several uncertain steps in Lady Katherine's direction, before she gave a low whimper and let herself fall. Lady Katherine was soon at her side.

"I do not feel well," Catrin said faintly. "I need to lie down."

Lady Katherine hesitated. "I could gather some cushions for you."

"Nay, I need my bed," Catrin said fretfully. "But I must get permission from the queen to leave."

"She will not give it — not today, when she is preparing for a feast."

"Please — please help me."

Lady Katherine gave in, and Catrin leaned heavily on her as they passed together into the bedchamber. The queen looked up from her book with an irritated frown, and Catrin squeezed her hand so that the note crackled.

The queen noticed, but she played along. "Lady Catrin, can you not stand on your own feet?"

"Nay, Your Majesty, I am faint. Prithee grant me permission to go lie down, and allow Lady Katherine to help me."

"Granted — I do not wish illness around me," the queen said sharply.

"Thank you, Your Majesty," Catrin said, and let her head loll against Lady Katherine's shoulder until they had passed back out through the royal apartments and were progressing slowly through the corridors. Then she stood upright so quickly that Lady Katherine squeaked with surprise, pinned the girl to the wall with a quick twist of her body, and held the letter directly in front of her eyes. "You know what this is."

Lady Katherine whimpered and wriggled, trying to escape, but finally gave in and nodded. "It is the seal of the Master."

Catrin blinked. Richard Verney had used the same phrase. He had told her that her mother had been killed on the orders of the Master. "Who is the Master?"

"I don't know. I swear! I don't know."

"Then who has been giving you your orders?"

"No one."

Catrin shifted so that her forearm was against the girl's neck. It was not ladylike, but with Lucy's life at stake — as well as Lord Robert's — Catrin did not care. "I do not believe you."

"It's the truth!" Lady Katherine gurgled. "I am not part of it — I was never part of it!"

"Then how did you know about this letter?"

Lady Katherine's gaze dropped in sorrow and defeat, and immediately Catrin knew the answer to her own question. Lady Amy's lyrics did explain it all, if she considered the whole verse together. *Bent fortune takes the chance away.* Bent … twisted … hunched.

"It's your sister Mary, isn't it?"

"She has been meeting with someone she calls the Master for months, but won't tell me anything about him," Lady Katherine said. "She just insists this person will give us our due."

"And what is your due?"

"The honour that was given to you!" Lady Katherine shoved Catrin away from her and straightened to her full height. "Under Queen Mary, my sister and I had great influence as ladies of the bedchamber. We helped make decisions that affected thousands of people. We had salaries, pensions, gifts from the queen — and, best of all, our own room, far away from those chattering maids who never — *never* — go silent." She slumped back against the wall. "Under Elizabeth, we are nothing."

"And how does your sister think the Master will restore you to the queen's bedchamber?"

"He promised that his most devoted follower would free two places by All Saints' Day." She twisted the lace of her sleeve around her wrist, tightly enough to make her fingers red. "The two places taken from us."

His most devoted follower … Catrin remembered how Sir Nicolas had shown such fervent adoration of the Master and knew it had to be him. And that revealed his role in this plot. Like the Branch, he planned to kill, and his quarry was clear.

She had to save not only Lucy's life, but her own.

Catrin stared at Lady Katherine for a long time, forming a plan in her mind. "Go and speak to your sister," she said at last. "Tell her that she has been discovered, and her only chance to save both of your lives is to help me."

Lady Katherine's eyes widened. "Do you really think our lives are in danger?"

"I do." Catrin held the letter close to the girl's face. "Because if the Master does not kill you, the queen just might."

CHAPTER THIRTY-ONE

Catrin dressed for the feast in rubies and crimson velvet, and her sleeves, her bodice, her hemline — even her slippers — were embroidered in gold. Her hood was lined with diamonds and pearls, and her night-black hair gleamed beneath it. In a way, the finery was not necessary, for that night she was looking for a killer, not a suitor. But somehow it felt right — like putting on armour before a battle.

She waited until a crowd had passed into the great hall before she entered, and paused in the doorway so that she glittered and gleamed in the warm glow of the torches. Lord Robert was the first to notice, but he was escorting the queen so he responded with only a quirk of the lip. The Earl of Bedford stared at her as he passed, with such intensity that he ran into a page boy and nearly toppled over. The Earl of Shrewsbury also looked in her direction, but turned firmly away. His son, Lord Talbot, noticed the gesture and smirked.

Sir Nicolas was nowhere in sight, and she could not stop a shiver of relief. She knew that any attack on her was unlikely until she had completed her task, but she could not help but feel the threat of it.

Catrin circled the room. She saw the Grey sisters standing next to a group of swarthy men who were surrounding the Spanish ambassador. They were both dressed in dark green, with tiers of pearls spilling down over their bodices. Lady Katherine was talking to some of the other maids, but Lady Mary stood alone. She caught Catrin's eye and tilted her head, then walked over to the ewery to wash her hands.

Catrin obeyed the silent summons, and as she drew closer, Lady Mary spoke with low, angry intensity. "Did you really think you could stop me by sending my sister to plead on your behalf?"

"It was a warning, not a plea," Catrin said. Her eyes fell upon Lady Katherine and suddenly another piece of the puzzle fell neatly into place. "'Greensleeves'. Of course, that is the tune you have been humming — in the maids of honour's chamber, and earlier, in the privy kitchen."

Lady Mary scowled at her. "What of it?"

"It was a hint from a good, brave lady, which I should have understood before now," Catrin said, and waved her hand. "But never mind; that is a tale for another day."

"And what if there will never be another day?"

Catrin kept her smile firmly in place. "Then others will know why, and you will suffer the consequences."

Lady Mary's face darkened. "If you have told the queen about our quest, Lucy will be dead before midnight, and you will soon follow."

"According to your sister, we will be dead whether I tell the queen or not."

"Perhaps. But I just heard Sir Nicolas begging the Master to spare your life, so you might not want to betray him just yet."

Catrin's fingers traced the line of her *stiletto* under her sleeve. "The Master is with Sir Nicolas right now?"

"Yes." Suddenly Lady Mary stepped closer and strained her bent back to look up into Catrin's face. "Are you brave enough to face him?"

"Are you foolish enough to let me?"

"It is no concern of mine." Lady Mary turned away, her lopsided gait making her pearls swing from side to side. "I have my own role to play."

It might be a trap. Catrin hurried away from the great hall, the pitter-patter of her slippers echoing in the corridors. Perhaps Sir Nicolas would be waiting with his sword ready, and she would die before she had a chance to draw breath.

Or it might be a chance. A chance to end the threat once and for all.

She slowed down as she approached Sir Nicolas' chamber, moving with the light-footed grace her father had taught her so that she did not alert anyone to her presence. But it seemed there was no one there to alert; the door hung open, and a strange rasping sound emanated from within.

It was dark inside, the only light a single candle burning low in its holder. It cast a gentle circle of light over Sir Nicolas, who lay on the bed gasping for air, his face pale and sweating. He was wearing only a shirt and hose, the shirt stained dark by a wet ragged circle.

And at the centre of the circle … the hilt of a knife.

"God help us," Catrin whispered. There was nothing she could do; it was clear to see that he was at death's door. But despite his treachery, she could not let him suffer alone.

She went over and took his hand, and he turned his head toward her. For a second his dull eyes flared with the light of recognition. "The lonely place," he whispered. "Flowers … in the lonely place."

Her heart ached. "Is that what you see before your eyes, Nicolas?"

"No … your mother … asked me to … tell you."

Catrin's heart skipped a beat. "When? When did she tell you that?"

He drew in a breath with an enormous effort. "Before I … gave her body … to the river Colne."

Catrin pulled her hand away with a cry. "*You* killed her?" This man who claimed to love her, who had promised to protect her, had killed her mother.

Tears shimmered in his eyes. "Yes. May God … forgive me."

"Why? Why did you kill her? She was my mother — she had done nothing wrong!"

He drew in a deep rattling breath. "For the master, I killed … the innocent … and the guilty … alike."

Catrin took him by the shoulders, all her compassion erased in a wave of rage. "Who else did you kill? Lady Amy Dudley?"

"No … the Master killed her. I do not know … why."

"Who is the Master?" Sir Nicolas' eyes fixed on a point above Catrin's head. "Nicolas! Tell me — who is he?"

"He … did this to me." He drew a deep rattling breath. "Because I refused to kill … tonight."

"Nicolas, I need to know his name. He has Lucy. I must find her — please tell me, Nicolas."

"My dove…" he murmured, and his hand went limp in hers.

A cry tore from her throat unbidden, and behind her a man's voice let out a crude oath. Catrin knew who was there; the reek of alcohol was enough to tell her. "Verney, what are you doing here?"

Richard Verney moved into view in the doorway, steadying himself with one hand against the frame. "The Master does not leave things to chance," he mumbled, his bleary eyes fixed on her. "I'm here to make sure you do as you are told."

She rose slowly to her feet. "And just how do you plan to do that?"

Verney drew his lips back from his teeth in a mocking imitation of a smile. "Have you forgotten Lucy?"

"No, of course not."

"Then you have a task to perform."

"I know that."

He leered at her. "And my task is to escort you back to the great hall."

Catrin sent him a scornful glance. "If you feel you must."

Catrin felt like she was drowning as she returned to the hall; her feet dragged and she could not quite catch a breath. It seemed quite unbelievable that everyone else was behaving so normally. She arrived in the great hall to find Lord Robert sitting by the queen, laughing at something the Earl of Norfolk had said. Lord Talbot was playing idly with his dagger as he waited for his food. Servants were coming into the hall by the dozen, bearing gleaming silver platters, jugs of ale, carafes of wine.

Catrin wove cautiously between them as she started toward her place, passing by the group of Spanish men who served the ambassador. They all appeared impressed with the pageantry of the food: each time a dish came out they gasped in fresh delight. One dish, a peacock with the feathers re-inserted so they formed a colourful halo around the roasted bird, set them all chattering with excitement in their own language. Catrin caught very little of it — only what Lucy had taught her.

"It's beautiful!"

"So big!"

"Ramos, look! That could feed your whole family!"

Catrin stopped. *Ramos.* Lucy had taught her that word. She knew what it meant, and she knew what a discovery she had made. She should send word to Lord Robert somehow, or warn the queen, or even go speak to Sir William, who was not far away. But she didn't. Instead, she walked right up to the man, who was tearing the flesh from a chicken leg with his teeth. "Ramos," she hissed in his ear. "That means 'the branch'. And that means that I know what you are here to do."

His face did not change, but he rose in one smooth motion and took her arm in a vice-like grip. She had no choice but to go with him out of the hall, and by then she had regained her senses. "I want to work with you," she said in her best Spanish. "I am part of —"

She didn't get to finish. His fist crashed against her head, and the world went black.

CHAPTER THIRTY-TWO

"Catrin, dearest, please wake up."

The whisper came with the gentle touch of small hands, cradling her head. Catrin tried to answer, fighting against the fog that held her, and the whisper came again. "Please, please, I beg of you. You were my only hope; don't leave me to face this alone."

Catrin managed to moan once, and the whisper became a cry. "Are you badly hurt? Can you wake up?"

Catrin forced her eyes open, but found herself still in the dark. An unfamiliar dark, that felt very damp and smelled of mould. The voice, though — the voice she knew. "Lucy?"

"Catrin!" Lucy started to laugh and cry at the same time. "I thought they had killed you. When they carried you in, I thought … I thought —"

Catrin sat up so she could pull her friend into a fierce hug. "I am fine, dearling, but for a headache," she said. "Please, tell me that you are not hurt."

Suddenly Lucy's voice sounded very small. "I am not hurt … just frightened."

Catrin wrapped her in her arms again. "I am so sorry — so very sorry — that you were dragged into this nightmare."

"So am I," Lucy said, and took a few shuddering breaths. "But here we are, and all we can do is find a way to end it."

"Indeed, dearling. So let us begin." Catrin sat up, straightened her hood and peered into the darkness. "Where are we?"

Lucy wrapped her arms around her knees. "I don't know. There is nothing to discover but wet and dirt."

"There must be more than that. See over there? A patch that is paler than anywhere else; perhaps it is a window." Catrin got up, swayed slightly when the room spun and then steadied herself with a hand against the wall. She felt around over the paler patch and found boards nailed haphazardly over shutters. So she pulled her *stiletto* out of her sleeve and slid it gently under a board, then pulled with all her strength. Something gave way with a crack, and Lucy gasped.

"The guard — he will have heard that!"

They both fell silent, but there was nothing from outside the door.

Catrin pried one of the shutters open, and let out a faint cry of surprise. "We're on the water."

Lucy struggled to her feet. "How can that be? There are stairs. I remember hearing the guard climb the stairs."

Catrin pursed her lips in thought, and the answer came almost at once. "It's a boathouse."

Lucy's lip trembled. "If they brought us here on boats, we could be a long way from the castle."

"Or not far at all," Catrin said. "Come, dearling. We have to find a way to get out of here. I am certain someone is going to try to kill Lord Robert at the feast."

"Is it Sir Nicolas?"

"No. Sir Nicolas is dead."

Lucy gasped, and Catrin shoved her knife back into its sheath. "Killed by the Master of this thrice-damned conspiracy."

"So who is the Master?"

"I am growing more and more impatient to find out." Catrin went over to the door and traced her fingers around the edge. "I wonder if we could pry this loose … or maybe I could break the lock with my —" She broke off at the sound of heavy footsteps approaching fast. And then the rattle of a key in the lock.

Lucy let out a cry of fear, and Catrin retreated from the door so she could shield her. She drew her blade again as the doorknob turned, holding it by the tip so she could fling it as soon as she had a target.

But the target did not appear. Instead, the door swung open under the weight of a man who fell forward, senseless, onto the floor.

"Sheath your weapon."

It was the last voice Catrin expected to hear at that moment. She sheathed her knife, bemused. "Lady Mary?"

"Yes." Lady Mary Grey shifted into view, standing over the man's prone form with a heavy cudgel in one hand and a key in the other. "I followed when they took you from the great hall."

Catrin raised one eyebrow. "Not long ago you were happily contemplating my death. I find it hard to believe that now you're saving my life."

"I am saving my own life." She kicked the prone man away from the doorway with surprising strength, considering her size. "My loyalty to the Master has come to a sudden and abrupt end."

"Why?"

"He told Richard Verney that he has plans for the throne, and Katherine is not part of them. That is not what he promised me."

"Name him, then," Catrin said. "End the conspiracy."

"Oh, no. Since my sister Jane was killed, I have learned not to share dangerous information. My silence may well keep me alive."

"And your help may well earn the queen's favour."

"Nothing will give me any more favour than I now endure; my bloodline ensures that. But some things can certainly take it away." She raised the hand that held the key. "So know now: I will lock you in again and run, if you prove unhelpful."

Catrin's eyes narrowed. "You are putting a price on our freedom?"

"I am. You must tell the queen of my role in your rescue, not my connection to the Master. That will keep me out of the Tower for a while longer."

Catrin considered. "Very well, but be warned: it is a condition I will soon forget if I find out that you are working against the queen again."

"You will not have the chance to forget," Lady Mary said dryly. "Next time, you shall be the last to know."

CHAPTER THIRTY-THREE

After a frantic scramble from the boathouse to the castle, Catrin and Lucy sped up the stairs to the queen's gallery, bursting in through the archway to find the space echoing and empty.

Lucy skidded to a stop. "There's no one here. Is this not where you were meant to bring Lord Robert? Are we too late?"

Catrin looked around, noting the floor's smooth waxed surface. "No; I see no signs of a struggle."

"Too early, then. The queen does not like to linger over her meal, but tonight she may have changed her mind."

Catrin went still. "Changed her mind…" she murmured. "Like Lady Mary did."

Lucy made a scornful face. "Lady Mary changed her mind only because the Master had his own plans for the throne."

"Exactly." Catrin strode around the space, her mind racing. "But how can he establish his own person on the throne, unless he first removes the queen?"

Lucy pressed her fingers to her lips. "Oh, woe. Lord Robert isn't his intended victim after all."

"No. The Master charged me to bring Lord Robert here to the gallery merely to get us both away from the queen. That is why there is no one here waiting." Catrin's fist clenched in her skirt. "His true goal is to kill the queen. I did not understand that before. And now … we may be too late."

"Or we might be just in time." Lucy took her hand and squeezed. "We won't know until we go to the great hall."

They ran together down deserted corridors, and Catrin wondered where all the yeomen of the guard had gone. The space was completely empty as she and Lucy flew down the stairs.

They were nearly at the bottom when Lucy cried out and tumbled to the floor below.

"Lucy!" Catrin jumped the last stair and dropped to her knees by her side. "What happened?"

"I — I slipped on something," Lucy said, and rose shakily to her feet. "Fret not; I am not hurt."

Catrin's heart pounded, for she could see that Lucy's gown was stained red with blood. "Oh, dearling, I think you are."

Lucy touched the patch with wondering fingers. "No, truly, I'm not. It is not my…" Her voice trailed off, and her face blanched white. "Catrin — look!"

Catrin turned around to see where Lucy was pointing. Streaks of blood marred the flagstones … chairs were upturned … a slash across a tapestry made it sag. And a man lay propped against the doors to the great hall, his guard's livery wet with blood.

Catrin went to him. His eyes were still clear, but she knew at once that he did not have long. She set a gentle hand on his shoulder. "What happened here, goodman?"

"Set upon," the man murmured. "Men dressed in our livery … false guards… Some … still inside."

Catrin's heart skipped a beat. "Did they attack the queen?"

"No — Lord … Robert."

So, it had begun. "Is he…?"

"Gone," the man said, and his head lolled to the side.

Catrin jumped to her feet. "Lucy, find Sir William. Tell him everything," she said, and shoved the doors to the great hall open. She was immediately blinded by the light of a hundred lanterns and strained her eyes, trying to see.

The feast was over, and the revellers were on their feet. Servants were moving amongst them, silent workers in the midst of a hundred conversations, sliding the tables against the wall and clearing the dishes away. At the front of the room, the queen's chair of state sat empty, gleaming faintly in the reflected light from the golden canopy above it.

Suddenly a recorder trilled to mark the start of the dancing and a cheer broke through the noise. The crowd thinned, moving to the edges of the room to clear the space and, to Catrin's great relief, the queen emerged into view. Lord Talbot was by her side, drawing her into the centre to dance.

But where was Ramos? It was nearly impossible to see one dark-haired man in the midst of such a crush, so Catrin jumped up onto the nearest bench. She started searching the crowd, but then her eye was caught by someone standing on the edge of it. He was dressed as a guard, but his gaze was not fixed on the queen as it should have been. Instead, it was following the tall figure of a man as he slipped through the crowd, drawing closer and closer to the queen.

Ramos.

The queen was dancing now, whirling around at the centre of a column of couples, and Ramos had nearly reached her.

Catrin leapt from the bench and darted through the crowd, ignoring the indignant cries and muttered oaths. She had failed to help Lord Robert, but she would not — could not — fail the queen.

A blade flashed in the lantern light. Catrin broke free of the throng and jumped forward, dragging the man to a stop and digging her fingernails deep into his arm. The knife clattered to the floor.

One of the dancers saw it and screamed. Ramos tried to flee but Catrin hung on grimly.

"Catrin!"

It was Lucy, pushing through the crowd. Behind her came Sir William, roaring orders. Fresh guards poured into the room, and at once the hall dissolved into chaos. All around her, men were running and women were shrieking. The music ended on a single discordant note. "Go to the queen, Lucy!" Catrin cried. "Make sure she's safe!"

Lucy nodded once and disappeared, and Ramos started to swear. It was a string of oaths in two languages, and most of them Catrin had never heard before. "Oh, my. That is very creative," she said wryly. "But if you want to save your life, you might consider saying something more helpful."

"I would not help you for all the gold in Spain," Ramos spat. "You have ruined a plan months in the making."

"Thank you," Catrin said. "Now tell me — who is the master conspirator?"

He sneered. "Do you really think I will tell you that?"

"I do," Catrin said. "If you are wise."

He glared down at her. She gazed back, unblinking, and uncertainty crept into his eyes. "What happens if I do tell you?"

"I will help you."

He considered a moment. "Perhaps —" he said, but then his body jerked forward and his eyes rolled back in his head. Suddenly, instead of using all her strength to hold him still, Catrin was taking all his weight. She could not do it and crashed to the floor. Ramos landed on top of her, and the wet sticky flow of his blood began to soak into her gown.

Above her, Richard Verney wiped his knife on a napkin, and winked at her before he melted into the crowd.

The queen was standing in the far corner of the antechamber when Catrin and Lucy arrived. Immediately she took their hands in a warm, firm grasp, and they formed a circle for a long moment. Standing together, shoulder to shoulder. None of them spoke, but they all understood.

Suddenly Lord Robert appeared, somewhat wild-eyed, with a cut on his forehead. The queen gave a low cry of relief and let them go so she could reach out to him. "Oh, Robin, I thought you were dead. We all thought you were dead," she said. "Could you not have sent me word that you were well?"

"I fear not, Your Majesty," he said, and kissed her hand. "As you know, Lord Talbot lured me from the hall. I intended to capture and question him, but as soon as I left the hall I was set upon and had to fight my way free. My men and I chased the blackguards through the great park, but lost them in the dark."

"Do you know who attacked you?"

Lord Robert lowered himself to a cushion, obviously too tired to stand. "No, but Sir William arrested some of the false guards who were supporting the Master's plans. He has them in the Tower, ready for interrogation," he said. "No one is talking yet, but the sight of the rack might yet persuade them."

The queen set her hands on her hips. "So we still cannot name the master of this conspiracy," she said. "After all this danger, all this risk, we have progressed no further."

"Nay, indeed, Your Majesty," Catrin said. "We know that Sir Nicolas ranked highly in the conspiracy, and we know he was killed by its master. We can look closely into his visitors for the hours between when I left him and when I returned."

"And we have identified another conspirator: Lord Talbot," Lord Robert said. "He escaped when Ramos failed, but there are men scouring the countryside looking for him. We will have him confessing his every sin within the month."

"Good news indeed; I shall be able to sleep more soundly in my bed come Michaelmas," the queen said tartly, and then relented. "Forgive me, Robin, you have done good work today and I give you thanks. As have you, my talisman, and little Lucy. I am so grateful that you were able to escape your captors."

"With the help of Lady Mary Grey, Your Majesty," Catrin said dutifully. "We do not often see eye to eye … and she has a terrible habit of humming 'Greensleeves' over and over … but she was certainly useful today."

"'Greensleeves'?" The queen repeated the word thoughtfully. "From what I remember, Lady Amy had a penchant for that particular song."

Catrin smiled, unsurprised that the queen had so quickly understood. "Aye, she did."

"Does Lady Mary regret her obsession with that … melody?"

"Very much, I would say. The assistance she gave tonight was her penance, so to speak."

"Hopefully it will be enough to earn our forgiveness, then. We shall have to wait and see." The queen rose to her feet and held out her hands to Catrin and Lucy. "Return now to the ladies' bedchamber to rest, both of you. I have let it be known that you are no longer in disgrace."

"Thank you, Your Majesty," Catrin said.

"You're welcome, dear ladies." The sunshine of her smile warmed them all. "And to you, too, my hearty thanks."

Poor Lucy fell so deeply asleep a thunderstorm would not have woken her, but Catrin could not find the same oblivion. She lay awake, staring out at the stars, until false dawn turned the sky a charcoal grey. Then she rose and put on a dressing-gown and slippers before she gathered what she needed and left the room.

The castle corridors were strangely crowded, with drunken courtiers lying haphazardly about. In the first antechamber she entered, the sounds of a lusty couple made her hastily retreat, and in the next an old man lay half-dressed and snoring loudly. She kept looking, and gradually her quest for a private space led her back to the royal apartments. The esquires let her in, and she crossed to the fireplace for better light. A page boy rose silently from his sleeping mat and added another log to the fire, and she thanked him with a smile, grateful for the heat as well as the light.

And then, at a small table, she started to decipher her mother's letter. First, the code key. *Flowers in the lonely place.* That was the hint her mother had given Sir Nicolas in her last moments on earth, and Catrin had known at once what it meant. Roses. Their secret place in the woods, where they had hidden from her stepfather and written sweet foolish messages to make each other laugh … it had always been filled with roses.

She added the code key at the top, then formed the grid. And then, slowly, carefully, with many errors and crossings-out, she made out the words.

Catrin, my own heart's root, my beloved child,
I need you to know that your father was no traitor. It was Roger, Lord Ashbourne, your father's best friend, who fell for Wyatt's lies. Your father

took the blame to save him. He knew Ashbourne was weak and easily led astray.

I married Ashbourne to give us security and to make sure he remembered what a sacrifice your father had made. I hoped it would make him a better man, but I now have fresh proof, if I needed it, that he is still a pathetic fool. And this time his betrayal could destroy an entire kingdom.

I overheard Ashbourne talking with two men — one was the leader and instigator of a group determined to overthrow the queen, and the other was his second-in-command, Sir Nicolas Swann.

Ashbourne had a letter from Swann, and I have saved the seal as proof. Sadly I have no proof of the identity of the leader, but I know him. The whole kingdom knows him — he is...

Catrin read the name her mother had written and gasped. Of course! It made perfect sense. No one had a better motive. But how to prove it? How to bring him out of the shadows?

"What is it?"

Catrin jumped. The queen stood in the doorway to the bedchamber, tall and slender, looking terribly young and fragile in her long white nightgown. "It is my mother's letter. I finally managed to decipher it," she said, and paused to clear the catch in her throat.

The queen frowned. "I thought I had commanded thee to close that particular book, young Catrin."

"As I promised, Your Majesty, I have not searched. Sir Nicolas himself told me the code key, and by doing so he has helped us immeasurably."

"How?"

Catrin held out the letter. "My mother named the master of the conspiracy."

The queen snatched the paper and her eyes flicked quickly over the words. Then her whole body went rigid. "We must prove it," she said with quiet intensity. "We must find a way."

Catrin smiled. "I have an idea."

CHAPTER THIRTY-FOUR

The Master walked out along the wharf at the break of dawn, when light shone over the castle but the Thames was still cloaked in darkness. Verney was there, skulking in the undergrowth. "I want my fee."

"The attempt failed," the Master said. "And you ran like a coward."

"But I rid you of Ramos."

The Master snorted. "I did not need to be rid of Ramos. He would have disappeared back to his own country before anyone even knew to look for him."

"They might have found out who he was."

"Even if they did, they would have blamed a foreign conspiracy and never known our connection. That was why we hired a Spaniard to begin with."

"I don't think it would have been worked that way," Verney said. "I heard him — he was about to confess."

"I doubt that. His reputation suggested a certain...ruthlessness that I appreciated."

"I fear it was exaggerated. So I took care of it." Verney stuck out his chest. "And that saves you his fee, so I think part of that should come to me, too."

"Perhaps it should," the Master said dryly, and took his purse from his belt. "Come and fetch it, then."

Verney cackled. "Do you think me dull enough to get within the reach of your blade? Nay, indeed. Throw it to me, my lord, if you please."

The Master let out an oath and threw the purse. Verney darted out to catch it, and then fled at top speed while the Master turned back to the castle.

Suddenly he noticed a golden hilt lying on the balustrade, and the sight made him swear so loudly that he frightened a swan into taking flight. He snatched it up and continued toward the castle, but then stumbled to a halt. Before him lay a doublet stitched with silver thread, with one square button missing and several scratches marring the sleeves.

The man took the doublet and marched onward, but just as he reached the castle a girl stepped out to meet him. A slender girl with eyes of cornflower blue and jet-black hair, and a smile that could drive a man to madness.

"Catrin Surovell." He spat out the words. "What are you doing out here so early?"

"Accusing you, my Lord Norfolk," Catrin said sweetly, and delicately set a charred piece of paper on the balustrade. "You said the man with the papers at Cumnor Place was Richard Verney, but it wasn't him, was it? You put this paper in the fire in the hall yourself, just in time for Gryse to draw it out."

"You have no proof of that," the duke snarled.

"Not of that, but of other things," Catrin said, and opened her palm. A small square button glinted in the morning light. "This matches yours, does it not? Much as another button, now lost, matched the ones on that doublet you carry." She sighed, shook her head. "I wondered why you wore such a light travelling-costume when we went to Cumnor, my lord. And now I see — it was because your heavier one had been damaged on your previous visit. When you killed Amy Dudley."

"She failed me," Norfolk said. "I went myself to collect the gold, because she said she would give it to no one else. And then, when I arrived, she did not have it."

"No, she didn't. She used the promise of gold merely to lure you into the open, because she was secretly working for the queen. Against you." Catrin wrapped her fingers around the button again, forming a fist. "The Master. The Duke of Norfolk."

"Yes. Yes! The only duke left in this cursed realm. The last of the old religion." He dropped the hilt and the doublet and reached instead for his sword. "The man who will be king, once all obstacles have been removed."

"Like my mother, who would have exposed you years ago? Like my stepfather?"

"Aye." He drew the sword and pointed its tip towards her. "Like yourself."

Catrin gazed at him without fear. He let out a roar and swung the sword wide, and suddenly steel clashed against steel.

Lord Robert had leapt out from the alcove where Catrin had hidden. Fury made him fast and brutal, and Norfolk had all he could do to defend himself. He danced, circled, parried, using Lord Robert's anger against him by forcing him to attack again and again. Soon enough Lord Robert began to tire, and for a short second his guard went down. Norfolk swung his sword with a vicious twist and Lord Robert's weapon flew out of his hand.

Norfolk let out a cry of triumph too soon. Even as he raised his blade to deliver the killing stroke, a *stiletto* flew towards him out of nowhere and buried itself in his wrist. He let his sword fall with a shriek of pain, and Lord Robert immediately pressed his advantage. He recovered his sword in one smooth movement and held the blade against the duke's throat.

Norfolk saw Catrin's arm fall and realized what she had done. "Damn you, woman," he snarled. "You have ruined me."

Catrin's smile was pure ice. "One can only hope."

Lord Robert looked over at Catrin. "I did not know you could use a blade with such skill, my lady."

She bowed her head in acknowledgement. "I use it only when under threat, my lord."

Lord Robert blinked. "So you have wielded it before?"

"Aye." Catrin's eyes glittered. "That is how my stepfather lost his earlobe."

EPILOGUE

27 September, 1560

The queen chose to go for her morning walk with only Catrin and Lucy as attendants. They walked slowly down to the end of the new wharf, and then the queen turned to gaze upon her castle.

"I wager you are wondering what has happened in the last few days, since you unmasked the Master," she said.

"Oh, yes, we are, Your Majesty," Lucy said eagerly.

"And I will tell you, if you promise to keep the secret."

"Of course, Your Majesty," Lucy said, her blue eyes wide. "We would never betray your confidence."

"Thank you, Lucy." The queen went over to the balustrade and gazed down into the water. "We have arrested the Duke of Norfolk — quietly. I do not want this scandal to become common knowledge."

"I admire your restraint," Catrin said. "It would be all too easy to send him to Tower Hill."

"Yes, it would, but I dare not." The queen sighed. "Royal blood flows in his veins."

"And what if he tries again?" Catrin asked.

"He will not have the chance. I will send him back to Norfolk and never trust him near my person again," the queen replied grimly. "And I will repress all knowledge of the truth of Lady Amy's death, so that no one knows how close I came to an ignoble end. Even the coroner's report will be hidden."

"It will be difficult to hide it all," Catrin said.

"Yes, it will. His conspirators tried so many ways and means to end my reign: hiring the Spanish assassin, Ramos. Printing that evil tract, which would have caused so much damage to my reputation in Europe."

Catrin looked out over the river and remembered the scent of primroses. "Lady Amy prevented both of those."

"Yes. Lady Amy, and others like her, have thwarted these conspirators again and again."

"Did the duke tell you that, Your Majesty?"

"Aye, he did, when he gave up a dozen names to save his own skin. Including Mistress Rose Kene."

Lucy clutched Catrin's hand. "What will happen to her?"

The queen's face hardened. "Prison — or death."

"Oh, no, please!" Lucy cried. "She is so young — she didn't understand what she was doing. Please spare her, Your Majesty — for my sake, if not for hers."

The queen tilted her head, gazing at her thoughtfully. "You have earned a reward for all you have done," she said. "I had another gift in mind, but…"

"I would rather you spare her," Lucy said earnestly, and clasped her hands together. "Please, Your Majesty."

"Very well. I will send her home to her family to learn some sense," the queen said, and the sternness in her face faded into a smile. "And I will save your gift for New Year."

Lucy sunk into a curtsy. "Thank you, Your Majesty."

The queen turned to Catrin. "And as for you, my talisman … you shall have to wait. I have something very special in mind."

Catrin smiled. "You always do, Your Majesty."

I am in London now, waiting for a carriage to take me to West Drayton where I will be safe until after the coronation. I long to come and see you, my sweet, but it is not safe for you to get involved in this. Once it is over, and I have uncloaked this conspiracy, I will come and see you at court in all your splendour.

Be strong. Be brave. Find where you belong and love the people there with all your heart. That will bring you the greatest joy, and help you create a life worth living.

Your loving mother,
Angharad Surovell, Lady Ashbourne

Catrin had read the message over and over, hungry for every word, grateful that at last she knew what her mother had wanted to tell her. At last she knew why her mother had disappeared, and why.

"Catrin! Are you coming?"

"Yes, yes," Catrin said, and rose to join Lucy and Lady Mary Sidney as they left the ladies' chamber. It was chilly that evening; she wore a shawl over her gown and longed to wrap it tight around her. But a certain elegance was expected; the queen had demanded a feast even though the last one was only a few days ago.

They entered the great hall as always, in order of precedence, and the tables gradually filled up. Catrin saw the Earl of Shrewsbury come in and was surprised when he sent her a tentative smile and a deep bow. She responded with a curtsy, but did not try to join him. It was a game she was not in the mood to play — that evening, at least.

Finally, everyone was seated, and the queen herself came in with a flare of trumpets. But she did not sit down under her golden canopy. Instead, she walked to a center point in front of her table and turned to address them all.

"As you all know, Roger Surovell, the Earl of Ashbourne, died recently," she said. Her voice rang clear and strong, resonant with authority. "The title reverts to us, and is purely in our gift to bestow."

A hush fell over the crowd, and all faces grew hopeful. "Therefore," the queen continued, "we give it to Lady Catrin Surovell, in her own right. She is now the Countess of Ashbourne, and holds all the rights and privileges of that rank."

There was a chorus of applause, and a rumble of discontent. A voice rose out of the crowd. "Your Majesty, no! This is unprecedented. Women should not hold such a title in their own right!"

"Unprecedented? Not at all," the queen said icily. "Do you not remember the Marquess of Pembroke?"

That silenced the rumblings, for the Marquess of Pembroke was the queen's own mother. "Of course, Your Majesty, of course," the voice muttered. "I do apologise."

"Accepted," the queen said, and suddenly her smile lit up the room. "What say you, Lady Catrin?"

Catrin looked around at them all, that whole glittering company, and suddenly they seemed very precious. Dashing Lord Robert, brilliant Sir William, sweet Lucy, clever Lady Mary Sidney. They were all hers — the family she had found, not been born into. And she belonged, because she served a good and generous queen.

She was free, and she was home.

Catrin sank into a curtsy, although she was truly unsure whether her trembling knees would allow her to rise again. "Thank you, Your Majesty. For everything."

A NOTE TO THE READER

Accident, suicide or murder?

On 8 September, 1560, Lady Amy Dudley, Lord Robert Dudley's wife, was actually found dead at the bottom of a staircase at Cumnor Place. After a few days of investigation, the coroner's jury came to the conclusion that it was an accidental death, but that didn't end the speculation. More than 460 years later, people are still wondering. Why did Lady Amy send all her servants away that day? Was she really ill with a 'malady of the breast'? Was someone slowly poisoning her?

New questions about her death came to light when the long-lost coroner's report was discovered by historian S.J. Gunn in 2008. That was when it was discovered that Lady Amy had had two 'dints' in her head, one of which was deep enough to fracture her skull. These injuries could have been the result of falling down stairs, but they could also indicate foul play. So what happened? How and why did she die?

This novel presents a fictionalized answer to that question. There is no indication that there was a conspiracy of this sort in play at the time, and even less indication that Lady Amy was involved in it. Her surviving letters indicate that she was a simple woman with a wry sense of humour and a keen fashion sense, who took care of the business of managing her husband's estates while he was occupied at court. It may have been purely accidental that she ended up at the centre of a great court scandal, and that is what makes it a great story. I can recommend Chris Skidmore's *Death and the Virgin* to anyone who would like to read more about it.

One more thing. It is not known what happened to Anne Boleyn's famous 'B' necklace after she was executed. There is a very faint possibility that Mary Boleyn managed to collect it before Anne died, and some people speculate that the necklace went back to King Henry VIII, who kept it out of sentiment. Others say that it went back to the royal collection with the rest of Anne's jewels and was taken apart, with some of the pearls ending up on the State Crown. And, finally, a few people suggest that Henry's last queen, Katherine Parr, ensured that the necklace was saved for Anne's daughter Elizabeth. That is the story I have chosen to tell.

I once went to see a singer who said the following at the end of his concert: 'If you enjoyed this, please tell all your friends to come. If you didn't, please tell all your enemies!' I feel much the same. I hope you enjoyed reading this novel, and thank you for choosing it. If you enjoyed it, please tell all your friends, and post a review on **Amazon** and **Goodreads**. Reviews are really important for authors, so it would be much appreciated.

Readers can connect with me **on Facebook (Angela Ranson Author)** and through **my website (Angela Ranson)**, which includes not only updates on the Catrin Surovell series but humorous thoughts on the quirks of life and the art of writing.

Angela Ranson

Sapere Books is an exciting new publisher of brilliant fiction and popular history.

To find out more about our latest releases and our monthly bargain books visit our website:
saperebooks.com

Printed in Great Britain
by Amazon

40026328R00165